ASHES
OF
BETRAYAL

THE ENFORCER'S BRIDE: BOOK TWO

JAYNE CASTEL

WINTER MIST
PRESS

Ashes of Betrayal, by Jayne Castel

Published by Winter Mist Press

ISBN: 978-1-991280-10-7 (Paperback)

Edited by Tim Burton
Cover design by Winter Mist Press
Cover images courtesy of Deposit Photos and generated by Midjourney
Chapter header images generated by Midjourney

Visit Jayne's website: www.jaynecastel.com

From the ashes of betrayal rises a love with the power to change everything. An assassin in disgrace. An enforcer gone rogue. A destiny that binds them. Dive into the thrilling conclusion of The Enforcer's Bride Fantasy Romance duology.

Bree was once the Raven Queen's assassin—a ruthless killer with the blood of many on her hands. However, when she returns home after her last mission, she finds herself sidelined … and it's not long before the chilling truth settles upon her.

She doesn't belong in Sheehallion any longer.

Nor can she forget the man she left behind in Albia.

Meanwhile, her husband, Cailean, is haunted by his own demons. His illustrious career is destroyed, and his brief and disastrous marriage to Bree has forced him to confront the ghosts he's long avoided.

But betrayal isn't enough to keep husband and wife apart—not when Bree makes a decision that propels her on a dangerous journey across the wilds of Albia.

A journey that brings her straight to Cailean.

Outlander meets The Witcher and Throne of Glass. ASHES OF BETRAYAL is Book Two in a Fantasy Romance duology with enemies-to-lovers, slow-burn delicious spice, redemption, and a dark and lush world inspired by Celtic myth.

*For anyone who has ever felt lost, yet still had the courage to begin again.
This story is for you.*

CONTENT WARNINGS

ASHES OF BETRAYAL is a fantasy romance set in a brutal Pict-inspired world. It's intended for mature (18+) readers and contains the following triggers:

Violence and gore

Beheading

Slavery

Stockholm syndrome

Graphic sex

Murder

Dark themes

Coarse language

THE REALM OF ALBIA
THE WESTERN ISLES
THE SEA OF SORROWS
THE BALEFUL SEA
THE UPLANDS
THE WOLDS
Harra
The Spine
Darkmere
Morar Barrow
Morae
Cannich
The isle of Laggan
Darkmere Barrow
Strath
Bracebell Barrow
Eothie
Crook Barrow
Loch Glass
Dunmorth Barrow
The Ring of Ard
The Goatfell Mountains
The Hallow Woods
Dulross
Doure
Baldeen
The Ring of Caith
Loch Caith
The Ring of Starke
The Isle of Arryn
The Shiel Range
Deeping Barrow
Dorne Forest
Golval Barrow
Duncrag
The Golval Woods
Loch Lethe
The Firth of Tallow
Dunharra Barrow
Farnoch
Strathnich Forest
Dingford
Ordsheen
Strathnich Barrow
The Galan Peninsula
Loch Ord
Gavich Barrow
Muirport
Inverwich
Troon
Braewall

MAP

Visit my website to view a larger version of the Realm of Albia map.

1: BURNED TO ASH

The Hallow Woods
The Realm of Albia

THE TIME TO seek justice had come.

Not for the dead who burned before him, but for a past that couldn't be silenced any longer.

Standing back from the large pyre, Cailean watched the flames devour the corpses of those who'd ridden north with him—Prince Kennan among them.

Although the afternoon sky was overcast, sweat trickled down his back. The heat of the fire was searing, and after spending most of the day dragging bodies into a mound, exhaustion dragged down at him, settling deep into his bones.

Yet, inside, he seethed.

Skaal sat at his side, watching the hungry flames. The fae hound, a huge dog—at least four times the size of a wolf—with a shaggy dark-green coat and glowing golden eyes, was his shadow.

Around them lay the ruins of the Marav encampment, tents trampled into the damp, peaty earth. After combing the dead, in the hope someone might have been left alive, he'd set all the horses free, leaving them to make their way out of the Hallow Woods. Dark, oily smoke wreathed up above the treetops. The druidic wards had long since fallen, and on the fringes of the clearing where he stood, the cruel whispers of The Slew tormented him.

Cailean ignored them. The Unforgiven were weaker in daylight, although the malevolent spirits wouldn't touch him anyway, for they fed on fear—and he wasn't afraid.

Instead, an old rage—one he'd ignored for too long—writhed in his belly.

And all the while, the fire sizzled and popped. The char of burning bodies made his bile rise, but he remained at the fireside.

He owed the dead that, at least.

The High King would seek reckoning against the Shee for this, yet Cailean was done with it. Enough. For years, he'd been Talorc mac Brude's servant, but no longer.

He wouldn't be going home this time. When the High King learned of his son's death, he'd be incensed, maddened by grief. He'd be looking for someone to blame, and Cailean wasn't going to offer himself up as a sacrifice.

Aye, his career was over. Everything he'd worked so hard for was gone. The pyre before him wasn't just incinerating bodies—but his old life.

It had taken this massacre to tear down the walls he'd spent two decades shoring up.

It had taken *her*.

He cut his gaze back to the fire then, his hands fisting at his sides.

Bree Fellshadow.

Heat swept over him, hotter than the blistering fire he stood before, as he recalled how thoroughly his wife had deceived him.

Until a few days ago, she'd been Fia—the Maid of Albia he'd ordered when the High King insisted that he take a bride—but then she'd tracked him into the Hallow Woods and taken off her mask. His wife was one of the Shee, who'd taken Marav form: an assassin sent to spy on the enemy.

He should have run her through with his sword as soon as she told him the truth. But instead, like a shit-brained fool, he'd taken Bree to The Ring of Caith, on this Mid-Summer Fire's morn, and sent her back to her people through the standing stones.

And, all the while, she'd known the Shee had already hit this camp and slaughtered everyone in it.

Cailean dragged a hand down his face before giving his head a shake.

He couldn't let himself think about that bitch, and how easily he'd fallen under her spell. There wasn't any point in trying to get even with her either. Bree was now back in Sheehallion, where she belonged.

Three large crows, drawn by the odor of roasting bodies, flapped down from the pale sky, perching on the branch of an old pine. Among druids, the sight of three ravens or crows together was a sign of new beginnings: the end of one chapter and the start of another.

He glared at the carrion birds. "You're too late," he muttered. "There will be no flesh for you to feast on today."

He waited there by the fire for a while longer, watching as the bodies burned to ash. Eventually, he cast Skaal another glance. She'd remained loyally at his side while the fire smoldered, silently waiting. Meanwhile, a few yards behind him his stallion, Feannag, also waited. His dog and his horse—they were all he had.

And the hunger for revenge that made his gut ache. It was time to deal out long-overdue justice.

"Are you ready to go north, lass?" he asked Skaal.

The fae hound cocked her head as if she understood him. Of course, she didn't though. Such a notion was ridiculous.

"Come on then." Turning, he strode across to his horse, skirting around a clump of listing gravestones. And in the shadows, back from the clearing that had once been the Marav camp, The Slew stirred, hissing at him.

Once again, Cailean barely heard them.

Instead, he mounted Feannag and turned him toward the overgrown path that wound its way north, where the shadows of great mountains rose into the sky: the heart of The Uplands. Skaal trotted at his side.

They left the dead behind them.

2: FOREVER ALTERED

Caisteal Gealaich
The Realm of Sheehallion

I SHOULD NEVER have returned.

Pulse hammering, Bree kept her gaze fixed on the gleaming moonstone floor of the throne room. The hard tiles dug into her knees, but she remained kneeling. Misery constricted her ribs, while around her, she was aware of the gazes of the Ravens—Mor's personal bodyguards—and the Raven Queen's two advisors, drilling into her.

Meanwhile, Mor had gone silent. Never a good sign.

Bree's skin prickled under the queen's stare, nervousness fluttering up. All the same, it was difficult to focus. Not when she knew, to the marrow of her bones, that she didn't belong here.

She belonged with her husband.

Her chest started to ache. *Shades, I thought I'd freed myself of this.* She'd been sure that going through the stones and becoming

Shee once more would restore the order of things. She'd be herself again: cold, detached, and pragmatic. The Raven Queen's favorite pet.

But the pain pulsing under her breastbone contradicted her.

"You were supposed to remain at Duncrag," Mor said finally, shattering the silence. "Why have you come back so soon?"

Swallowing, she raised her chin, meeting the queen's black gaze.

Mor sat upon a throne carven from moonstone, her lovely face stern with disapproval. She wore a storm-grey gown that hugged her lean frame and a heavy jet necklace that gleamed against the deep umber of her skin. As always, her messenger, Eagal, the raven, perched upon her shoulder. The bird watched the queen's assassin, unblinking.

"I had to, My Queen," Bree answered, steeling herself for what was to come. "I was compromised."

Mor's full lips pursed. "How so?"

Bree drew in a deep, steadying breath. On the journey back to Caisteal Gealaich from The Ring of Caith, she'd tried not to dwell on what she'd just lost. Instead, she'd planned what she'd say to her queen. It had provided a welcome distraction.

She had to be careful. Only a fool underestimated Mor. Despite that Bree had served her faithfully for over two centuries, this mistake could send her to the pit—a cavern under the fortress where the ravenous wyrm dwelt.

She wasn't keen to wrestle with the serpent.

"The chief-enforcer was suspicious of me from the start," she began, choosing each word with care. "The High King had *forced* him to take a wife. He was hostile and determined to be married in name only." Her heart kicked then as she recalled all the times they'd clashed over the past moons. His coldness. His rudeness. And yet, she'd persisted, working her way under his skin like a thorn.

In doing so, she'd awoken something within him—within them both.

And now, she was forever altered.

Grief gripped hold of her throat then, its rough fingers squeezing tight, choking her.

Cailean.

She couldn't believe she'd never see him again. She'd never hear the low rumble of his voice, or see the glint in those woad-blue eyes when she vexed him. She'd never feel his hands on her skin. Her throat started to ache viciously, and she blinked, wrestling to maintain her self-control.

"The chief-enforcer was vile and abusive," she continued, wishing her voice wasn't a rasp. She also tried not to remember the strain in Cailean's face, his shadowed gaze, as they'd said goodbye before The Ring of Caith. He hadn't wanted her to go either, but he'd thought he was doing the right thing. "With the manners of a goat."

Mor's expression didn't change. So far, Bree's tale wasn't hitting the mark.

Panic washed over her. *Concentrate! You can do better than this.* Clearing her throat, she pushed on. "His temper was explosive … and his favorite trick was to shove me up against the wall and shout in my face."

An image rose unbidden, of Cailean's body against her back as he pressed her up against the wall of their alcove. The husk of his voice in her ear. The hunger that clenched her belly as she sagged against him. She started to sweat then; she could feel it under her arms and trickling down her back under her tunic.

Meanwhile, Mor's lip curled. "I expected you to be prepared to deal with the brute," she replied coldly. "Not whine about it."

Bree's pulse took off once more. "I did … as best I could," she assured her queen. "But locked in a weak body … and impersonating a sniveling Marav … meant I had to be careful. Subtle."

That was an irony. Her brother would attest that there was nothing subtle about Bree. Mor had sent an assassin to do a spy's work, and right from the first moment she'd locked stares with the man she'd wed, her days at Duncrag had been numbered.

A chill silence settled over the throne room. Meanwhile, Bree's pulse thumped in her ears.

Mor's gaze had narrowed, while Eagal's beady eyes felt as if they were slicing right through her.

"He started using his fists on me," Bree continued, shattering the brittle hush. Yet again though, her mind betrayed her. Images of that torrid night they'd shared, of how good his touch had felt, flooded over her. Clenching her jaw, she tried not to think about Cailean buried deep inside her. *Iron smite me, this isn't the time!* "I weathered his violence for as long as I could," she plowed on, desperate now. "But on the eve before he departed on his mission to the north, he cornered me … and so I fought back."

Mor's mouth thinned.

"I punched the bastard in the throat and slammed my knee into his balls," she said, recalling how quickly he'd deflected her attempts to maim him on that fateful evening. Aye, she'd fought well as a Marav woman, but she was no match for the realm's most powerful warrior-druid. "A servant interrupted us … or I don't know what might have happened. However, before leaving Duncrag, mac Brochan warned me that he'd 'deal with me' upon his return."

Her spine straightened then, her confidence returning. Aye, she could get through this—if she held her regret at bay. She only had to keep up the act for a short while longer. Once she was alone, she could let her shields down.

She could rail at herself for coming back here.

"I had to kill two guards to gain access to the dungeon so I could find Bryce … and after speaking to him, I ended his life too," she went on. "After that, my cover was blown … so I left the fort while I was still able. The High King enjoys torture. He'd held Bryce in the dungeon for moons, slowly carving him up before he revealed our secrets. I couldn't let the same thing happen to me."

The Raven Queen didn't answer immediately. Mor leaned back, her long slender fingers drumming upon the armrests. She then shared a veiled look with the two sharp-eyed females, clad in long silver robes, who stood to her right—Nell and Sage, Mor's most trusted advisors.

Both females were frowning.

Mor shifted her attention back to Bree. "Being married to the chief-enforcer would have been a trial," she said coolly. "But I sent my best to Duncrag for a reason. Now I have no ear in Talorc mac Brude's household."

Bree swallowed. "I gained much that was valuable from Byrce, did I not?"

It was foolish to speak thus to Mor, yet Bree could feel anger quickening, momentarily eclipsing her misery. She'd put her neck on the line for her queen. A little gratitude would have been nice.

Mor inclined her head. "Aye … we were ready for them at Sheathan." The queen's eyes, the color of a moonless night, glinted. "Thanks to your warning, we *ambushed* the enemy … slaughtering the entire warband."

Bree's heart dropped to her belly.

The entire warband …

"You killed *all* of them?" she whispered, struggling to keep her voice even.

"Aye … even the prince. I watched him fall too. He was brave enough, coming at my Ravens with an iron blade in each hand. But it wasn't enough to save him."

Bree's pulse took off.

The urge to ask the queen about the chief-enforcer surged through her, yet she swallowed it. Instead, she exhaled slowly, trying to calm down.

Careful.

"When did the attack take place?" she asked, with exaggerated slowness, as if the answer mattered not.

"Shortly before dawn."

Weakness flooded through her, and she was grateful that she was kneeling, or her legs might have given way under her.

He's alive.

Cailean hadn't been at the camp just before dawn. Instead, he'd taken her south to The Ring of Caith and watched while she walked through the stones at sunrise. He would have returned to the woods, and the camp, to find everyone dead.

A chill skated down her spine then, the brief surge of relief draining from her.

He'll think I knew … that I lied to him.

He would, but she couldn't dwell on that now. Not when she could almost feel the wyrm's hot breath on her back.

"Unfortunately, though, we found no sign of the chief-enforcer," the queen added. "The bastard must have gone off on patrol."

Bree didn't answer immediately. She had to be very wary now, for suspicion glinted in the queen's dark gaze, while her sinister-looking raven continued to stare Bree down.

Her breathing grew shallow, her limbs prickling in warning.

Mor could never learn about what she'd done—that she'd raced to the Hallow Woods and warned her husband about the coming attack.

"What now, My Queen?" Sage, one of Mor's advisors, asked as the silence between them grew brittle.

"We've had a victory against the Marav … but things will not end here." Mor's fingers increased their tempo, a sign that anger thrummed inside her. "Too long has the High King hunted our people. Once, the Shee could roam freely in Albia, yet now we are pushed to the fringes. High Kings of old let us be, but not this royal line." Her fingers wrapped around the armrests, squeezing hard. "Mac Brude and his father … and his grandfather before him … have increasingly persecuted us." She leaned forward on her throne, a muscle feathering upon her jaw. "Aye, the High King has lost his son and half of his precious enforcers … but that isn't enough. I will make him rue the day he ever sought to avenge himself upon me."

Bree stilled.

She should have been relieved that Mor wasn't currently focusing on her—but misgiving feathered down her nape at the ferocity on the queen's face. She'd seen that expression before, after one of the queen's brothers, Grae, had attempted to take the throne. In response, she'd sent Bree to hunt and kill him.

Once Mor fixed her mind on something, or someone, she wouldn't be thwarted.

Talorc mac Brude had now drawn Mor's full attention—a foolish thing indeed.

Someone cleared their throat then, and Mor glanced over her shoulder to see that it came from the captain of the Ravens, Gavyn Frostshard. His handsome face wore a hard, hungry, look. "What do you have in mind, My Queen?"

Mor lifted her chin, scowling at the intrusion. "We shall talk of my plans soon enough, Frostshard," she replied, her tone sharp. "But for the moment, you shall exercise patience."

Mor glanced back at Bree then, her eyes narrowing. She had a gaze that could melt iron.

"What do you ask of *me*, My Queen?" Bree asked, her throat suddenly parched.

"Nothing," the Raven Queen replied, her voice as cold as an Albian winter. "Your failures outweigh your successes. You ignore instructions and lie when you find yourself backed into a corner ... aye, don't take me for a fool. I haven't lived two thousand years to be so easily taken in."

Bree broke into a cold sweat. "My Queen," she gasped, ready to do whatever it took to save her skin. "I—"

"Enough," Mor cut her off. "One more insincere word and you'll be feeding the wyrm at sunset." Mor halted then, a chill silence rippling across the throne room. "Now get out of my sight ... before my merciful mood passes."

3: ON EDGE

A EWER OF chilled apple wine in one hand, and two silver goblets in the other, Bree gingerly made her way down the winding stairs. Her boots whispered on stone, while around her soft light reflected off the white walls.

In the aftermath of her audience with Mor, her legs were unusually shaky. She'd left the throne room in a daze, stumbling out into bright sunlight and warmth. Quite frankly, she was lucky to be alive. The Raven Queen's wrath could be deadly, yet she'd survived it. For the moment, at least.

As tempting as it was to lock herself away in her tower, and rage at her stupidity, she'd descended into the bowels of the fortress instead—to the archives.

Bree found her brother up a ladder, rifling through a stack of rolled parchments on the top of one of the high oaken bookshelves that lined the huge space.

"Greetings, Gil," she said with a breeziness she didn't feel.

He stilled at the sound of her voice before casting a narrow-eyed look down at her. "Bree," he replied coolly. "Back so soon?"

"That's right." She held up the ewer and goblets, even as she noted the tremor in her hands. "Care to celebrate with me?" Her chest clenched then. She had little to celebrate this afternoon, save avoiding the pit, although here she was pretending otherwise.

Gil's tawny eyebrows drew together. "What … *now?*"

"Aye … we should hurry up though" —Shades, it was hard keeping her mask in place— "you don't want the wine to get warm."

Nearby, grey-robed males and females cast the queen's assassin censorious looks. Meanwhile, Gil wore a pained expression as he slid down the ladder and turned to face her. "We don't drink or eat down here," he told her sternly.

She forced a brittle smile. "In that case, take a break and we'll have our drinks upstairs."

A short while later, brother and sister sat on the terrace outside Gil's quarters. The mid-afternoon light was dazzling, and kites wheeled across the cloudless arch of the sky. From here, they had a view east over the meadows that stretched down to a glittering estuary. The scene was lovely, yet Bree barely noticed it.

Fidgeting, she crossed and uncrossed her legs, trying to get comfortable in her seat. Brilliant sunshine reflected off the white stone, and her eyes smarted as she poured the wine. "Iron," she muttered. "Everything is so bright."

Gil gave a soft snort. "Compared to Albia, you mean?" He screwed up his face then. "That foul place."

It isn't as awful as you think, she corrected him silently. *Aye, Albia is grey and misty, yet it has a beauty that steals your soul.* However, she said none of this. There were some things her brother wouldn't understand.

Bree still couldn't relax. Her booted foot kicked rhythmically against a table leg.

Meanwhile, Gil observed her, his expression wary.

She didn't blame him. As younglings, she'd been protective of her younger brother, but with the passing of the years, and the centuries, he'd grown wary of her. He hadn't approved of her choice of profession, and she'd sneered at his lowly one. Fellshadows were warriors. *Violence* was in his blood, not scholarly pursuits. She wasn't sneering now though. It surprised her to realize that three turns of the moon apart from Gil—living amongst the Marav—had made her view him in a different light. He wasn't weak, just different from her.

Picking up her goblet, she held it aloft. Shades, she wished her hands would steady. "To surviving Duncrag."

Still eyeing her as if a powrie had just leaped over his balcony and was sitting across the table from him, Gil lifted his own goblet. "I thought the queen wanted you to stay a while?"

"She did … and she's not happy to see me back … but the situation took a turn, and I had to leave."

He raised an eyebrow. "The chief-enforcer wasn't charming then?"

"No," she replied quietly, even as her stomach twisted. Every time she thought of Cailean—and the last time she'd seen him—it felt as if someone had kicked her in the guts.

"I heard about the attack you warned us of … you saved many lives," her brother said after a pause. "Everyone in Caisteal Gealaich is talking about it."

Bree nodded, even as queasiness washed over her. *And condemned many Marav to death.* Of course, Gil wouldn't care about that. And she shouldn't either. But curse her, she did. She cared about many things that had once left her cold. "Aye, but Mor was tempted to throw me to the wyrm, all the same," she replied huskily. "I think I'll lie low for a while."

He grimaced at this and took a sip of wine.

She followed suit, sighing at the crisp sweetness. She then raised the goblet to her lips again and took a deep draft. Damn it, she needed something to take the edge off. She was aware then that her brother was watching her steadily, his golden eyes—the same hue as her own, with slitted cat-like pupils that were so different from those of the Marav—slightly narrowed.

"You're on edge," he observed after a beat.

She snorted, even as anxiety fluttered through her. "Aye … well, it wasn't an easy job, and I've just weathered Mor's wrath."

"It's more than that though," he replied, his gaze drilling into her. "What happened to you in Albia?"

She took another gulp of wine, welcoming the warmth that pooled in her belly. "Maybe I was humbled."

He huffed a laugh. "You?"

"Aye … me."

"What was it like … living among the enemy?"

"Difficult," she replied, before adding. "And surprising." Nerves fluttered once more. She couldn't open up to her brother. No one here could discover her shame.

His eyebrows lifted, encouraging her to continue.

"They're irrational, flawed, and overly emotional compared to us," she continued, aware of her brother's rapt attention. "Their lives pitifully short." She shrugged, desperate to end this conversation now. "But maybe that's what makes them live more intensely than we do."

He inclined his head. "An interesting view." He leaned back in his chair, stretching his long legs under the table as he swirled his apple wine before him. "I never thought about it that way … and yet, it makes sense. When you live as long as we do, you must guard your emotions or you'll burn yourself out, like a candle that flares too bright."

"Perhaps," she replied, wishing they could talk about something else. Anxiety was flapping like a caged raven under her ribs now. If Gil ever learned what she'd done—that she'd warned the chief-enforcer of the coming counterattack and saved his life—he'd look at her in an entirely different light.

Some secrets were too dangerous to share.

Silence fell between brother and sister. A sweet, musky scent, from the roses that climbed the walls of Caisteal Gealaich, wafted over the terrace then, and Bree drew the perfume deep into her lungs. It was the smell of Sheehallion. She'd missed it over the past moons, and yet it couldn't unravel the tangle inside her.

"There's definitely something amiss with you," Gil said eventually. "Ever since we came up here, you can't seem to sit still."

Bree stopped kicking her foot against the table leg and cut him a frown. "There's nothing wrong," she lied, even as her pulse leaped into a gallop. She'd thought seeing her brother again would settle her—but she wasn't in a fit state to converse with anyone right now. She was a twisted, knotted mess.

Gil's tawny eyes glinted. "If you say so."

4: CAST ASIDE

Two moons later …

SWEAT RAN DOWN Bree's back as she went through her drills. Blades out, she sliced at the air, swiveled, and high-kicked with her right leg. She then repeated the drill but led with her left leg this time. These daily training sessions, atop the castle walls, kept her sane. She pushed herself until her muscles trembled from fatigue, until her lungs burned from the exertion.

Until she stopped thinking.

And she'd reached that point now. Breast rising and falling sharply, Bree halted, sheathed her knives, and staggered across to one of the merlons that ringed the training terrace. She always chose this time of day—while most of the inhabitants of Caisteal Gealaich were consuming their noon meal—for she usually had this space to herself. A soft, rose-scented breeze feathered her skin as she leaned against the merlon.

The stone was warm from the sun, and for a few moments, she closed her eyes. The thud of her heart in her ears was nearly deafening, but after a while, it eased. Eventually, she opened her eyes once more and pushed herself upright.

And then she surveyed the army amassing beneath the fortress.

Steel scale armor glittered in the bright noon sun, gold and silver cloaks fluttering in the breeze. Even from up here, she spied the long hunting daggers, swords, and pikes the warriors who moved around the camp sported. Their steeds—elks, and stags—pawed the ground and bellowed at each other.

Bree's chest started to ache then, not from over-exertion this time though, and she lifted a hand to rub at her breastbone. Her ribs felt as if an anvil sat upon them.

Muttering an oath, she dragged her other hand over her face. She'd hoped her longing for Cailean might fade. But it hadn't.

Mor hadn't called for her again since her return, and in the meantime, Bree had kept herself busy: training until she nearly dropped, and then taking Tivesheh out on long rides in-between, where she'd try to outrun herself.

She never managed to do so though.

Meanwhile, her people were readying themselves for war, and the Marav would likely be doing the same. No one told her anything these days, but she had eyes—and she'd watched over the past two turns of the moon as warriors poured in from every corner of the realm. The Raven Queen had raised *The Tannith*— the Shee call to battle.

Mor had said Talorc mac Brude would pay for his long campaign against their people, and it seemed he would. Over two centuries had passed since the Marav and the Shee had locked blades in open battle—a war that had claimed the lives of both Bree's parents. Since then, she'd watched relations worsen between the two races once more, waiting for the tipping point.

It had now arrived.

And Cailean will be in the midst of it.

Queasiness rose then. Aye, he'd be in the Marav front line.

Enforcers were deadly—and the High King had spent years readying himself for this battle—but Mor was gathering a huge force too.

As formidable as he was, it was likely Cailean wouldn't survive the coming conflict, especially with so few enforcers left now. And all the while, she was stuck here. Useless. Cast aside. Split between two worlds.

It galled her that she was unable to stop this, unable to save him.

"It's been a while, Bree."

She turned from the wall to see a tall, lithe male with long pale hair, clad all in black, emerge from the stairwell behind her.

Halting, Captain Frostshard sketched a mocking bow.

Bree fought the impulse to scowl. Crossing paths with Gavyn reminded her how little she cared about her ruined career. She never wanted to kill for Mor again. "Aye," she replied coolly, trying to ignore the glint in her former lover's storm-grey eyes. "I've been busy."

He raised an eyebrow. "Doing what, exactly?"

Bree pursed her lips, refusing to take the bait. She didn't want to talk about herself. "That's quite an army down there," she replied casually, gesturing to the view.

"It is."

"She must be readying herself for an attack?"

He shrugged. "It'll come soon enough."

Pretending his deliberate vagueness didn't vex her, Bree mirrored him with a shrug of her own. "Which barrows will you go through to enter Albia?"

A beat of silence followed this question. She'd asked it with an offhand tone, as if she didn't care about the answer. However, the truth was she *burned* to know.

She checked herself then. *What will you do with such knowledge? Warn Cailean?* Her pulse quickened. *Maybe.*

Gavyn's gaze sharpened. "Such details are reserved … for those in our queen's inner circle."

"What … you can't share them with *me?*" She flashed him a smile, hoping it would soften him. He'd cared for her once; surely, a spark of that old affection remained.

Unfortunately, he was unmoved. "No."

An awkward silence followed. Heat ignited in her belly, her temper rising.

Curse them all. She'd helped Mor. She'd risked her neck to give the Raven Queen what she needed so she could surprise the Marav in The Uplands, so they could ambush them at Dunmorth Barrow. She'd had victories because of Bree. But because her spy had disobeyed orders and come home instead of lingering at Duncrag and putting herself in even greater danger, Mor had now shut her out.

The rejection was galling, humiliating, and bitterness flooded her mouth.

"You've finished with the terrace, I take it?" Gavyn asked then.

"Aye," she replied between gritted teeth, her gut burning.

"Good." He crossed to the center of the space and began a series of stretches. He moved with the loose-limbed, supple grace that only Shee possessed.

Bree didn't shift from her spot by the merlon, and eventually, Gavyn glanced at her over his shoulder. "Don't mind me," he said with a half-smile that made her want to punch him in the mouth. "Why don't you move along now … and get on with your busy day?"

A golden gloaming was settling over the world when Bree sought out her brother.

Usually, when each interminable day ended, she retreated to her tower and soaked up to the chin in a hot bath to ease her sore muscles, a ewer of ice-cold wine within easy reach. But today, she broke with routine.

She found Gil with the other archivists, taking their seats in the dining hall on the lowest level of the fortress, where the lesser-ranking individuals at Caisteal Gealaich ate their meals.

Her arrival drew stares.

Ignoring them, she strode toward Gil's table.

The archivists seated with him saw her coming and leaped up as if scalded, moving to another table. Meanwhile, Bree slid onto the bench seat opposite her brother.

Gil's raised tawny eyebrows. "You're popular these days."

She pulled a face. "Don't start."

He smirked. "If I want some time on my own … I just need to invite my sister to supper."

"You didn't invite me."

"No, I didn't."

Their gazes met, the moment drawing out as servants appeared bearing platters of soup, cheese, and bread. Since her return to Caisteal Gealaich, she and her brother hadn't spent much time together. It wasn't as if she didn't have a lot of time on her hands. However, Gil had a way of probing into things best left alone.

Her emotions were close enough to the surface these days without him stirring her up. Nonetheless, this evening, she wished to talk to him.

Maybe he knew what Mor was planning.

Gil broke their stare first, picking up a ewer and filling the empty goblet in front of Bree. "Mor still hasn't called for you, I take it?"

"No."

"Just give her time … our queen's focus is elsewhere at present."

A female servant placed a tray in front of Bree before darting away. Glancing back at her brother, she found him watching her.

"So, to what do I owe this visit?" he asked finally.

Frowning, she helped herself to a bread roll, ripped a piece off, and dipped it into the soup. "Aren't I allowed to look in on my little brother?"

Gil raised an eyebrow, his expression easy to read. *You never cared before.*

Popping the bread in her mouth, Bree chewed and swallowed; these days, she ate more out of habit than enjoyment. "Have you heard any whispers about what Mor's up to?" she asked finally.

To her disappointment, her brother shook his head. "Archivists are always the last to know."

"No word has reached you about when and where the attack will come?"

His features tightened. "None."

Curse it. Swallowing her frustration, Bree hurriedly veiled her expression, for Gil was giving her one of his penetrating looks.

Around them, conversation filled the cavernous dining hall. Nonetheless, she caught the sidelong glances and whispers of those nearby. Having the Raven Queen's 'shamed' assassin join them was indeed causing a stir. She ignored them.

"What will you do now?" Gil asked, still observing her over the rim of his goblet.

Bree's belly clenched, and she cut her gaze away. "I don't know," she admitted softly.

Shades, she'd once been so sure of herself, so secure of her place in the world. Yet now, she was adrift and battling with a longing that threatened to drag her down, like an aughisky—a vicious water spirit—into the depths of a deep, dark loch.

"But you can't linger here forever, hoping Mor will forgive you."

"I know." Steeling herself, she looked at him then, her skin prickling under the directness of his stare. "But where would I go? I gave my life to serving my queen, to killing for her. Who am I, if I'm not her assassin?"

5: PINING

GIL'S EXPRESSION SOBERED at his sister's admission. "Shades," he murmured. "I didn't realize you were so unhappy."

Bree's fingers clenched around the stem of her goblet. "Aye, well … I'm not in the habit of showing my underbelly to anyone."

He gave his head a rueful shake. "I can't believe you are now."

Bree swallowed. "You've all I've got, Gil … and let's face it … we aren't close."

Aye, that was the truth of it. Three centuries she'd lived, and a strained relationship with her brother was all she had to show for it.

And a broken marriage to the chief-enforcer.

Her throat constricted painfully.

Shit. Maybe it wasn't a good idea to speak about how she was faring. She was in danger of losing her hard-won control.

But now that she'd started talking to her brother, she couldn't hold back the tide. "Ever since I came home, I feel as if I don't belong here any longer." She broke off there, pushing aside her bowl of soup. "Living in Albia changed me … and I don't know what to do about it."

"There *is* something up with you." Gil's tawny eyes narrowed. "If I didn't know better, I'd think you were *pining*."

Bree's heart started to pound. Iron flay her, how had he guessed?

Her brother shook his head ruefully, before taking what looked like a fortifying gulp of apple wine and fixing her with a level stare. "Come on then … you might as well be frank with me."

Dizziness swept over her. "I've got nothing to say," she whispered.

He snorted. "Don't make me pry it out of you."

"There's nothing—"

"It's the chief-enforcer isn't it," he cut her off, his patience faltering. "You've *bonded* with him."

The dining hall wheeled around Bree, and she gripped the edge of the table to steady herself. "No." Her voice was unnaturally high and panicked.

"Aye, you have. There's no point in lying to me … it's now written all over your face."

"Iron," she gasped. "Please, tell me it isn't."

Her brother's silence was damning. "Ancestors, Bree," he said eventually. "What have you done?"

The sweat that bathed her body chilled.

If only he knew.

Silence fell between them, while the rumble of conversation ebbed and flowed like surf upon a shingle shore around them.

Their exchange had turned treasonous. Fortunately for her, none of the other archivists were sitting close enough to overhear. "I didn't mean to," she whispered. "I couldn't stand him at first … but then, somehow, with the passing of the days, and the turns of the moon … things changed."

Dizziness assailed Bree once more. She couldn't believe she was admitting this.

Gil had gone silent again. Bree's admission made her feel sick. It was foolish to be this vulnerable.

Flexing her fingers around the stem of her goblet, she slowed her breathing and waited for his anger to splinter the heavy silence that now swelled between them. But Gil didn't speak, and finally, she cleared her throat. "Will you tell the queen?"

Her brother's mouth thinned. A moment later, he folded his arms across his chest. "No."

"Why not?"

His eyebrows drew together. "Is your opinion of me really that low?"

She stared back at him, nausea churning in her gut.

Gil muttered a curse under his breath and pushed himself up from the bench seat, rising to his full height. His grey robes made him look older, more censorious. For the first time, he reminded her of their father. "We're blood, Bree," he replied. Leaning forward, his gaze seized hers. "Do you think I want my sister thrown to the wyrm?"

She stared back at him. "But I've done something unforgivable," she said huskily. "I've fallen for a man who has hunted and killed countless Shee. You should hate me."

Gil raked a hand through his mane of golden hair. He abruptly sat down once more, another oath gusting out of him. And then, to her surprise, he reached out and caught her hand, gripping it tightly in his. "Of course, I don't," he muttered before grimacing. "However, I *do* question your taste."

Alone in her tower, watching as the sun slid behind the mountains to the west, the sky ablaze, Bree waged a silent battle—with herself.

Confiding in Gil had been idiotic.

Aye, she pined for the man she'd left behind. Knowing that Cailean lived and breathed on the other side of the veil, where she couldn't reach out and touch him, was slowly breaking her apart. How she longed to hear his voice, to watch him eat supper while they bantered. How she yearned to see her husband stalk across the yard before Duncrag broch, Skaal at his side, to watch shadow and light chase each other in his eyes.

But admitting it to herself was one thing—telling her brother was another.

She was losing her mind.

Leaning her palms upon the windowsill, she continued to stare at the fiery sunset.

Gil had surprised her earlier. His reaction to her shame revealed that he was a better person than she would ever be. And he was loyal. More loyal than she deserved.

Throat tight, she dragged her gaze from the sky, lowering it to the meadows far below her tower, to the swathe of pavilions.

She didn't know when the army would mobilize, but surely it would be soon.

Her breathing grew shallow.

I must be with him.

Bree's fingertips dug into the slippery moonstone ledge. And as the heavens faded to indigo and then black, the hearths on the meadow below glowing like fireflies, she let her choice settle deep into her bones.

And it felt right.

She'd been wrestling with the decision for a while now. She could tell herself that she had to warn Cailean, yet the news she'd bring to Duncrag wouldn't surprise her husband. He knew about the brewing conflict between the Marav and the Shee.

The truth was, they had little time left, for soon war would sweep across Albia. But she'd take whatever The Great Raven gave them.

She'd see him again, even if it was the death of her.

A heady mix of hope and despair wrapped itself around her chest as she turned from the window and went to the table where her large collection of steel blades lay. Deftly, she strapped them on.

Despite that she hadn't worked since her return to Sheehallion, she wore her hunting leathers and high boots. As she trained daily, these were the garments she'd always been the most comfortable in. Readying herself took just moments, for Bree was used to traveling light. Before leaving her chamber, she cast a cloak around her shoulders—Fia's blue mantle—and grabbed her quiver and bow.

And then, without a backward glance at the chamber that had been her home for the best part of two centuries, Bree departed. She descended the thousand steps from her quarters before stalking through a network of corridors and exiting the keep.

Outdoors, standing within the inner ward, she breathed in the sweet, balmy air.

Nearby, guards stood rigidly to attention. However, they ignored her.

The irony wasn't lost on Bree. Ever since her return, she'd chafed at being treated like a ghost. But now, the fact that no one cared where she went or what she did made it even easier to slip away.

Not halting to consider her choices, she strode under an archway into the outer ward.

More guards stood before the closed gates, their scale armor gleaming silver in the moonlight.

"Let me out," Bree ordered as she approached.

The guards both regarded her frostily before sharing a long look.

Watching them, she bristled. It was an effort not to let her hand stray to the pommel of her longsword, to issue a silent warning to them. She might no longer kill for the Raven Queen, but these two would mind her.

Moments passed, and then, reluctantly, the guards moved, opening the gates just wide enough for Bree to slip through. She did so without thanking them, stalking down the causeway beyond. To her right spread the meadows, where a sea of tents, the smoke from cookfires blurring the night sky like mist, lay.

Bree whistled. The sound, high and shrill, carried through the balmy night air.

And then she waited.

Her heart was racing now, yet every sense was sharp, and the heaviness that had dogged her steps for the past two moons lifted. Her belly now pitched as if she were on the deck of a ship in high seas. She couldn't believe she was doing this—that she was walking away from her home. Her people.

All to be with one of the hated Marav.

If Mor discovered where she'd gone—and she likely would, for the Raven Queen had eyes everywhere—she'd put a price on her head.

Was she ready for this?

Bree glanced over her shoulder at where Caisteal Gealaich's curtain wall reared above her.

Aye, she was.

Worry fluttered up then like a sack of released moths. *What about Gil?*

Her gaze continued to linger upon the great fortress where she'd lived for most of her three hundred years. Surely, Mor wouldn't punish him for her misdeeds? Gil was a talented archivist. She wanted to say goodbye to him, but there was no time.

It was safer though, for her to leave without Gil knowing, as Mor would question him.

Tensing, Bree turned away from the walls. Urgency coiled in her belly. She had to leave. Now.

A pale shape appeared ahead then, emerging from the darkness. A great white stag.

Relief weakened her limbs. *Tiv.* Her mind touched his. *Are you ready for another adventure?*

Always.

Are you sure? This one will take us into Albia ... and we won't be returning.

Tivesheh drew up before her and dipped his large head. *I will take you wherever you wish.*

A lump rose in her throat. Stroking his nose, she swallowed. Tivesheh had been her faithful companion on so many journeys. Once they crossed into Albia, they'd depend on each other for survival.

Vaulting up onto his back, she nudged him gently with her heels, making her urgency clear. *We ride for Golval Barrow … fast.*

Tivesheh pivoted on his haunches and leaped forward into the darkness. An instant later, they were bounding northwest, away from Caisteal Gealaich.

6: RETURN TO DUNCRAG

THEY REACHED GOLVAL Barrow just as dawn was breaking. Drawing her stag up in front of the large grassy mound that rose before a stand of sycamores, Bree glanced nervously over her shoulder.

She shouldn't worry yet—for Mor hadn't placed any restrictions on her movements and was focused on preparing for war at present—although she was on edge, all the same.

Sliding down from Tivesheh's back, Bree cast her gaze around the barrow. As always, her skin prickled at being so close to one of the portals that bridged the veil between this realm and Albia. A faint buzzing sound filled her ears.

Are you ready, Tiv?

The stag snorted, letting her know that he was.

Placing a hand upon his warm, damp neck, she moved forward. *Follow me then.*

They hadn't often traveled through the veil together over the years, for most of Bree's marks had been in Sheehallion.

However, there had been a male—one of Mor's servants, who'd tried to poison her—whom she'd hunted in Albia. The servant had been working for Mor's brother Grae.

Vyan, that had been his name. He'd begged for mercy in the end but hadn't received any.

Bree's mouth thinned. Some memories were best not dwelt upon.

She strode toward the barrow's entrance, a stone archway that was just big enough for Tivesheh to follow her through. It was a bottleneck—and one that only admitted travelers at dusk and dawn. Indeed, when Mor's army was ready, it would take a while for all the warriors and their beasts to travel through the portals their queen chose.

Entering the barrow, Bree breathed in the damp, musty air before whispering, "Sleeping dead, let us pass. We tread lightly."

And her people did. The Shee walked in long, gliding steps and could blend with the shadows when it suited them—an ability that would come in useful when she emerged in Albia.

Nonetheless, the fine hair on the backs of her arms prickled as she walked along the passage that led through the heart of the barrow. The dawn light only reached inside a few feet, and after that, the darkness was impenetrable. It was always tempting to bring a torch, to light the way, but that was ill-advised.

The wights that dwelled here didn't like to be disturbed. Aye, they suffered the Shee passing through their resting place— whereas none of the Marav with their heavy tread, bright torches, and rough voices had ever managed it. These barrows, tombs of the Ancients, resisted druidic magic too, something else that kept the Marav away.

The buzzing in Bree's ears increased, the deeper she walked into the barrow. It wasn't a pleasant sensation, yet it wasn't like when she'd passed through The Ring of Caith. That had been painful, especially on the second occasion.

Her boots whispered on smooth stone as she walked, and the air became ice-cold. Behind her, the gentle thud of Tivesheh's hooves broke the silence, and the hot blast of his breathing feathered across the back of her neck.

Bree touched his mind. *Just a little longer.*

The dead are waking up.

Aye, but they won't touch us.

Around her, the hiss and wheeze of labored breathing filled the darkness, followed by the rattle of bones.

"Sleeping dead, let us pass," Bree murmured once more. "We tread lightly."

She kept walking, ignoring the thin whispers that now echoed against the stone, and gradually the chill of the tomb eased. And then, up ahead, light beckoned.

Bree quickened her pace, hurrying toward it, and moments later, she emerged into a grey Albian morning.

Mist wreathed through the surrounding oaks and elms, which were all losing their leaves, and the clouds hung low overhead. Wonder wreathed up as she cast her gaze around, taking in the fiery cloaks of gold, bronze, and red the trees wore this time of year.

It struck her then that she'd never ventured into Albia in this season.

Gateway, the Marav celebration that heralded the start of winter, was no more than a moon's turn away now. Behind the barrow, she spied the dark waters of Loch Caith. Tivesheh drew up next to her and tossed his head, clearly relieved to leave the suffocating darkness of the barrow behind.

Raising her face to the soft rain, Bree's breathing hitched. A savage joy twisted deep inside her chest.

I'm back.

Her time away from Albia had felt like an eternity. She was now breathing the same air as Cailean mac Brochan, and just three days' journey away from setting eyes on him again.

Bree's breathing quickened, anticipation drawing a tight knot in her stomach.

Cailean was in there. *So close now.* Shades, she *ached* to see him again.

Sitting astride Tivesheh, she looked up at the broch perched at the summit of the promontory. Made of stacked stone, windowless, and shaped like a beehive, Duncrag cast a shadow over the surrounding hills.

But things weren't as she'd expected at Albia's capital—for a large army, one that equaled the size of that before Caisteal Gealaich—camped on the hills outside the fort.

The knots in her belly twisted.

Mor hadn't been the only one making plans. The High King had also been busy. *Both* sides were preparing for imminent war.

Talorc mac Brude had reacted swiftly when he'd learned that the warband he'd sent north—to slaughter his enemies—had been massacred. That the heir to his throne was dead. Over the moons Bree had resided in this fort, she'd marked the High King's complex relationship with his only son—both close and combative.

She wouldn't have been surprised if grief, and an intricate web of guilt, had added fuel to the need for revenge.

Bree's brow furrowed. She had no sympathy for the High King of Albia. After all, he'd persecuted her people for years—and if the bastard had his way, the Shee would be banished from this realm forever.

And yet, you've fallen for his right hand. Something twisted deep in her chest. Aye, she had, and she wasn't sorry.

It was early morning, not long before sunrise. Ever since leaving Golval Barrow, she had been careful. They'd traveled swiftly, but once they left The Uplands behind and entered the lowland area known as The Wolds, she'd slept during the day and journeyed at night.

It was safer to travel shrouded by darkness, for a white stag with a rider would only draw unwanted attention. The Marav didn't ride stags and elk as her people did. As one of the Marav, she'd have been cautious of traveling after nightfall, for that was when the most dangerous of the faery creatures roamed. But as one of the Shee, they left her alone.

Sliding down from Tivesheh, Bree glanced around. She'd deliberately stopped a safe distance from the fort, on the edge of a birchwood. They were far enough away from the tents that spread out beneath Duncrag. Nonetheless, she'd been cautious. Amongst the silvery trunks of the trees, she caught sight of flickering lights.

Corpse candles, spirits that drew the unwary into bogs and swamps.

But as a Shee, she was impervious to them. The sight of the golden flames reminded her of just how much had changed since the last time she'd been here. It felt odd to be standing before Duncrag once more—this time, in her real form.

Her chest tightened as she considered her situation.

She was a Shee female in the heart of the Realm of Albia. The last time she'd entered Duncrag, she'd been one of the Marav. But she hadn't traveled through the stones on this journey. She couldn't have anyway—for they only allowed her kind to pass through at equinoxes and solstices—even if she'd wanted to, which she didn't.

She was stronger and faster as a Shee, and yet there was a part of her that quailed at the thought of meeting her husband again.

Suddenly, Bree was unsure of herself.

What if he prefers my Marav form? The woman he'd married was shorter and curvier—comely, but not as beautiful as she was now, in her opinion. Once, Bree's lip would have curled at having to compete with one of the Marav, yet it felt strange to compete with … herself.

Shaking herself free of confusing, and troubling, thoughts, she turned to her stag then and patted his shoulder. *I don't know how long I'll be.*

It doesn't matter … I'll be waiting.

Her heart kicked hard then. Duncrag loomed before her; she needed a plan. There was a good chance Cailean wouldn't be pleased to see her—especially after returning to The Hallow Woods that morning only to find his warband slaughtered.

He likely thought she'd deceived him.

Misgiving tightened her chest. Aye, she had to tread carefully here.

The High King couldn't know she'd returned either, for she'd departed suddenly and left three dead bodies behind her. And if mac Brude had been cruel before the death of his son, he'd be vicious now.

Mastering her nerves, Bree moved to Tivesheh's head and ran an affectionate hand down his long face. As always, she was loath to be parted from her stag. *Hide yourself in the trees. I will whistle if you're needed.* She paused then. *But if I don't reappear within a turn of the moon, you are to make for Golval Barrow … and return home.*

Tivesheh dipped his head, acknowledging her.

7: A MEETING AT MARKET

BREE STEPPED BACK from her stag, watching as he moved off into the trees. Then she turned, her gaze traveling east, where the sky was lightening behind the broch. The serrated edges of the Shiel Range, the mountains that thrust up to the north, weren't yet snow-capped, although the Sharp Billed Wind that gusted in from those peaks bit into her cheeks.

Shivering, she pulled her cloak close. Then, jaw set in determination, she headed down the hill toward the tents that barred the way into the fort.

Before she reached them, she flicked her fingers at her side, glamoring herself as a tall woman with straw-colored hair and a long, plain face—a stranger that no one here would recognize. She pulled her cloak tighter still around her, to disguise the sword and the dagger she carried, and rounded her shoulders to make herself look beaten down by life.

She was fortunate this morning, for it was Market Day. A crowd of farmers and merchants was making its way inside

Duncrag along the road that cut through the camped army. Once a moon, the fort held a bustling market that attracted vendors from the outlying villages.

Her timing was a stroke of luck, indeed, for Princess Lara usually ventured beyond the high walls encircling the broch on Market Day. If Bree could get close enough, she could plead with her to arrange a meeting with Cailean. It would be safer than trying to get inside the broch.

Bree's pulse quickened then. Lara would be wary of her now—after her mysterious disappearance in the summer—but she was also a friend. If she was still living at Duncrag, she'd help her. Of course, Lara was betrothed to King Dunchadh of Braewall and their handfasting would be looming.

Weaving through the press of tents, Bree noted the standards bearing the different sigils of Albia's kingdoms. Amongst the High King's wolf's head banner were those bearing a leaping black stag and an iron shield: Braewall and Baldeen.

Warriors gathered outside hide pavilions, some warming their hands over fires while others handed out wooden bowls of porridge.

A couple of them glanced Bree's way, but they quickly lost interest.

She swallowed a smile.

Good. Her glamor had been well-chosen.

Taking care to make her stride less fluid, her step heavier, she followed the crowd of vendors through the gates. What a difference a few turns of the moon made. The first time she'd entered this fort, she'd been impersonating a demure young woman schooled to become the perfect wife and had been paraded up to the broch to meet her future husband. But today, she slipped inside the fort unnoticed. Her current guise was one she was more comfortable with, for, as an assassin, she was used to blending with the shadows.

Bree made her way across the dirt-packed square, where a lass threw grain for a gaggle of honking geese and a group of rough-featured warriors stood in a knot, arguing. She recognized these men; they were all members of the Fort Guard.

Ignoring their disagreement, she headed up The Thoroughfare, past the open doorways of the forges. The stench of hot iron wafted across the wide road, and she stumbled, slapping a hand over her mouth.

Ancestors, the reek of it stuck in her throat and made her eyes water.

She'd have to keep her distance from it.

She spied Mirren first—a small woman with a riot of curly peat-brown hair and sky-blue eyes, weaving through the crowd.

Her breath catching, Bree resisted the urge to push her hood back and call out to her. Shades, she'd missed Mirren. They'd gone through much together during Bree's stay at Duncrag.

But to draw attention to herself now would be idiotic.

She reminded herself then that she no longer looked like Fia, the chief-enforcer's estranged wife. Mirren wouldn't recognize her.

Bree's attention shifted to the regal, auburn-haired woman in an emerald fur-lined cloak, who walked just ahead of Mirren. Lara stopped to survey the wares of a leather merchant—coin purses, belts, and gloves—on display. The vendor, delighted to have caught the princess's attention, fawned and smiled.

However, Lara didn't smile back.

Watching her heart-shaped face, Bree frowned. The princess loved Market Day, and on the occasions when she had accompanied her, Lara's eyes had shone with excitement, her mouth curved into an easy smile. But even from yards away, her tension, her shadowed mood, was evident.

Bree's belly tightened. Lara would still be grieving her brother. How would she react if she knew her friend was responsible for his death? Her heart started to pound as she imagined hate darkening Lara's pine-green eyes.

As always, four of the Fort Guard shadowed the princess and her maid. Stern-faced men with domed iron helmets, they walked a few feet behind Lara, hands upon the pommel of their swords.

Wary of them, Bree pulled the edge of her hood lower and edged closer.

The women had stopped before a jewelry stall now, and Lara had picked up a jade brooch.

Seizing her opportunity, Bree sidled alongside, pretending to peruse the wares as well. Then, closing her eyes, she summoned an image of what she'd looked like as Fia—a woman with lush curves and gentle features, with knowing hazel eyes, long oaken-colored hair, pale skin, and a scattering of freckles across the bridge of her nose.

She then flicked her fingers gently at her sides.

A shiver passed over her as her guise changed.

It was dangerous to take this form, for Fia mac Callum wasn't welcome at Duncrag any longer, but it was necessary. Lara and Mirren wouldn't talk to her otherwise. Of course, there was the risk that her friends would betray her, yet she had to hope they wouldn't.

Halting just two feet from the princess, Bree's gaze went to the green brooch she was now holding up to the light. Drawing in a deep breath, Bree pushed back her hood just a little so that her shadowed face was visible.

"A fine choice, Your Highness," she murmured. "It will match your eyes."

Lara's gaze snapped to her.

Their eyes met, and shock rippled over the princess's pale face. Relief swiftly followed. "Fia," she breathed, warmth igniting in her eyes. "What are—"

"Careful, princess." Bree edged close, bowing her head as she pretended to examine a pair of amber earrings. "I shouldn't be here."

A heavy pause followed, and when Lara replied, the joy in her voice was tempered. "No … you shouldn't." She put down the brooch and reached for the earrings Bree was staring at. Picking them up, she then exclaimed. "Aren't these lovely?"

"Aye, Your Highness," Mirren replied, oblivious to whom the princess had just met. "Honey-colored amber … the same color as your handfasting tunic."

"Thank you, Mirren," Lara muttered, "as if I need reminding."

"You're not yet wed to King Dunchadh then?" Bree asked.

"No," Lara replied, a nerve flickering in her cheek. "The ceremony is tomorrow." Her brow furrowed then, and she leaned closer. "Where have you been, Fia?" she whispered. "After you disappeared, I sent word to your parents in Braewall, but they said you never returned home." Her eyes narrowed then. "Two guards and a prisoner died on the day you disappeared … did you have anything to do with that?"

"I'll explain everything later," Bree replied, her own voice lowering urgently. "Right now, I—"

"Father has put a price on your head," Lara cut her off. "You need to get out of the fort … while you can."

"I can't," Bree whispered back. "I must see Cailean."

"Fia!" Mirren stepped in between the princess and Bree then, her voice choked. The handmaid's blue eyes glittered. "Is that you?"

Bree's heart leaped into her throat. "Aye," she muttered, even as the urge to enfold Mirren in a tight hug reared up. "But keep your voice down."

Ignoring her, Mirren clutched at her wrist. "Why—"

"Mirren!" The imperious edge to Lara's voice made the handmaid release Bree's arm as if scalded. The princess then picked up another pair of earrings and held them up, making a show of comparing them with the first ones. "What do you think?" she said loudly. "The dark or the light amber?"

"The light, Your Highness," Mirren replied, even as her gaze remained upon Bree's face. Her lips parted, her eyes burning with questions.

"The dark is beautiful too though," Bree added, playing along while casting Mirren a warning look. The lass had an impulsive nature that could get them all into trouble if not checked. All the same, warmth kindled deep in her chest.

Shades, this was almost like old times. She'd felt so alone over the past two moons without these women.

The guards had stopped a couple of yards back from the stall, and she could feel the weight of their stares upon her back. If she turned now, one of them was sure to recognize her.

"Can you arrange a meeting with my husband?" Bree asked, regaining her focus.

Both Lara and Mirren's faces changed then. Her heart lurched. Why were they staring at her like that? Why did pity shadow their gazes?

Moments slid by, and then Lara's throat bobbed. "I can't … he's dead."

Dead.

Bree's heart slammed hard against her ribs, and she grabbed the edge of the stall to steady herself. Suddenly, the world tilted, and a roaring began in her ears. "No," she croaked.

That couldn't be right. Cailean was supposed to be here.

Lara's fingers wrapped around her forearm, squeezing tightly. "I'm sorry … he fell in The Barrow Woods." The princess broke off there, her eyes gleaming. "My brother too."

"They all did," Mirren whispered. "When the warband didn't return, the High King eventually sent scouts north. There, they found nothing but the charred remains of the enforcers and warriors."

"Aye." Bitterness roughened Lara's voice then. "It appears that after the Shee massacred our men, they threw them onto a great pyre."

The roaring in Bree's ears dulled as realization dawned.

The Shee never burned their dead. The hills of Sheehallion were filled with grassy barrows; only the Marav built funeral pyres.

Her breathing grew shallow then. *Cailean* had burned those bodies. But after doing so, he hadn't returned to Duncrag as she'd thought.

Another wave of dizziness assailed her, and she placed her hand over Lara's, squeezing tightly.

Of course. She should have considered that, after being the sole survivor of a massacre, Cailean *couldn't* go back to Duncrag. The High King would have held him personally responsible.

But if he hadn't returned to the capital, where was he?

Hope burst through the fatalism that had dogged her steps since leaving Sheehallion. She'd told herself that Cailean would soon be taken from her. He was the High King's chief-enforcer, after all. But if he'd gone rogue, he wouldn't take part in the coming conflict.

He'd survive.

And she'd find him—even if she had to scour this realm from one end to the other.

Aye, he'd snarl at her initially. He'd likely blame her for ruining his life, yet she was tough enough to weather his anger. He'd recover from it, in time.

Instead, she had to remember the look in his eyes when they'd parted at The Ring of Caith, and the fact that he'd saved her life when he could have dragged her back to the High King.

He wanted her as much as she did him.

"Fia." Lara's husky voice drew her back to the present. She was aware that both the princess and her maid were watching her, their expressions stricken. "I'm so sorry."

Bree heaved in a deep breath. "Just give me a few moments," she replied, the catch in her voice unfeigned.

She became aware then that the jewelry vendor was staring at them, his expression expectant.

Clearing her throat, Lara raised her chin haughtily and thrust the two pairs of earrings at him. "I shall take both."

A delighted smile flowered across his face. "Of course, Your Highness. Six silver pennies, if you please."

With a snort, the princess dug into the coin purse at her waist. Usually, Lara would haggle, yet she was too distracted to do so today. The vendor took the coins eagerly and set about wrapping up her purchases.

Meanwhile, Lara glanced Bree's way once more. Her brow furrowed then. "You grieve him?"

"Aye."

Lara's expression turned searching. "If you care for Cailean … why did you run off?"

"I panicked."

Bree started to sweat, resisting the urge to glance over her shoulder at where the princess's escort still waited. Surely, they'd be getting suspicious now, wondering whom Lara was talking to in such a furtive tone.

Her throat constricted. Her friendship with Lara and Mirren was built on lies. If they knew who she really was, what she'd done, they'd run shrieking. They'd call for the guards to run the 'Shee fiend' through with their iron-tipped pikes. But Lara didn't know the truth, and so she watched Bree expectantly, waiting for her to elaborate.

Swallowing hard, Bree took a step back. Now she knew Cailean wasn't in Duncrag, urgency coiled in her chest. She had to find him. "I should go."

"Here, Your Highness. Many thanks for your custom!" The jewelry vendor handed Lara a neatly wrapped leather package.

The princess took it, although her gaze remained upon Bree's face.

Meanwhile, Mirren impulsively reached out and grasped Bree's hand tightly in hers.

Guilt twisted under her breastbone. Iron smite her, she didn't deserve the lass's kindness.

It was time to leave.

"Goodbye, Mirren." Her gaze then flicked to the princess. "Lara." She paused then. "Thank you both … for everything."

Her friend's gazes clouded in confusion. They didn't want her to go—instead, they wanted answers.

Gently, she extracted her hand from Mirren's. Then she pulled her hood down, shadowing her face once more. And, without giving either of them time to stop her, she slipped away into the crowd.

8: A BLESSING AND A BANE

Twenty days later …

"I DON'T WANT any trouble in here."

Cailean cut the big man with the stained apron an irritated glance before focusing on the mercenary seated at the long table in the ale-hall once more.

"The fight master," he growled. "Tell me what he looked like."

The mercenary—a wiry man with close-shaven black hair—curled his lip. "Give me another silver penny and I might."

Heat swept over Cailean, his temper rising swiftly. He didn't have time for this horseshit. He needed to know where Eilig was. The whoreson was a hard man to find. Years earlier, the fight master had been successful enough to have left a clear trail behind him. But these days, he'd turned into a ghost.

Cailean had started to wonder if Eilig was dead, when he'd learned a group of traveling fighters had stopped here at Rothie.

He was onto something, yet this greedy bastard had already taken two of his rapidly dwindling coins and told him little in return. After the first coin, he'd revealed that he'd indeed attended a fight and spoken to the man in charge. And after the second coin, he'd admitted that the fighters had all borne iron collars, which marked them as slaves.

His jet eyes gleamed now as he stared up at Cailean.

The mercenary could smell his desperation.

And he *was* desperate. He'd waited far too long to go after Eilig, although now he had, all he could think about was revenge. It kept him awake at night and drove him from fort to fort. This search was getting to him. He was tired, irritable, and sick of sleeping rough.

This mercenary had the information he needed. But unless he emptied his coin purse, the man wasn't talking. Finally, he had a lead, but this dog humper thought he could play with him.

He was out of patience.

Reaching out, Cailean knocked the wooden tankard out of the mercenary's hand. "You're not getting any more silver," he ground out. "Tell me what I want to know."

The amusement on the mercenary's face vanished, and he shoved himself up off the bench seat, unfolding his long, lean body. The man's movements had a fluidity that warned Cailean he was dangerous.

He didn't care.

It had been a while since he'd had a fight. Some violence might improve his mood, might release the anger that had simmered in his gut ever since he'd walked away from that pyre in The Hallow Woods. It might even clear the bitter taste that Bree Fellshadow had left in his mouth.

"Prick!" the mercenary snarled, reaching for the blade strapped to his thigh. "You'll buy me another drink."

"No fighting!" The proprietor of the ale-hall—a narrow, rectangular building lined with long tables, where men in oilskins drank and diced—bellowed. His meaty hand grasped Cailean's arm, but he shook him off.

Instead, he reached out, grabbed the mercenary by the collar of his vest, and hauled him into the aisle between the tables. He then grabbed the man's wrist, just as he went to draw his knife, and headbutted him in the face.

Reeling back, the mercenary lifted a hand to his bloodied nose. He went still then, his gaze narrowing. "You'll regret that, *enforcer.*"

Cailean favored him with a hard smile that showed his teeth as he flexed his hands at his sides. Aye, he was enjoying himself. Hopefully, this opponent would prove to be a worthy one. And after he'd spilled some blood, he'd get him to talk. "Will I?"

Of course, this man knew what he was—the tattoos that covered his arms and snaked up his neck made it hard for him to hide in a crowd. His size too, the muscle that he'd spent years putting on, marked him as a warrior-druid.

The men surrounding them were mostly locals: men who'd just finished work in the fields outside the fort or sold the last of their catches on the wooden docks below and were enjoying a cup of ale before going home to their wives. They scattered, clearing a space in the center of the ale-hall. Muttering followed as they started to lay bets.

"Enough!" the proprietor roared, wading in. "You won't—"

However, he never finished his sentence, for the mercenary whipped out the knife from its sheath upon his thigh and slashed it across the ale-hall owner's throat.

Eyes snapping wide, the big man staggered, his hands clasping where the blood now pumped out of his neck.

Cailean's mouth thinned, his anticipation of a good, bruising, fight shattering. "There wasn't any need for that," he growled. "Your problem was with me."

The mercenary's gaze glinted. "Aye … and it still is."

He struck then, his blade flashing for Cailean's throat.

Reeling back, he avoided the lethal move, even as he felt the whisper of the dagger blade, too close to his skin.

Cailean had enough iron strapped to his body to make a Shee warrior shriek, yet he didn't draw the dagger at his hip or one of the knives sheathed on the belt across his chest. If he did that, this maggot would be dead within moments.

And he needed him alive.

It was unfortunate that the only person he'd spoken to over the past three moons who had anything useful to tell him was a grasping mercenary with a vicious streak.

That couldn't be helped though.

Dodging another swipe of the gleaming blade, Cailean grabbed his opponent by his wrist and drove him backward. Violence ignited in his blood, the earth magic that slumbered there crying for release. He ignored it.

Grunting a curse, the mercenary reached for another dagger with his free hand, this one hanging from his belt, but Cailean drove his knee into his groin.

An agonized wheeze followed, but now wasn't the time to play fair. He was dealing with a killer, and he had to disable him if he was ever going to get what he needed.

Nonetheless, even with a broken nose and injured bollocks, the mercenary wasn't going down easily. Twisting out of Cailean's hold, he tried an eye gouge. In response, Cailean grabbed his wrists once more and gave him another, brutal, headbutt.

The two men toppled sideways onto one of the tables, sending earthen cups and trenchers flying.

The mercenary writhed and twisted under Cailean, harder to keep hold of than quicksilver. The Warrior's balls, it was like fighting an eel. Once again, earth magic surged in his veins. He could have called upon it, yet he was wary of doing so. Ever since leaving The Hallow Woods, he was aware that sacrificers were few and far between in The Uplands. There would be some in Cannich, but elsewhere, should he drain himself of The Warrior's strength, he likely wouldn't be able to replenish it through a blood-letting ceremony.

But, as the fight continued, and Cailean became dimly aware of the rough shouting outside the ale-hall that was gradually getting louder, his already stretched patience grew thinner still. Aye, given more time, he could best the mercenary—but time wasn't on his side. Soon, the local chieftain's warriors would interrupt them, and he'd never find out if Eilig had been in Rothie.

Heat and strength surged through his muscles, and suddenly, the man he fought was snarling curses at him, pinned hard to the tabletop.

His temper simmering, Cailean pushed his forearm, where the woad tattoos inked upon his skin now glowed silver, against the mercenary's windpipe. The man's dark eyes bulged, his fingers biting uselessly into Cailean's arm.

"The fight master," Cailean said between gritted teeth, out of patience. "Give me his description."

The mercenary struggled a little longer, but as his face started to turn purple, and his mouth gasped soundlessly, Cailean spied the fear in his eyes.

Lessening the pressure on his throat, Cailean allowed him to rasp his answer.

"Big. Short silver hair. Grey eyes. Walks with a bad limp."

A limp. Eilig hadn't been lame the last time he'd seen him. However, it had been a long time ago.

"Did he bear a scar?"

His opponent wheezed a curse, and Cailean applied pressure once more. Moments later, when he eased his arm off the mercenary's windpipe, the man's face had gone the color of liver.

"Aye," he choked. "A thin one … upon his left cheek."

Cailean's mouth tugged into a victory smile. Eilig was still alive, still traveling The Uplands with his band of slaves. And just a few days ago, he'd been here—which meant he'd catch up with him soon. Cailean's pulse quickened in anticipation.

Finally.

"One more question," he said, keeping a warning pressure on the mercenary's neck. The shouts and thunder of feet were louder now. At any moment, warriors would throw open the wattle door behind him and surge into the ale-hall. "Where did they go?"

"Go fuck your mother," the man croaked, his dark eyes glittering.

"Cease!" A deep, angry voice sliced through the ale-hall, and then an instant later, rough hands gripped hold of Cailean and yanked him off the mercenary.

Warriors clad in leather and fur, their faces grim, surrounded Cailean and his opponent.

Shrugging them off, Cailean raised his hands, palms exposed, in surrender. Then, meeting the eye of one of them—a massive brute with a shaven head—he nodded to where the mercenary rolled off the table and straightened up. The man's chest was heaving, yet his expression was murderous.

"He's the one you want," Cailean said calmly. "He sliced the ale-hall keeper across the throat without provocation."

The bald warrior eyed him, a blend of respect and suspicion in his eyes—a reaction Cailean was used to, for enforcers garnered a mix of responses from people. His gaze cut to where the dead man lay, face down upon the reed-strewn floor, and his mouth thinned. "So you say."

"It's true!" A man wearing an oilskin cape, one of the fisherfolk who lived outside the walls of the fort, stepped forward. He then pointed to Cailean's opponent. "He killed Iain. We all saw it."

The warriors converged on the mercenary then and dragged him from the hall.

Not without a fight though. The man's hoarse shouts of rage took a while to fade as the warriors hauled him up to the broch to face the chieftain's justice.

Glancing around, marking the mess he and the mercenary had made, Cailean's gaze then settled upon the dead ale-hall keeper.

His elation at getting the details he needed, and the hunger for reckoning that beat like a drum in his chest, faded. The strength that had pulsed through his veins drained away, weariness replacing it. A chill then settled into his bones.

Shit. That was unfortunate.

Cailean clenched his jaw, watching as his tattoos faded. It had been a few moons since his last blood-letting, when he and his wife shared blood under the full moon outside Duncrag. If he continued to draw upon his magic, he'd be disadvantaged in a fight against Eilig when he found him.

An enforcer's magic was both a blessing and a bane. Cailean was powerful indeed when his druidic magic was at its height, but vulnerable when it ebbed, for it was tied to his mortality. Without blood-letting, he'd eventually die.

Remembering the last blood-letting ritual, the sight of Fia's—no, *Bree's*—lovely face frosted by moonlight as they clasped hands, made his pulse quicken.

Anger surged then, blistering him.

The Gods damn her.

She'd worked him like a puppeteer, right until the end.

Over the past moons, he'd had too much time to think about that fateful night—and now he was certain that she'd *known* he'd spare her life, that he'd take her back to the stones and see her safely through. And while he lingered at The Ring of Caith, watching her go, her people had ambushed his camp back in The Hallow Woods.

She'd spared his life but doomed everyone else.

Don't think about her. With effort, he pushed thoughts of his Shee imposter wife aside, turned, and headed toward the door of the ale-hall.

After drawing so much attention to himself, it was time to disappear.

A crowd still lingered around the fringes of the space, whispering together and casting him wary looks. Aye, everyone would have seen the tattoos on his neck and arms glow as he'd fought the mercenary. Enforcers weren't a regular sight here, and the locals would be curious as well as wary. Another reason why he had to go.

On his way out, he noted a woman standing close to the wall. Wearing a blue cloak, she was tall and long-faced with straw-colored hair peeking out from under her hood. The woman's eyes gleamed shrewdly as she tracked his path.

Cailean's stride faltered. There was something oddly familiar about her—and yet he couldn't remember where their paths might have met.

It didn't matter though. He wasn't interested in pausing to find out.

Cutting the woman a warning scowl, he ducked under the door's low lintel and left the ale-hall behind him.

9: SHOW ME WHO YOU REALLY ARE

BREE'S HEART POUNDED as she watched Cailean mac Brochan leave.

Shades, the man had a glare sharper than an ax-blade.

He hadn't recognized her though, for she still bore the guise she'd adopted since Duncrag. It served her well. Her face was plain enough for men to leave her be, and her tall and strong body didn't give her a weak appearance either. She looked like a hardy farmer's wife, a woman who could slap a man's face hard enough to leave a bruise.

Only, Cailean had stared right at her, and she'd caught the flicker of confusion in his eyes before he scowled. He'd been distracted, or he'd have marked the glamor that shrouded her—all druids could.

As Bree's pulse settled, elation tingled through her body. A heavy, relieved sigh then gusted out of her.

He looked rougher than the last time she'd seen him. His hair was longer, curling against his scalp, and stubble shadowed his jaw. His clothing was travel-stained. Cailean's face had a slightly haggard look to it, indicating that he slept poorly these days.

Aye, the strain was showing, but that didn't matter. She'd found him.

The Great Raven had favored her today, for after nearly a turn of the moon searching, it had dawned on her that the High King's chief-enforcer might not want to be found. Over the past days, worry had started to gnaw at her. If Cailean had gone into hiding, it could have taken her years to discover his whereabouts.

Since leaving Duncrag, she'd traveled deep into the misty mountains and dark forests of The Uplands, stopping at each village, every fort, and asking if anyone had seen a tall, muscular man with short dark hair, blue eyes, and enforcer tattoos. She'd also mentioned that he might be traveling with a fae hound. She'd worked her way up to Harra—where he'd told her he was from—and then down again.

No one had seen him, or Skaal, until she reached Rothie.

She'd arrived at the fort the day before and discreetly asked if anyone matching Cailean's description had been seen here. A woman selling live fowl at market had told her that a braw warrior had bought a pie from the stall next to hers a day earlier.

"A fine-looking man he was too," the woman had added with a wink. "Is he yours?"

He *was*, Bree had thought as she'd shaken her head. Her stomach had pitched then, a blend of nerves and excitement sweeping through her.

And he would be again.

Nonetheless, her gut clenched now at the thought of confronting him.

You're not letting him get away, she reminded herself. *And you haven't traveled all this way just to watch him from a distance.*

Pushing herself off the wall, Bree followed him out of the ale-hall.

On the dirt street outside, which led toward the gates of the fort, she spied Cailean's broad-shouldered figure ahead. His fae hound was nowhere to be seen this evening—understandable, for Skaal would draw even more attention to the enforcer. He carried a broadsword strapped across his back, and a fighting dagger knocked against his thigh as he strode. Head bent, she drew her cloak hard around her—for this far north, The Sweeper had teeth—and hurried after her husband.

And as she walked, she altered her glamor.

For the first time since she'd spoken to Lara and Mirren, she smoothed her features into those of the woman that Cailean had taken as his wife. Her hair darkened from yellow to oak, and her body became smaller and softer.

This woman, Cailean *would* recognize, although she had to ready herself for his reaction when he did.

Quickening her pace further, for it was hard to match his long stride, Bree crossed the wide space before the gates, where the wind blew up dust and scattered straw. The light was poor and the shadows long. The gloaming was upon them now; the days drew in as Gateway approached.

Rothie wasn't a large fort, barely a quarter the size of Duncrag, yet it had the same layout—a wide space used for meetings and markets just inside the gates and a main street that curled its way up to the crown of the hill, where a stumpy broch crouched against the darkening sky.

The warriors at the gates barely glanced at Cailean, although they both favored Bree with lustful looks as she walked by.

She ignored them, even as irritation stabbed her. Aye, this was why she'd chosen a plainer face whenever she guised herself. It was best to be forgettable.

Meanwhile, Cailean strode down the rutted road outside the high stacked-stone walls of the fort, past the wooden docks where fishing boats bobbed with the tide. The Sweeper had whipped the Sea of Sorrows up into whitecaps. Usually, the Isle of Laggan—a barren, low-lying island—was visible to the northeast, but not so this evening, for dark clouds had lowered over the horizon. The wind had spits of rain in it.

A wooded glen, thick with birches and dark spruce, spread west of the fort, and the road—which stretched northwest into the heart of The Uplands and toward Cannich—cut through the woods.

Cailean didn't follow it.

Instead, he veered left, disappearing into the trees.

Bree broke into a jog, desperate not to lose him now. She ran easily, covering the ground with Shee swiftness. It was safe enough to do so, for no one was watching her. However, whenever she was surrounded by the Marav, she took care to slow her stride and movements.

The resinous scent of spruce greeted Bree as she stepped into the woods, a springy bed of needles underfoot.

There he was, just a few yards ahead, moving through the trees. And now that they were alone, it was safe to call out to him.

"Cailean!"

He halted, his body stilling. He'd recognized her voice.

Bree also stopped. Straightening her spine, she inhaled slowly and deeply. However, her pulse had now gone wild. Shades, she'd been so sure of herself when she embarked on this journey, but now she was terrified. What would she do when he turned around?

Talk to him, Bree. He's just a man.

Her mouth quirked, remembering the advice she'd given herself all those moons ago. *Aye, no match for you.*

For a moment, he stood there, as motionless as the birches that grew around him, the last of their leaves hanging from spidery branches. And then, slowly, he swiveled to face her.

Pulse still bounding like a bolting hind, Bree met his eye.

In return, Cailean's gaze narrowed. No, he wasn't overjoyed to see her again.

Her gaze roved over the grips of the knives sheathed upon the belt across his chest. *Iron.* The man was covered with it. Even standing a few yards away, she could smell its metallic tang, and her skin prickled.

Body still as taut as a bowstring, her husband moved slowly toward her. "Do my eyes deceive me?" His voice was low and rough.

"I'm afraid so, Cailean," she replied softly. "I've glamored myself so you'd recognize me."

He halted, his gaze sweeping over her cloaked form. A muscle then feathered in his jaw. This close, the strain and exhaustion on his face was more evident. There were dark smudges under his eyes, and deep grooves bracketed his mouth. "You were inside the ale-hall." A flinty edge crept into his tone, and Bree started to sweat.

"Aye," she whispered. "I've been looking for you for nearly a moon's turn now. I tried Duncrag first … but everyone there thinks you're dead."

He continued his path toward her then, stopping when they were around five yards apart. There was no warmth on his face, and his gaze glittered.

Bree swallowed to loosen her suddenly tight throat. Shades, where were her nerves of steel?

"Why?" His voice was harsh now, the blunt question falling heavily. "I sent you back to Sheehallion for a reason."

Bree wet her dry lips with the tip of her tongue. "You did." A pause drew out between them, swelling like a rising wave before she forced herself to continue. "But the moment I stepped through the stones, I knew it was a mistake." She broke off then, raising a hand to rub at her breastbone with her knuckles, where a familiar ache had risen. "I've missed you, Cailean."

He didn't answer. Her heartfelt admission hadn't moved him in the slightest. His expression was still hard; only the nerve flickering under one eye hinted at the emotion roiling beneath. His hands, which hung by his sides, flexed as if he wished to grasp her by the neck and throttle her.

Bree's pulse quickened. *You knew he'd be hostile … don't give up at the first hurdle.*

"You shouldn't have come looking for me," he said eventually. His voice was like iron being dragged over stone.

"Whether you wish it or not, we are bonded," Bree replied, stubbornness rising.

"You betrayed me," he snarled as his hands bunched into fists. "You knew the Shee would attack before dawn. You *knew* and didn't warn me."

"No," she countered, relieved he'd brought this up, so she could put him right. "I had no idea that Mor would attack early. I swear it."

"By what?" he shot back. "The Great Raven? Your God means *nothing* to me."

He took a threatening step toward her, and without meaning to, Bree moved backward, raising her hands to warn him from advancing farther. His dark brows knitted together at her reaction, and she exhaled shakily.

"It's the iron," she replied, resisting the urge to reach for the steel blades she carried—a survival instinct that was difficult to fight. "Take the blades off," she whispered, a plea creeping into her voice. She wasn't one to beg, but she couldn't talk to him with iron biting into her flesh, its odor searing the back of her throat.

His blue eyes glinted. "Show me who you are ... your *true* form ... and I might."

Bree stilled. It wasn't an unreasonable request. After all, she'd deceived and manipulated the man throughout their entire, albeit short, marriage. She didn't blame him for wanting to see who she really was.

And yet, she hesitated.

It was ridiculous really. Shee women were beauties, and Bree was no exception.

But Cailean hadn't bonded with Bree Fellshadow. He'd fallen for *Fia mac Callum*, who looked altogether different. Maybe he preferred smaller, softer women with hazel eyes, freckles ... and curves.

Maybe he wouldn't find her attractive.

It was a humbling moment, one of many she'd weathered over the past few moons, but she sat with it.

And then, as the silence between them deepened, Bree finally nodded.

10: NOTHING WAS REAL

CAILEAN STARED AT his wife. Only, she wasn't the woman he'd wedded. She was an imposter. A liar who'd fooled him one too many times. The urge to draw one of the blades in his knife belt and lunge at her pulsed in his gut.

Clenching his hands into fists at his sides once more, he fought the impulse.

Watching him, her hazel eyes bright, Bree swallowed. He could see the glamor upon her—as most druids could—as if he were looking at her through a sheet of rippling water.

Aye, she still looked like the woman who'd haunted him ever since he'd watched her walk through the stones, yet there was something insubstantial about her.

Moments passed, and then Bree bowed her head, her fingers flicking by her sides.

And before his eyes, she grew taller, leaner. Her pale skin took on a honeyed hue, and when she raised her chin, a stranger looked back at him.

A beautiful *Shee* stranger with long pale-gold hair that hung over one shoulder in a thick braid, and tawny eyes with elongated pupils. Like many of the Shee he'd seen over the years, this one had high, prominent cheekbones, and a haughty look about her.

Cailean's breathing caught in his chest, even as he checked the urge to take a step back. He was used to trusting his own eyes to tell him friend from foe—but it came as a shock to learn that the woman he'd married didn't exist at all.

Nostrils flaring, he wordlessly unstrapped the knife belt from his chest and cast it aside, before doing the same with the fighting dagger at his hip. He then unsheathed his sword and stuck the iron blade into the peaty ground. It was an aggressive, challenging gesture, but she didn't flinch.

Bree's golden eyes tracked every movement, and then, to his surprise, her mouth quirked into a half-smile. "I should pay you the same courtesy, I suppose." With that, she pushed aside the blue cloak she wore and removed her sword belt, fighting knives, and dagger, tossing them onto a patch of ferns.

They stood then, watching each other, unarmed.

However, Bree's attempt to lighten the mood between them washed off Cailean. He wouldn't let his wife distract him. He moved toward her then, stalking her, although Bree didn't back away this time. "Shades, husband," she murmured, the smile fading. "That glower of yours could sour milk."

He growled a curse under his breath. Did she have any idea of the self-restraint he was exercising right now?

Reaching Bree, standing so close he could smell the faint scent of rose that enveloped her, Cailean met her eye. "So, this is who you really are?"

Rage beat against his ribcage like a hammer, although the anger wasn't just directed at her—but at himself. He'd let himself be thoroughly duped. Had he been that lonely, that easy to mold? All his years of toughening his hide, building walls no one could scale, and all it had taken was three moons married to this … spy.

"Aye," she whispered back. "But does my appearance matter so much? Inside, I'm still me."

Cailean's lip curled. It did when she'd used a false identity to trick him. He wanted to snarl at her, yet something checked him. Indeed, although she didn't look like the woman he'd married, recognition flickered to life inside him. The shell was different, but it was still her.

All the same, seeing her real form shocked him. It made humiliation burn even hotter.

Nothing was real.

Clenching his jaw, he raised his hand and encircled her throat. He felt her pulse now, fluttering against his palm, and tried to ignore the tingle that shot up his arm at the contact.

He'd expected the Shee's skin to be cool, but it was warm and damp with sweat.

Pushing aside the observation, he tightened his grip—and those tawny eyes widened, their slitted pupils contracting. And yet, her gaze didn't stray from his face.

"What will you do now?" she whispered, a challenge glinting in her eyes. "Crush my windpipe?"

"I could."

"I know … but you won't."

Anger writhed in his gut. He'd forgotten how aggravating his wife could be—how she liked to push him. "Why won't I?" he growled.

"Because I'm yours."

His fingers clenched against her skin. "No, you aren't. You're a fucking liar."

A tawny eyebrow rose. "Aye, I'll not deny what I did." To his shock, she lifted her hand then, her long fingers gliding across his cheek to the line of his jaw. Cailean froze, heat igniting in his belly at her touch. Her gaze shadowed, and she swallowed once more. "But I'm sincere in this, Cailean. I want us to be together again. I know you're angry … and that you don't trust me. But trust can be rebuilt … stone by stone. Let me prove to you I'm worthy of it."

Cailean stared into her eyes, glimpsing tenderness and compassion in their depths—and it made an ache rise in his throat. It hit him then that she understood what her deception had done to him and was sorry. Fighting the urge to soften, he reached up with his free hand, curled his fingers around her wrist, and drew it firmly away from his face. He couldn't have her touch him. "You wield words like a bard, Shee," he ground out. "Are you trying to enchant me?"

She huffed a laugh, the sound vibrating against the palm that still pressed to her throat. "You credit me with too much power," she replied, her mouth curving into another wry smile. "We can't ensnare Marav into doing our bidding. We'd rule Albia if that were the case."

Cailean's gut cramped, his fingers flexing against her throat once more. He then yanked his hand away, trying to ignore the tingling in his palm as he did so. "Enough," he snarled. "You've had a wasted trip. Crawl back to Sheehallion, where you belong."

"It isn't my home any longer." Her expression sobered, her jaw setting in an expression he'd come to know well in Duncrag. Despite that she'd dropped her glamor, this female's expressions reminded him of the woman he'd married. "And you won't get rid of me that easily, mac Brochan."

"Fine. Go wherever you want … but it's over between us, *Bree*." A familiar sourness flooded his mouth as he moved back from her. "None of it was real, anyway."

Heat flared in her eyes. "Aye, it was. You know it."

Ignoring her comment, even as his stomach clenched once more, he picked up his knife belt and fastened it about his chest. He then buckled on his dagger at his hip and yanked his broadsword from the damp ground, sheathing it behind his left shoulder in one easy movement.

Without another word, he turned on his heel then and stalked off through the woods. The scent of fir enveloped him, and around him, The Sweeper made branches creak and groan. A few yards on, the trees opened up into a small glade, where Feannag cropped grass, and Skaal reclined by the ashes of the previous evening's fire.

Upon spying him, the fae hound rose smoothly to her feet.

Her golden gaze glinted then, disturbingly like Bree's, and he knew he'd been followed. And when the fae hound's tail started wagging, he snarled a curse. Heart kicking against his ribs, he cut a glare over his shoulder. His wife was, indeed, just a few yards behind him.

He whirled around to face her. "Get—"

"Tell me whom you're hunting, Cailean," she cut him off, a husky edge creeping into her voice. "Maybe I can help."

"You can't," he grunted. "And it's none of your Gods-damned business, anyway."

Heat flared in Bree's tawny eyes. "Pig-headed bastard," she muttered.

"Deceiving bitch," he shot back.

Their gazes fused, and the fury that simmered like a pot on the boil inside him started to spit and bubble. His patience had reached its limit. "Go," he ground out. "Before an iron blade lodges itself in your throat."

The words were vicious, but he was desperate now. He needed her to leave.

He didn't need any distractions in his life—especially now he'd finally picked up Eilig's trail—especially from the Shee spy who'd made a fool out of him.

A heavy silence fell before Skaal gave a low whine. The sound was almost pleading, and it made Cailean grind his teeth.

The moments drew out, and then Bree's lovely face veiled. It was like watching the sun slip behind a cloud. A shadow fell over the glade where they stood.

Bree's throat bobbed then, the only sign his words had wounded her. Stepping back, she pulled her cloak around her. And then, without another word, she turned and disappeared into the trees.

Her departure was so abrupt, so swift, that Cailean blinked, staring into the dark firs.

Behind him, Skaal whined once more.

Raking a hand through his close-cropped hair, Cailean cast the fae hound a glower. "Disloyal beast," he growled. He then turned away and moved over to the fire pit. A stack of kindling and firewood sat next to it, ready for this evening's campfire. Hunkering down, he withdrew a flint from a pouch on his belt and focused on coaxing the dry tinder into flames.

However, when he marked the slight tremor in his hands, he stilled. This was new—a sign that more than just anger seethed inside him this evening. His wife's reappearance had torn open a wound that had just started to scab, and he was raw in the aftermath. "The Mother's tits," he muttered. "What has she done to me?"

11: IRON CIRCLE ME

CAILEAN WANTED TO saddle up the following morning and ride as if a host of pike-wielding powries were pursuing him. He needed to get away from the devious Shee female he'd wed, and from his dangerous response to her.

But he wasn't leaving Rothie just yet.

After a restless night—during which he'd lain by the glowing firepit, one hand on the hilt of his dagger—Cailean rose in the early dawn. Stepping over the ring of salt he'd scattered before retiring—for it was wise to take precautions when sleeping rough, especially in the wild north—he slaked his thirst with a few gulps of ale and kicked dirt over the smoldering embers of the fire.

Leaving Feannag saddled and ready to go upon his return, and Skaal to keep watch over his stallion, Cailean strode back into the fort.

He emerged cautiously from the woods, bracing himself to find Bree waiting for him.

But she wasn't.

He was both relieved and unsettled by her compliance, although his gut told him, he hadn't seen the last of her. His wife was as stubborn as he was. She wouldn't give up that easily.

Smoke wreathed up from turf roofs, blending with an iron-colored sky. The air was damp and cold, yet he paid little attention to the weather. Instead, his thoughts were on the mission he'd set himself.

Where had Eilig gone? Three roads struck out from the fort. The first led south to Doure—this was the highway he'd recently traveled, so he ruled that one out—while the second stretched northeast to Cannich, and the third led up the coast north to Harra.

Harra. Cailean's stride faltered. He hadn't been back to his birthplace since childhood. But if Eilig had led his band there, he would return. Heat kindled in the pit of his belly then. It would be fitting to face that shitweasel in the place where everything had kicked off all those years ago.

As he approached the gates, Cailean's gaze settled upon a grisly sight: a head upon a pike. The mercenary's expression was set in a grimace, his once coppery skin ashen in death. Flies were buzzing around his mouth and nose.

Cailean's lips thinned. He wasn't sorry he was dead, for he'd been tempted to end him the day before. However, the sight of the mercenary's head reminded him that he'd drawn far too much attention to himself.

It would be best to be discreet this morning.

As usual, a busy produce market was in full swing in the wide dirt space within. Not wasting time, Cailean wove through the press—mostly local women bundled up in cloaks with wicker shopping baskets looped over their arms—to the pie seller he'd spoken to a couple of days earlier.

"Back again." The man flashed him a gap-toothed smile. "My pies are that good, eh?"

"Aye," Cailean replied, digging into his coin purse and handing over two copper pennies. "Two more." He wasn't hungry this morning, although he'd need food for his journey.

"I have another question about the fighting band that stopped here the other day," Cailean said as the pie vendor wrapped his purchases up in a square of oiled cloth.

The man glanced up. "I told you I didn't go to any of the fights."

"Aye, but did you hear where they went after Rothie?"

The man's brow furrowed. "No." He glanced then at where a plump woman standing before a stack of cages filled with live fowl was watching his customer intently. "Do you know, Ina?"

She nodded eagerly, smoothing her frizzy hair as Cailean focused on her. "I heard they were going to Morae." Ina paused then. "Apparently, there was a poor turn out here … so they were hoping for a warmer welcome from the crannog dwellers."

"Piss-poor entertainment, if you ask me," the pie vendor said with a snort. "Watching idiots hack at each other."

"Aye," Cailean replied. He couldn't agree more. He favored Ina with a half-smile in thanks, anticipation coiling under his ribs. Morae was just over a couple of days' journey from here. He'd catch up with Eilig sooner than he thought.

Reckoning was so close now, that he could almost taste it.

"A woman was here the other day … asking after you," Ina said then, continuing to primp her hair.

Cailean stiffened. *Bree.* "How do you know it was me she wanted?" he replied gruffly.

Ina grinned. "There aren't many men matching your description, handsome." She winked at him. "Friend of yours, is she?"

"No," he snapped. With that, Cailean turned on his heel and stalked away.

I'm coming for you, Eilig.

Sheets of icy rain swept over Cailean as he rode away from Rothie, taking the highway northwest toward Morae. The vicious Gales of Complaint barreled in from the northeast, bringing with them a chill that cut straight to the marrow. Feannag bowed his head, and even Skaal flattened her ears back and tucked her tail between her legs.

But the foul weather couldn't douse the hunger for vengeance that smoldered like a lump of peat in Cailean's belly. It was a fever in his veins now, like earth magic, pushing him on.

The highway between Rothie and Morae was rutted and muddy, yet well-traveled. They passed merchants traveling to the coast and farmers with wagons piled high with neeps to sell at Rothie's bustling market. And every traveler he saw stared at Cailean as if a wulver had just appeared on horseback. Unfortunately, the tattoos that crept up his neck and the fae hound that padded at his side made it impossible for him to blend in with his surroundings.

As he traveled, he cast the odd glance over his shoulder.

He'd expected Bree to tail him, yet there was no sign of her.

Even so, when he finally made camp at the day's end, in the driving wind and rain, Cailean readied himself for his wife's reappearance.

Surely, she was too pig-headed to stay away?

He'd stopped under the sheltering boughs of an old, twisted pine, where he tied his stallion up. There was no grass in this spot for Feannag to graze upon. Instead, he fitted his horse with a nosebag of oats before settling onto the damp, pine-needle-strewn ground, and leaning his back against the trunk. Meanwhile, icy rain slid down his face and the wind bit at any exposed skin.

The Mother's tits, he was tired of sleeping outdoors in all weathers. What he'd give right now to crawl into a soft pile of furs. But his coin purse was getting alarmingly light these days, and traveling with a fae hound made finding accommodation difficult.

Skaal slipped away—off to hunt—while Cailean unwrapped one of the pies he'd bought that morning.

He hadn't eaten all day, and his belly was now hollow and rumbling.

However, after a few bites, his appetite deserted him. Rewrapping the remains of his supper, he cast a sharp look into the gloaming.

Where is she?

Clodhead, he cursed himself. *Disappointed, are you?*

No, he wasn't. He'd wanted rid of her, and he'd gotten his wish. Bree wasn't as dogged as he'd thought.

Jaw clenched, Cailean dug into the salt pouch he carried at his waist and sprinkled a circle around the base of the trunk. Through the veil of rain, lights flickered in the trees to his right, and he stilled. It was hard not to stare at the beguiling golden flames that glowed warmly. However, he knew how to deal with corpse candles.

Cailean closed his eyes, his fingers flexing as he called forth his earth magic. His skin prickled, his tattoos glowing faintly as he built a mental ward between himself and the call of the beckoning flames. Years earlier, when he'd been an initiate druid upon the Isle of Arryn, a young woman who'd been set to take the bard's path had followed the lights one eve. She'd walked into a peat bog and was never seen again.

Ever since, he'd never underestimated the lure of corpse candles. Beautiful yet deadly—like most things that came from Sheehallion.

Like his wife.

Cailean's mouth twisted.

He needed to stop thinking about her.

I want us to be together again.

Her voice whispered to him then, husky and sensual, and his chest constricted, his breathing growing shallow. Even now, those words had a primal effect on him, but he'd managed to keep his reaction hidden. Aye, his wife was dangerous. To his sanity.

Nonetheless, this was a fight he'd win, even if it killed him.

Cailean's skin prickled then, and he emerged from his brooding, his gaze sweeping the dark glade where he rested.

Someone *was* out there, after all.

He stiffened, his pulse quickening.

A figure emerged from the trees to the south of the clearing then, and as it moved toward him, he made out a tall and lissome form.

Cailean's lips thinned. Curse her, he wasn't in the mood for this.

But as the figure approached—and a sudden shaft of moonlight, which pierced through the heavy clouds above, illuminated her—he realized it wasn't his wife.

It was a woman though, beautiful with pale skin and long wavy hair. She wore a flowing tunic and cloak, frosted by silvery light. Seeing him watching her, she favored him with a slow, sensual smile.

Lust, sudden and swift, ignited in the pit of Cailean's belly, heat sweeping over him. His reaction to this strange woman caught him off guard. He wasn't the sort of man to be led by his prick—or he hadn't been before Bree crashed into his life—and his body's response unsettled him.

"Lonely?" she greeted him in a low and honeyed voice that made his mouth go dry. "I can keep you company."

Cailean's breathing grew shallow, his groin hardening painfully.

Gods, he *was* lonely. His stomach ached from it. He longed to sink into softness and heat, to wrap himself around a lover.

However, underneath the haze of lust, something warned him. He didn't know this woman, and yet with each gliding step she took toward him, he could feel his self-restraint unraveling.

Heart leaping into a gallop, he drew one of the knives strapped across his front and thrust it before him.

The stranger's step faltered, the smile fixing upon her lovely face. "There's no need for that, lover," she murmured, her eyes dark, limpid pools. The chill of her breath feathered over him. "I only wish to keep you company this night."

"Iron circle me," Cailean rasped. "Keep light near and darkness afar. Iron circle me. Keep peace within and evil out." It was a protection charm—one his mother had taught him as a child, lest the botach crawl out of the smoke vent and try to steal him away. He hadn't spoken it in many years, yet the words had stayed with him, long after the memory of his mother's face had faded.

The woman halted, tension rippling through her slender body.

And then her smile slid into a snarl, two sharp canine teeth glinting in the pale moonlight. The woman hissed, her hands clawing at him. Her fingernails were long and sharp.

But she wouldn't come any further though. Salt wasn't enough against some of the faery creatures that stalked the Albian night—but iron *and* a protection charm were another matter.

The woman whirled then, the cloak and long tunic she wore billowing around her—and Cailean caught sight of the cloven hooves protruding from the hemline.

His heart lurched. She was one of the bavaan.

With a shriek of rage, the vampiric faery fled, just as clouds covered the moon once more and darkness fell across the clearing.

Breathing hard, Cailean lowered his knife.

Leaning against the rough trunk of the pine, he stared out into the murky darkness, heart pounding.

His mouth twisted then. Even surrounded by salt and clutching an iron blade, he wouldn't sleep easily, not after such an encounter. Bavaans usually preyed on hunters, seducing them before slicing open their throats with those talon-like nails and drinking their blood. Cailean had traveled from one end of Albia to the other over the years yet had always avoided these creatures. They were usually drawn to lonely men, ones that were easily duped by a pretty face.

It galled Cailean that the creature had smelt vulnerability on him.

Had Bree also marked his loneliness? He'd cloaked it well, but she was capable of seeing past his bitterness, anger, and lust for revenge.

Cold sweat bathed his skin as he railed against his weakness. He swore then that neither his wife nor a blood-sucking bavaan would catch him unawares again.

Time drew out, and eventually, exhaustion dragged at his eyelids. By this stage, the lashing rain and wind had numbed him, and he fell into a fitful doze. At some point, he was aware of Skaal joining him, her warm, wet body pressing up against his. Only then did he relax. The fae hound was wet and stank of blood and offal, but he didn't care. Sinking against her, he finally slept.

12: WARY OF STRANGERS

IF CAILEAN HAD been paying attention, he wouldn't have found himself this close to Bracehell Barrow at dusk.

But he'd been distracted. Instead of scanning his surroundings as he usually did, he'd been imagining the shock in Eilig's pale-grey eyes, followed by agony, as he twisted a blade in his guts. He'd lean over the shitbag then and whisper. "For my family."

It was only when he passed a marker—a stone laid by druids to warn passersby not to stray off the road—that he jerked from his vengeful thoughts. The marker indicated that the barrow lay around twenty-five furlongs to the north. Too close.

"Dung-brained fool," Cailean cursed himself as he stared down at the lump of mossy spearhead-shaped stone thrusting from the roadside. A muddy puddle surrounded the marker, for the weather had worsened further as the day lengthened. Sheets of rain slashed in horizontally now, and the bitter Gales of Complaint chafed his skin.

Gods, by this stage he'd forgotten what it was like to feel dry.

The weather had turned against him. He felt as if he were riding through the Underworld—a dark and hostile place where winter storms lashed for eternity. Unlike the Otherworld, where most people went when they died, the Underworld was for those whom the Gods spurned. After the life he'd lived, Cailean had always believed he'd end up there.

And after this blunder, his arrival might be quicker than anticipated.

He couldn't believe he'd been so careless. The night before, he'd sworn that he wouldn't be caught off guard again, and now here he was, far too close to a barrow at sunset. The time before dusk and dawn was the most dangerous to linger in these places, for that was when the Shee crossed into Albia.

Cailean's jaw tightened. What the fuck was wrong with him? Time was, he'd never have made a novice mistake like this. An enforcer didn't let emotion drive him; he knew that. But the restlessness that had seized him as he stood in The Hallow Woods, watching his people burn, and his bitterness and anger toward Bree were affecting him.

He needed to rein the emotions in. When he faced Eilig again, he wanted to be dispassionate. In control.

He angled his gaze forward, to where the rutted road cut between two stands of tall pines. And all the while, the rain streamed down his face, stinging his eyes.

An instant later, he stilled, his hand straying to the hilt of his dagger.

Dark shapes crouched upon the road around ten furlongs distant.

Cailean's pulse quickened as he squinted through the murky gloaming. Had the Shee come out to play?

His lips flattened then. If they had, they wouldn't be expecting an enforcer laden with iron. Drawing the blade, he urged Feannag on.

But as he approached, he realized the Shee weren't waiting for him. Instead, he made out a listing wagon and four struggling figures, who were attempting to free it from the mud. Meanwhile, the garron that pulled the wagon grunted under the strain as it valiantly tried to heave the cart forward.

The family—a man and woman and two sons of no older than twelve winters—wore thin woolen cloaks and were all soaked to the skin. Mud splattered their strained pale faces.

Upon noting his approach, they halted their efforts, their eyes widening nervously. And as expected, their gazes slid from him to the massive hound at his side. Skaal's ears had pricked, and the ruff on the back of her neck lifted.

Like him, she was always wary of strangers.

Sheathing his dagger, Cailean drew up his stallion, his gaze flicking to the wagon. Its left wheel was stuck up to the axle in mud. "Need some help?" he asked curtly. He really was tempted to ride on, to leave this foolish family to their fate.

However, he found he couldn't.

"Aye," the man, who had the ruddy complexion of someone who drank heavily and spent a lot of time outdoors, rasped, out of breath from attempting to push the cart free of the mud. "It's stuck good and proper."

"You shouldn't be traveling the road at this hour … so close to Bracehell," Cailean pointed out.

The man grunted, before lifting heavily muscled shoulders in a shrug, and knuckled the rain out of his eyes. "And neither should you."

The light was fading fast, and Cailean had pulled up the collar of his cloak. They couldn't see his tattoos, although his size and the fae hound made them wary. The family clustered together now, like a mob of skittish sheep, as if they were expecting trouble.

Moments passed, and then Cailean huffed a deep sigh. Swinging down from the saddle, he squelched through the mud toward them. "Right," he muttered. "Let's see if we can get this wagon unstuck."

"Thank you," the woman replied, her gaunt face lighting up.

Cailean moved around to the back of the listing wagon. He then nodded to the family. The two lads were staring at him like startled rabbits, and their parents hadn't moved.

Uneasiness shifted inside him, his gut tightening. Something in their gazes made the hair on the back of his nape prickle—and when the husband and wife shared a look, his instincts flared. *Shit.* He shouldn't have stopped to help this lot.

Shouts echoed across the road then, cutting through the drumming rain.

Swearing, Cailean swiveled on his heel, his gaze going to the line of trees behind him, on the northern side of the road. A swarm of warriors, men and women clad in fur and leather, their bare arms smeared with woad, was hurtling toward him—murder in their eyes.

Watching from the safety of the trees on the southern side of the road, Bree hissed a curse.

Behind her, Tivesheh snorted in agreement. *He's done for.*

Her pulse leaped into her throat. The stag wasn't wrong.

She was soaked to the skin, and the wind felt as if it were knifing through her leathers. However, her discomfort was forgotten as she witnessed the warriors streaming onto the road. The moment Cailean had dismounted, Bree's stomach swooped. Surely, he realized how suspicious it was to find a family out here, so close to Bracehell Barrow?

All the same, they'd been a pathetic sight, drenched and muddied, their faces hollow with hunger. And despite the face her husband presented to the world—that of the pitiless chief-enforcer—she'd seen his protective side a few times now.

Something jolted painfully in her chest.

Aye, Cailean mac Brochan was a man of contradictions, but his decision to stop and help this family had been the wrong one.

Warriors surged out of the woods and converged upon him, howling as they came.

Her husband reacted with enforcer speed, drawing his broadsword in one easy sweep and dropping into a fighting stance as the first of them swung an ax at his head.

With a snarl, Skaal launched herself into the fray, barreling into two women who were charging at Cailean with lethal iron-tipped pikes. The warriors screamed as the fae hound attacked, the sound choking off as Skaal dealt with them.

And as Cailean faced off against four warriors at the same time, his tattoos flaring bright in the gloaming, curses rang across the road. "Enforcer!"

Aye, it had been too dark for them to realize whom they were dealing with. Not that it mattered though. Enforcer or not—and even with Skaal's help—Cailean was vastly outnumbered.

Meanwhile, the family he'd stopped to help had shed their pathetic expressions. The two lads ran off into the trees while the couple advanced on Cailean's stallion. It was a fine beast and highly valuable. However, the horse bared its teeth, its neck snaking and huge hooves kicking, as the man tried to grab its reins.

Its teeth sank into his arm, and he gave a rough shout of pain. The stallion then swiveled on its muscular haunches and kicked out, bringing the man down. His wife shrieked, reeling back as the stallion took off into the trees, crashing past where Bree and Tivesheh still looked on.

Bree's heart started to pound, urgency twisting under her ribs.

I must help him.

Go then.

Bree drew two fighting knives, her gaze narrowing as she surveyed the fight taking place just yards away on the road.

Cailean was surrounded now—and although he cut down warrior after warrior, and Skaal mauled anyone who came within reach of her teeth and claws, it wasn't a fight the enforcer and his fae hound would win.

A crowd of warriors grew thick around man and beast now, more of them emerging from the trees.

She hesitated then. *That's a lot of iron they're wielding.*

Aye … but you've got Sheehallion steel. Move fast enough and the iron won't bite.

Bree grimaced.

Tiv was right. She'd fought the Marav before. She'd do so again.

Bursting from the trees, she raced across the muddy ground, her strides long and fleet. She gave the warriors no warning, cutting those nearest down from behind, before slashing her way into their midst.

Something stung her right arm as she drove a dagger through a man's throat and kicked him in the guts, sending him reeling backward. But ignoring the fire that now raced up her bicep, she fought on—until she was at Cailean's side.

His tattoos lit up the gloaming like silver corpse candles, and he fought viciously, the blade of his broadsword slick with blood. Beside him, Skaal had turned frenzied, her jaws wet with gore as she fastened them around the throat of the man she'd just brought down.

Teeth and claws weren't a fae hound's only weapons though. Their blood-curdling howl, when issued three times, could stop a Marav's heart from terror. Yet, Skaal couldn't wield it. The fae hound's howl wouldn't hurt Bree, but it *would* harm Cailean.

Her husband cut a glance sideways, his eyes widening at the sight of her. His skin was slick with sweat, and his chest was heaving. He was drawing on his reserves now.

Bree flashed him a harsh smile, sheathing one of her knives and drawing her longsword with her right hand. The rasp of razor-sharp Sheehallion steel echoed across the road, and a few of the warriors growled oaths.

"Shee!" Someone shouted. "The Gods help us!"

"Come on then," Bree shouted back. "Which of you wants to die on my blade first?"

To their credit, they were brave. Many a Marav fighter would have turned and fled at the sight of a heavily armed and enraged Shee slicing through their ranks. But not these warriors.

Desperation turned them savage, even as—one by one—they fell upon Bree and Cailean's blades, and as Skaal ripped her way through them.

The proximity of iron made her skin buzz and muscles twitch, yet battle lust made it easier to push the discomfort aside.

Finally though, when their numbers dwindled, some of them did run, stumbling into the trees, and leaving a trail of dripping blood behind them.

Trying to ignore the vicious burning that now covered her entire right arm, Bree watched them go. She then glanced over at Cailean. He too stared into the trees, where Skaal bounded after the fleeing warriors, before digging his blade into the ground and leaning upon the hilt. His chest rose and fell sharply now, and his tattoos had faded to their usual dark swirls upon his skin.

A chilling howl split the wet air, and Cailean sagged.

Bree cut a surprised look toward the trees. It appeared Skaal was determined to deal with the stragglers. However, despite that he wasn't her intended victim, Cailean could still hear the hound.

Another howl followed, slightly fainter yet no less frightening.

Cursing, Cailean fell to his knees in the mud, a shudder going through his big body.

Panic surged up Bree's throat, protectiveness swiftly following. If he heard another, his heart would stop. Squelching over the churned-up ground, she slapped her hands over his ears and whispered a Shee protection charm—just as a third howl shattered the gloaming.

Another shudder passed through him, yet Bree squeezed her eyes closed, repeating the charm over and over, until Skaal's final howl faded.

Night had fallen now, and she wagered that none of the warriors who'd tried to retreat were still alive.

13: ALL THIS IS

"CAN YOU HEAR me?"

Blinking the rain out of her eyes, Bree removed her hands from Cailean's ears and lowered herself to a crouch before him. She then surveyed his face, her belly tight with worry. Sometimes, if the fae hound's howl didn't stop a Marav's heart, it turned them witless with fear. And sometimes, the terror remained.

Her husband stared back at her, his eyes glazed. Mud splattered his face, and the rain plastered his hair to his scalp. His expression had turned slack.

Bree drew back her arm before hesitating. "Forgive me." She then slapped him hard across the face.

Cailean jerked, his eyes snapping wide. And when she met his gaze again, Bree glimpsed recognition—and ire—in their depths. Reaching up, he massaged his jaw. "Fuck," he ground out. "That stung."

Bree let out a relieved breath, the tension in her gut easing. She started shivering then, as the thrill of battle faded and she became aware once more of just how wet and cold she was. "Sorry," she said, rising to her feet and holding out her hand. "But I had to do something to bring you back."

Cailean hesitated a moment before allowing her to help him up.

"Some appreciation would be nice," she muttered, releasing his hand and taking a step back from him. "After all, I just—"

"Thank you," he cut her off sourly, his scowl deepening with each passing moment.

Bree's brow furrowed in response. She hadn't expected him to grovel at her feet for coming to his aid, but his attitude was starting to vex her. Shades, her teeth were beginning to chatter now. She wasn't used to spending prolonged periods out in such foul weather.

She was about to tell him so when Cailean's gaze lowered then to her right arm. "You're hurt," he observed tersely.

Bree glanced down to see that, indeed, a cut was visible. The rain-drenched sleeve of her tunic had torn, and the bracer on her lower arm glistened with blood. "Cursed iron," she muttered, wincing. She'd been so focused on the fight and helping Cailean that she'd almost forgotten the wound. "It burns."

Unfortunately, as quick as she was, Bree hadn't been able to emerge from that skirmish unscathed. There had been too many of the bastards, and they'd all been skilled with their vicious iron blades.

"Will it need treating?" His tone was still rough, making it clear that his concern for her was grudging.

"Aye … later." She looked around then. "We're not safe out here, Cailean."

As the dusk deepened, she felt Sheehallion magic in the air. The howling wind now brought a distinctive smell with it: the scent of rose mingled with the smell of mud and the iron stench of blood. It was risky for *her* to linger here as well. With war looming, Mor would start sending scouts out through the barrows.

Still gently massaging his jaw, Cailean nodded. He then gave a low whistle. A few moments later, his horse emerged from the trees.

Bree's mouth quirked, and she let out a whistle of her own.

A great white stag followed the stallion onto the road. The mud squelched under their hooves, and both beasts lowered their heads and flattened their ears back in the face of the wind that swept down the highway.

She glanced Cailean's way to find him eyeing her. "Show off."

Bree's smile widened as she crossed to her stag. "This is Tivesheh."

"Ghost?"

"Aye … he knows how to disappear when it suits him."

Bree vaulted lightly onto the stag's back, waiting while Cailean sheathed his broadsword over his left shoulder. He trudged across to the stallion, stroking the horse's neck to soothe it. The beast's nostrils were flared, its eyes wild. "All is well, Feannag," he murmured.

He then led the stallion over to where the pony was still attached to the broken cart. The poor garron was soaked and trembling. The beast gave a nervous snort as Cailean unshackled it. Removing the pony's bridle, he then slapped it on the rump.

Tossing its head, the heavyset pony trotted away, disappearing into the trees.

Cailean then mounted his stallion.

Sitting atop her stag, Bree surveyed the bodies littered across the muddy road. The falling rain stippled the mud and washed the woad off their skin.

"Who were these warriors?" she asked.

"Druthen most likely," he answered. "They're a reclusive tribe that dwells in this area of The Uplands."

Bree pulled a face. "Well … they decided to come out of hiding this evening."

"Aye, like the other Upland tribes, they have little respect for the authority of our High King or his overkings. They've become unruly and unpredictable, of late." Cailean cast a narrowed gaze over the dead. "Although they just got more than they bargained for."

Bree nodded, her gaze traveling to the tree line where the fae hound had bounded after the fleeing warriors. "What about Skaal?"

"She'll find me," Cailean replied, urging Feannag into a canter. Mud and water splashed up behind the horse's large hooves.

An instant later, he was thundering along the highway, heading west. Irritation surged in Bree's breast as she watched him go. "*Me?*" she muttered, rounding her shoulders as a particularly vicious gust of wind buffeted her. "How about 'us'?"

No, he wasn't getting rid of her that easily.

Come on, Tiv. She leaned forward and placed her hand on the stag's slick neck. *Follow him.*

The last of the light had faded and darkness crowded in by the time Cailean drew his mount up. Unfortunately, the Gales of Complaint still howled, and the rain continued to lash down as if the end of the world were upon them.

Bree was right behind him.

Swinging down from Feannag, Cailean's brows crashed together. "I didn't invite you along."

"No." Bree slid lightly onto the muddy road before jogging on the spot and rubbing her hands together to try and warm them up. "But I assumed it must be an oversight on your part. Even *you* couldn't be so rude."

A muscle feathered in his jaw, although a moment later, a mutinous expression settled over his face. Oh aye, he could be.

Spine stiffening, Bree wrapped her arms about herself and faced him. "Let me spell this out. I saved your hide back there, mac Brochan. The least you can do in return is let me share your hearth tonight. I swear, that wind cuts to the marrow."

His lips parted as if he was about to argue with her. However, a moment later, he shut his mouth firmly, swallowing whatever unpleasant response he'd been about to utter. He looked as miserable as she felt: dripping with mud and rain, his face pale with cold. "Very well," he finally answered, biting each word out. "One night ... and then we go our separate ways in the morning."

Bree's jaw clenched, even as she nodded. The man was proving to be frustratingly obstinate. But at least she had until dawn to get him to soften toward her—and she'd do her best, once she got out of this driving rain and warmed herself by a fire.

Is this wise? Tiv's mind touched hers then. *Pushing yourself in where you're not wanted rarely ends well.*

Bree stiffened. Her stag didn't usually question her, and his behavior caught her off guard. *I know what I'm doing.*

Cailean turned then and led his stallion away from the highway and into the oakwood.

Wordlessly, Bree and Tivesheh followed.

In the woods, the trees had lost all their leaves. Nonetheless, the heavy boughs would provide some shelter overnight. It wasn't much, but off the road, the sharp edges of the Gales of Complaint were blunted.

"I'm going to hunt for dry wood for a fire," Cailean announced brusquely. "Make yourself useful while I'm gone and see to my horse."

Bree snorted. "Good luck with that … these woods will turn into a loch soon if it doesn't stop raining."

Not bothering to answer her, he strode off, leaving Bree glaring after him.

She knew what he was doing. He thought if he made her angry, she'd leave. A thin smile tugged at her lips then, stubbornness knotting under her breastbone. "You'll have to do better than that, mac Brochan," she muttered between chattering teeth, "if you want rid of me." Even so, she found herself silently simmering as she crossed to Feannag. The man's ingratitude was galling.

Working quickly, even if her numb fingers kept fumbling, she unsaddled the stallion and rubbed him down. Digging around in the saddle bags, she found some oats and a nosebag and fed him.

Like that, do you, lad? She gently touched minds with the stallion as he munched.

Aye, came his gruff response. Horse and rider were similarly taciturn it appeared. *Better than sour grass.*

She was rolling out a square of leather on the ground under the broadest of the oaks when Cailean returned with firewood. He ignored her as he laid the hearth, and Bree held her tongue. It was wise to let the tension ease slightly before attempting to converse with him again.

A short time later, a small fire smoked before them. Thank the Ancestors, the rain had lessened a little now, and the bough above them kept them dry enough. Sighing, Bree warmed her tingling hands over the tender flames. She'd never been so happy to sit by a fire. Her wet clothing was clammy and chafed her skin, but there was nothing she could do about that. At least, warmth now seeped into her chilled body.

Wringing water out of her long braid, her gaze flicked then, to where Cailean had sat down, cross-legged, and was feeding twigs into the fire. His face still gleamed with rain in the firelight.

Eventually, he glanced up, meeting her eye. His features were strained now, his gaze guarded. "I'd have fallen back there if you hadn't appeared when you did," he admitted tersely, raking a hand through his wet hair—a move that left it spiky and in disarray. "Thank you."

The admission was a reluctant one, each word dragged up, but the tension in Bree's chest loosened, nonetheless. She inclined her head and favored him with a half-smile. "Just as well that I was following you then."

He made a noise in the back of his throat. "Don't make a habit of it."

"I wouldn't … if you'd let me ride with you."

Their gazes fused, her challenge hanging in the air between them.

To Bree's surprise, he didn't flatly refuse her. *Finally, some progress.*

Clearing his throat, Cailean broke the stare first. Retrieving his sodden cloak, he wrung as much water as he could from it before using it to wipe his face. He then glanced her way once more. "Are you hungry?"

"Aye." And she was. All she'd eaten today was a few handfuls of brambles.

Digging into a pack, he withdrew a leather-wrapped package and handed it to her. "It's a pie."

"Thank you."

Meanwhile, Cailean unwrapped his own package and took a bite out of a pie that looked as if he'd already started it. Wordlessly, Bree ate her supper. The pie was pork and herb, and surprisingly good—for Marav fare.

The meal was a silent one, tense. Despite her small victory, Bree was wary of him. Cailean was as prickly as a thistle these days. One flippant word could shatter what little ground she'd gained this evening.

Steam rose between them as they ate, as the heat of the fire started to dry their clothing and the cloaks they'd hung up next to it. The air smelled of wet leather and wool.

After they'd eaten, he handed her a skin of ale. Without thinking, Bree took it with her right hand. She then stilled, her breath hissing between clenched teeth.

Cailean frowned. "Your arm?"

"It's all right," she replied, lifting the skin to her lips with her left hand. It wasn't really, but it was best not to complain. She'd deal with it after supper.

Moments passed, and then Cailean muttered a curse under his breath.

Bree stiffened, surprised by his outburst. "What?"

Pushing himself to his feet, he moved around to her side of the fire. "Let me see it."

Frowning, she reluctantly held out her arm, watching as he unfastened the leather bracer covering her forearm. He then rolled up the sleeve of the close-fitting woolen tunic she wore underneath.

Bree's lips compressed into a grimace when he revealed the cut beneath. It was deeper than she'd realized and already inflamed. However, it was difficult to concentrate on her injury, for the scent of him—leather, woodsmoke, and a hint of spice—overwhelmed her senses. He knelt close enough that she could see the thick black stubble on his chin.

"What do your people use to treat iron wounds?" Cailean asked.

"Usually crushed whin … when it's in flower," she replied, trying to concentrate. This late in the year, the scented yellow flowers weren't available. "Otherwise, moss will do. I'll go looking for some shortly."

"I'll do it." He got up and fashioned a torch out of a bundle of twigs.

Bree watched him work, her pulse thudding against her ribs. "What a paradox you are, Cailean," she said softly. "One moment you're snarling at me … the next you're tending my wounds. Admit it, you *do* care."

He shot her a sidelong glance, his gaze hardening. "Don't look for things that aren't there," he muttered. "You were injured because of me … and I intend to put things right. That's all this is."

Not waiting for her response, he strode off into the darkness.

14: TWENTY YEARS TOO LATE

REMAINING BY THE fire, Bree watched the flames dance. Cailean's response had been a slap to the face, one that still stung.

It was a lie too, for she'd seen the concern flare in his eyes about her injury.

She was still brooding—and trying to come up with a way to get him to thaw toward her—when he returned with a handful of moss a short while later. Stopping off at one of his saddlebags, he extracted a small wineskin before kneeling in front of her once more. He then proceeded to clean her wound with what smelled like strong wine, using a scrap of moss as a cloth before applying some to the wound. After that, he tore the bottom of her sleeve off and used it as a makeshift bandage.

She watched him work, noting the deft movements of his hands.

However, the silence between them grew more awkward by the moment, and she was desperate to smooth things over.

"You know some of the healing arts, I see," she said finally as he secured the bandage with a knot.

Cailean glanced up, meeting her eye. "All druids are taught how to tend to minor injuries. My skills end here though." He moved back, putting some distance between them once more. "You'll need to dress it again and put on a clean bandage tomorrow."

Bree nodded. "I will … thank you."

He cut his attention away, focusing on feeding a branch to the flames. In the ruddy firelight, his face looked tired—a sign that he'd drawn too deeply on his magic during the attack earlier.

"Will you tell me where you're heading?" she asked after a spell. Aye, she risked angering him again, but she didn't want to pass the evening in silence.

He hesitated a moment, his eyes dark in the firelight as he looked at her, before replying, "Morae."

"Will the man you're looking for be there?"

His mouth pursed.

Bree huffed a deep sigh, her frustration spilling over. The man could be as immovable as a mountain when he wanted to be. "Shades, Cailean. I know you don't believe it, but I'm on your side."

His mouth twisted, a dark brow rising. "Really?"

"Aye." Bree leaned forward, her gaze never leaving his. "Really."

They stared at each other for a moment longer before he reached for another stick for the fire. Adding it, he glanced up at her once more. "The fight master's name is Eilig."

"And why are you searching for him?"

"We have an old ... debt ... that must be settled."

Bree frowned. She hated it when others spoke in riddles. "What did he do?"

Cailean's face hardened, and for a few moments, she was sure she'd pushed things too far. However, after a moment he replied, "he destroyed my family."

A long silence pulsed between them before Bree cleared her throat. "He killed them?"

His mouth twisted. "As good as."

"Will you tell me what happened?"

Cailean glanced away, dragging a hand down his face. He had the look of a man who was about to have a rotten tooth extracted.

Bree decided to be patient.

She'd asked him about his past before, at Duncrag, but it had been like butting heads with a stone wall. No, she couldn't force this out of him.

She needed to wait until he was ready to speak.

The fire crackled, and a large shadow appeared between two oaks a few feet away.

Bree tensed, her hand straying to the grip of the knife strapped to her thigh. However, a massive dog with a shaggy moss-green coat and glowing golden eyes padded across the sodden ground to the fire, sinking down next to Cailean.

Have you two made it up, yet? Skaal's mind touched hers.

Bree stilled in surprise before her mouth curved into a smile. It was a relief to be able to communicate with the fae hound like this; in her Marav form, it had felt as if she'd had a limb cut off. *Not quite. Give me time, and I will.*

Fear not, he'll forgive you ... eventually.

"Are you two having a private conversation?" Cailean interrupted them, his gaze narrowed.

"Aye," Bree replied, her smile turning rueful as their gazes met. "What's wrong … were your ears burning?"

His frown deepened, his lips parting as he started to respond. However, Skaal nudged Cailean in the ribs with her nose and gave a low whine, as if apologizing for her howls earlier.

Sighing, he reached out and put his arm around her neck. "I'm all right, lass," he said roughly. "Bree shielded me from the worst of it." His attention flicked once more to where Bree sat observing them.

"My home … Harra … was attacked by slavers," he said finally. "We were all taken … my parents, my elder sister … and me. They sold us to a man who led a traveling band of fighters. Eilig." He ground out the man's name like a curse. "My father then spent the next few years fighting in the arena, while the rest of us toiled in other ways. It was my chore to empty the turd buckets and scrub them clean … and run errands for him."

The glint in Cailean's eyes made Bree still. She could almost taste the hatred he bore this man.

"My mother died of the bloody flux during our second winter on the road." He glanced away, his gaze unfocusing. "My father changed after that. He was Eilig's best fighter, but he became reckless in the arena, and then … around six moons after Ma died … he fell."

"How old were you?"

"It was my tenth summer." Cailean picked up a stick and poked at the embers, sending a shower of sparks high into the night air. "Eilig started training me to be a fighter shortly after Da died. He was a harsh tutor, and his lessons often ended with him beating me senseless … but I learned quickly, and upon my thirteenth spring, he pushed me into the arena."

Bree frowned. "That's young."

"Too young. I barely survived my first few fights, although I killed each opponent. Word spread of the boy warrior who could bring down a fighter twice his size." He halted then, his features tightening. "About that time, Eilig raped my sister."

Bree stilled as she realized where this tale was heading.

"Enya was just two years older than me," Cailean continued, "but I'd noticed the fight master watching her as she changed from a lass to a woman." Iron crept into his voice then. "When I realized what he was doing, I attacked him. It was an idiotic act, for despite my growing strength, he was still a much better fighter than me. He beat me so badly I didn't wake up for days … and when I did, he warned me that he'd slit my sister's throat if I ever challenged him again."

He broke off then, his gaze shadowing. "It nearly killed me to know he was mauling her every night … and that I was too weak to stop him."

Skaal growled in Bree's mind. *Why do the worst ones always rise to power?*

Turds float, of course, she replied. Cailean didn't realize it, but the fae hound understood every word he uttered.

Skaal whined then and pushed herself against Cailean. He reached up once more and stroked her shaggy back.

"A few moons later, we were at Baldeen for the Mid-Summer Fire festivities, and the local overking had pitted some of his own slaves against Eilig's," Cailean continued, his gaze turning inward now. Bree didn't dare interrupt him; she'd never heard her taciturn husband speak so lengthily. "Folk from miles around came to watch the fights. One of them was an enforcer from the Isle of Arryn. He watched me best one of the overking's slaves … a seasoned fighter … and approached Eilig afterward." His mouth twisted into a bitter smile. "Apparently, he'd sensed 'the gift' in me."

"And the fight master let you go?" Bree asked, incredulous.

"Aye, once the druid handed over a bag of gold coins."

"He *bought* you?"

"He paid for my freedom," Cailean corrected her. "Enya pleaded for me to take her with me. I tried, but the enforcer refused to buy her as well." He looked away, the firelight dancing across his face. "I promised Enya I'd return for her" —he paused then, swallowing— "that as soon as I was able, I'd be back to kill Eilig … and free her."

A heavy silence settled over the campfire following this admission. Bree finally shattered it. "But you never did?"

"No." He was staring into the flames again, lost in the past. "I meant to … but my new life upon the Isle of Arryn, and the training they put me through, was intense, all-consuming. I had to prove myself, again and again. I was never given any time off … and I didn't start earning any coin until I entered the High King's service." His face was haggard in the glow of the flames. "By then, a decade had passed, and it was too late."

"She might still be alive," Bree pointed out softly.

A muscle flexed in his jaw. "Aye, although it's unlikely. I'm twenty years too late." He paused then, his blue eyes glinting. "But Eilig still breathes … and I intend to make him bleed for what he did to us."

Nodding, Bree wrapped her arms around her knees to ward off the cold and damp that had seeped into her bones despite the fire's proximity.

"The High King would have given you leave over the years … you could have gone after your former master at any time," she said after a lengthy pause. "Why now?"

Cailean's mouth curved into a humorless smile, his eyes darkening. "I thought I'd done such a good job of locking away my past in an iron strongbox and throwing it into a deep, dark loch … but then I took a wife, and she dredged it up from the depths and tore the lid off."

Bree stared back at him, her pulse quickening.

"Don't look so surprised," he muttered. "This is all your fault."

She swallowed. "Maybe I did you a favor," she whispered.

His jaw tightened. "I knew the day you arrived at Duncrag that you were trouble." His mouth twisted then. "By the time I realized you were keeping secrets, it was already too late."

Bree licked suddenly parched lips. "Too late?"

"You'd somehow gotten your claws into me."

She frowned. "It wasn't like that."

"Wasn't it? You were sent to deceive me, by whatever means."

"Aye … but I never intended to *bond* with you."

She tightened her grip on her knees then. This conversation had taken a swift turn. It was easier when the focus had been on him. But now that they were talking about *her*, she suddenly felt as if she were standing on the edge of a parapet, with the Sharp Billed Wind pushing at her back. One hard gust and she'd tumble.

"That's why I came to you in the Hallow Woods," she admitted, wishing her voice didn't sound so husky, so desperate. "I couldn't let you walk into an ambush … not after what we'd shared."

His frown slid into a scowl, and he leaned forward, glaring at her across the fire. "No, you let the rest of my warband die instead."

"I repeat … I didn't know that Mor would attack so early," she replied, her pulse thudding in her ears now. "Let me also remind you that in delivering a warning, I betrayed my people."

They continued to glare at each other, tension shivering in the air between them.

Skaal shifted next to Cailean, her golden eyes flicking from the enforcer to Bree. *Well … this is friendly.*

15: ASK ME AGAIN IN THE MORNING

CAILEAN BROKE THEIR stare first. Jaw clenched, he fed some more wood to the fire and waited for the tightness in his chest to ease.

He couldn't believe he'd spilled his guts to her.

To a Shee spy.

By The Hag's nails, he wanted to hate her. Instead, he'd told her about his past, about his family, and about his thirst for revenge that wouldn't be quenched until Eilig was dead.

Bree had suggested that Enya might still be alive, but twenty years with Eilig would have broken her. The fight master was more likely to have killed her, or she might have died birthing the whoreson's child.

Ice washed through Cailean's veins at the thought.

Meanwhile, the silence between him and Bree drew taut, like a bowstring.

The tension in his chest didn't loosen as he'd hoped. There wasn't the sense of relief that usually came after unburdening oneself.

Drawing in a deep breath, he fixed Bree with a penetrating look. Enough talking about him. It was his wife's turn. "How did you find me?"

"I traveled from place to place, asking if anyone had seen a huge enforcer traveling with a fae hound." Her mouth quirked. "You were harder to track down than I thought you'd be."

Cailean snorted, eyeing her. "What happened when you returned to your people?" he asked brusquely.

Bree pulled a face. "I went before the Raven Queen and lied. She was pleased that I'd warned her of your planned attack at Sheathan, but angry I'd left Duncrag without her leave." Resentment crept into her voice then. "Having eyes in the High King's broch was important to Mor."

Cailean snorted. "You made a terrible spy, Bree."

She winced at this yet didn't argue with him. "Aye, well … I've made a living by letting a sharp blade and quick reflexes do the talking. I wasn't prepared for all the sneaking and pretending."

"Did Mor punish you?"

"No, she merely cast me aside. I didn't see her again. Granted, she's been busy … amassing an army."

Cailean tensed at this admission, and marking his reaction, Bree's mouth curved into a humorless smile. "Aye, you can't be surprised. The High King has a sizable force camped at his gates too … the war that has been building for some time will begin soon."

Suspicion flickered to life in Cailean's gut. Was his wife withholding things from him again? "Do you know when and where the Shee will strike?" he demanded, his voice hardening.

Bree shook her head, irritation flaring in her golden eyes. "I told you … Mor ignores me these days." She grimaced then. "I did ask around … but no one would talk to me."

Cailean's lips flattened. If she expected sympathy, she'd be disappointed.

Feeding more wood to the fire, he then considered what she'd revealed. "Your people will strike before the snows come," he said finally. "Before it gets too cold."

"Aye. Golval and Deeping are the closest barrows to Duncrag … I imagine Mor will send her warriors through there."

Cailean met her gaze again, noting her guarded expression. It likely mirrored his own. She was on edge, awaiting further accusations from him. Aye, Bree had seemed sincere when she told him that she hadn't known that the ambush in the Hallow Woods would come early, but Cailean's suspicion that she was holding things back lingered. The Shee were as cunning as they were beautiful. Many Marav tales told of how they could be kind one moment and cruel the next. And the female seated across from him was an assassin.

Something occurred to him then, and he leaned forward, searching her features. Firelight played across her gilded skin and made her tawny eyes glow like Skaal's. "How old are you, Bree?"

Her lips lifted at the corners as if she'd been expecting him to ask this eventually. "Three hundred and two."

Cailean straightened up, something clenching deep in his chest. He shouldn't have been surprised—for he knew that Shee could live for thousands of years—but the knowledge that she'd been born around the time of his great, great grandsire made uneasiness stir inside him.

No wonder, even as a Marav woman, her eyes had been so knowing.

The moment drew out before Cailean broke their stare. He then cleared his throat. "It's been a long day … we'd better get some rest." Indeed, he was bone-weary. Traveling through howling wind and rain and then fighting for his life had drained him—as had this conversation. And even the glow of the fire couldn't warm the chill that had settled into his bones.

"Aye," she replied softly. "Cailean … can I accompany you to Morae?"

He glanced up to find Bree watching him, her lovely face solemn, her eyes pleading.

His chest clenched. Gods, he wished she wouldn't look at him like that. "Why?" he asked roughly.

"I know you still don't trust me," she went on, her throat bobbing, "but I'd like to help you find this Eilig. When you do … you might need someone to watch your back."

His first impulse was to tell her he didn't need her help. Yet, the sudden vulnerability in her eyes checked him. That, and he didn't have the energy to argue with her any longer.

"We'll see," he grunted, wrapping his still-damp, heavy fur cloak about him and rolling onto his side, next to where Skaal had stretched out her long body. "Ask me again in the morning."

Bree slept badly. Cailean had built up the fire, yet the cold still gnawed at her. Halfway through the night, the rain started again.

Curled up under her sodden woolen cloak, she listened to it patter around her. In the meantime, her mind turned over the things Cailean had told her, examining them from every angle.

The riddle that was her husband had been solved. Now she understood why he was such a hard bastard, why he'd been determined to cut himself off from others.

She'd cracked his shell—because of her, he'd set off on a quest for vengeance.

She had to stay with him. They were meant for each other. And with time, he'd realize it too.

Eventually, dawn broke, grey and misty, and Bree rolled to her feet. Her damp clothing itched her skin, and the morning's chill dragged at her lungs. Ignoring her discomfort, she turned to face her husband.

Cailean was kicking earth over the smoking ruins of last night's fire. The rain had done its best to put it out, yet he was making sure. Unlike her, he looked as if he'd actually slept; his face was fresher and less strained, his eyes brighter.

"Well?" she asked huskily. "What is your answer?"

Cailean glanced up, his gaze glinting. "That's an abrupt way to start the day," he replied. "How about a 'good morning' first?"

Bree swallowed. "Good morning."

She tracked him as he shifted back from the fire and moved over to his stallion. Feannag nudged him with his nose. Stroking the horse's noble face, he slipped on its bridle. "Very well," Cailean spoke the words so quietly that Bree almost missed them. "Although you aren't to interfere in my business … is that clear?"

"It's clear." Bree's heart kicked against her ribs. "So, that's an 'aye'?"

He shot her a warning look before nodding.

"You won't regret this."

He pulled a face and stooped to retrieve Feannag's saddle. "I already do." Swinging the saddle onto the stallion's back, he then set about tightening the girth. "Morae crannog is half a day's ride from here." He cast a glance over his shoulder at where Tivesheh stood, his white coat gleaming even in the morning's dull light. "However, the road will get much busier from this point on … you can't ride in on your stag."

"I'll travel with you then?"

His shoulders tensed in reply before he gave an abrupt nod.

Bree's stomach fluttered. Shades, this was awkward.

Not pushing her luck any further, she moved across to Tivesheh. *Follow us … but keep yourself hidden.* She stroked Tivesheh's smooth neck. *White stags are rare in Albia … I don't want a hunter finding you.*

They'll have to be fast to catch me. Tivesheh tossed his head. *Whistle and I will come.*

Bree smiled and slapped him on the shoulder. *Go then.*

Turning swiftly, the stag bounded into the trees. She watched him go, a familiar sense of loss tugging at her chest.

"I've always wanted to be able to do that." The rumble of Cailean's voice drew her attention then, and she glanced over her shoulder to see that he'd mounted Feannag and was watching her.

"Do what?"

"Touch minds with animals." His gaze flicked to where Skaal sat a few yards away, waiting for them to depart. "What do you and Skaal talk about?"

Her lips quirked. He sounded almost jealous. "That's between two lasses."

Cailean harrumphed, although a rare flicker of mirth softened his gaze. "Have it your way then."

"Skaal understands you," she said then.

Cailean cut the fae hound a sidelong look. "Really?"

"Aye … she just can't answer back."

He shook his head slowly. "Gods," he murmured. "All the times I've ranted at the poor beast."

Skaal made a sound in the back of her throat, halfway between a growl and a yelp, and Bree swallowed a laugh. *Aye, he's a grumpy prick.*

Cailean's gaze flicked between them before his mouth pursed. He then jerked his chin over his shoulder, making it clear she was to get up behind him. "Enough talk. Let's get moving."

Bree moved forward and vaulted up onto Feannag. The moment she was astride the stallion, she stiffened. The heat of Cailean's back was a furnace, and she quelled the urge to lean into him. Instead of looping her arms around his waist though, she rested her hands upon her thighs.

Her nostrils flared as the heavy tang of iron assaulted her senses. A tremor then rippled through her. The blades he wore strapped across his chest were uncomfortably close. Fortunately, he'd taken his broadsword off his back and strapped it, and the dagger he usually wore at his hip, to the front of the saddle.

Nonetheless, the proximity to iron made her break into a sweat.

Feannag moved off then, springing into a jolting trot. The movement threw Bree's body up against Cailean's—and the feel of the strong muscles of his back and the scent of leather and woodsmoke triggered memories.

Of Duncrag. Of the one night they'd spent in each other's arms.

Pushing thoughts of that encounter to the back of her mind, she attempted to settle properly into the saddle and adjust herself to the horse's stride. The harsh reek of iron caught in the back of her throat, and she coughed.

Shades, she'd have to put up with this all the way to Morae.

You wanted this, she reminded herself then. *It's too late for regrets.*

16: IN SEARCH OF EILIG

BREE AND CAILEAN didn't speak during the journey to Morae. Their silence wasn't companionable, but strained.

She wondered if he already regretted allowing her to accompany him to the crannog. Bree didn't question him about it though. Best to let his decision settle. She'd find a way to make herself useful at their destination so trust might bloom between them.

All the same, worry tugged at her, as did a nagging voice in her head. *Pushing your way into his life won't work*, it whispered. *Coming back to Albia was a mistake.*

Quiet. Bree shut the voice down firmly. *Just give me time.* In returning here and searching for her husband, she'd followed her gut. She just hoped it hadn't steered her wrong.

As they traveled west, the road became increasingly busy; it had been wise for her to send Tiv into hiding. From the moment the first traveler approached, a bent-backed farmer with a cart full of noisy caged fowl, Bree glamored herself.

However, she didn't choose the guise she'd used when she'd traveled alone through Albia—that of the stern-faced farmer's wife with straw-colored hair—instead, she glamored herself as the Marav woman she'd once been: Fia mac Callum.

The thick woodland drew back, and villages—scatterings of turf-roofed cottages—popped up like mushrooms on either side of the highway. Men, women, and children worked the fields, hoeing the dark earth, and harvesting the last of the cabbages and neeps before winter.

Many of them glanced up as Feannag thundered by, their gazes tracking the large crow-black stallion with its two riders—and the huge fae hound that ran at the horse's side, tongue lolling.

They reached Morae at noon. Skaal left them shortly before they did, disappearing into the hazelwood that hugged the shore of the loch. Bree wasn't surprised; she'd marked how Cailean left Skaal behind when he ventured into Rothie. Tales of the High King's chief-enforcer and his fae hound were no doubt far-spread throughout Albia. It made sense not to draw more attention than was necessary to himself.

After all, he was supposed to be dead.

A scattering of squat round huts with conical roofs encircled the lake edge, where women were bringing in washing and children played knucklebones in the dirt.

"No sign of the company of fighters out here," Cailean muttered, breaking the long silence between them. "Yet." His tone was all business, making his focus clear.

"They'll be residing inside the crannog then," she replied. "What should we be looking out for?"

"An enclosure with a banner … cheering."

"They should be easy to find."

He grunted in reply. "You'd think so."

They rode onto a wooden causeway. Peering over Cailean's shoulder, Bree's gaze settled upon the turf roofs within the crannog—a large island encircled by a high wooden palisade—in the midst of the wide loch. The blunt-edged Ben Morae rose to the north, a majestic peak with deep-green and purple slopes, reflected in the still waters beneath.

He raised a hand then to acknowledge the pike-wielding guards who flanked the gates on the way in. Bree noted the respectful nods they answered him with. Despite that he'd walked away from his old life, Cailean carried a commanding air about him that others couldn't ignore.

He angled Feannag toward a long, low-slung building to the right of the guard house, threw his leg over the pommel, and slid off his horse. He then strapped on his weapons. Bree was also about to dismount when he turned. His gaze sharpened as it traveled over her then, taking in her glamored form.

"I chose this face because we're both familiar with it," she murmured, even as her pulse took off. Iron bite her, this man's glare could flay the skin off a boar's hide. "Do you have a problem with it?"

"No," he replied brusquely. "One face is the same as another."

Anger pulsed to life in Bree's belly. His mood had been tolerable at dawn, but it seemed the ride to Morae had soured it. Aye, he was impatient to go in search of Eilig, but that didn't mean he had to be a prick about it.

Bree slid off Feannag's back to find herself standing too close to Cailean. The iron strapped across his front made her ears buzz in warning. Edging away from him, she waited while he unstrapped the saddle bags and handed over a bronze coin to the lad who emerged from the stables.

After making sure the lad would rub Feannag down well and feed him a generous nosebag of oats and plenty of hay, Cailean turned on his heel and strode out onto the wide street. Bree followed him.

Her husband walked with long, purposeful strides. He bristled with impatience, his shoulders tense. Of course, even without his hound, Cailean drew stares—many of them from women. His tattoos, size, and bearing made it impossible for him to pass unseen.

A company of warriors marched by then. Armed with iron-tipped pikes and axes, they were a sign of the unrest that had plagued The Uplands of late. Their rough voices mingled with the clucking of fowl that pecked at grain outside the dwellings, and the squeals of children chasing each other through the wynds that led off the main thoroughfare. At the far end of the isle, Bree spied the conical roof of the chieftain's roundhouse, where smoke drifted lazily into the pale sky.

They walked down the main street, gazes sweeping left and right as they looked for a fighting enclosure or a banner announcing the next duel. However, when they reached the large dirt square before the broch, there had been no sign of either.

After that, Cailean scoured the crannog, lane by lane, with Bree walking silently at his heel. And as the afternoon inched by, she watched her husband's face gradually darken. By the time they found themselves back at the gates leading out of Morae, a deep scowl creased his face.

"The Mother's tits," Cailean growled, stopping before the stables where they'd left Feannag. "He isn't here."

Bree winced, sympathetic to his frustration. He'd been building up to facing Eilig all day, and the man had eluded him. "What now?"

Cailean huffed an irritated sigh, raking his fingers through his hair. "I need to ask around … and find out if he was here, and if so, where the bastard went." He glanced about him then as if he'd only just noticed that dusk was settling. "But first, I'd better get us lodgings for the night."

An elderly couple rented them a lean-to behind one of the tightly packed cottages within the fort and promised to provide clean furs to sleep on, hot water, soap, and drying sheets.

However, embarrassment swept over Bree when Cailean made sure that there were *two* sleeping nooks inside—a request that earned a surprised look from the old woman. Of course, she'd assumed they were a couple, and Cailean had just made it clear they weren't.

Cheeks burning, she ducked inside the lean-to, glancing around the dim interior. Cailean entered a moment later, and she avoided looking at him.

The elderly woman bustled in then, bringing fresh drying sheets and soap, followed by her husband shortly after, with two large buckets of water. "We'll heat these in the cauldron over the fire," the old man instructed before lighting the logs waiting in the fire pit. His wife then tipped the water into the cauldron.

"Just ask if you need anything else," his wife sang out as they departed.

In the cramped lean-to, Bree eyed the iron pot full of water that now simmered over the flames. "Curse it," she muttered. "I can't escape iron."

"You won't in Albia," Cailean replied. "But I'll pour the water into the washbowl when it's ready."

Bree nodded, still avoiding his eye. Nonetheless, she was grateful he wasn't being obstructive.

She let her glamor fall then, for they were alone now.

Feeling his gaze upon her, she shrugged off her cloak and hung it from a hook on the wall. She then moved over to a stool, pulled it back from the hearth—so she wasn't too close to the iron cauldron—and waited. As awkward as this situation was, it was a luxury to have proper lodgings for the night.

Once the water was warm enough, Cailean used the thick leather gloves the elderly couple had left to heave the pot off the flames and pour some steaming water into the earthen washbowl on the nearby table.

Bree watched the way his heavily muscled arms rippled as he swung the pot around as if it weighed nothing. The sight made her chest grow tight. In the past, she'd never thought the brawn of Marav males was attractive. But that was before *him*.

Cailean hung the pot back up over the fire and headed for the door without a backward glance. "I'll be back later."

The wattle door rattled shut behind him, and Bree let out a deep sigh. She then rose to her feet and started to undress. The clipped edge to his voice warned she wouldn't see him for a while. In the meantime, she'd bathe and look at the wound on her arm.

He agreed you could accompany him as far as Morae, a voice whispered to her then. *But what will you do if he continues without you tomorrow? You can't keep stalking the man.*

Bree's breathing grew shallow. No, she couldn't. Instead, she had to find a way to convince him he needed her at his side.

"Aye, the fighters were here." The smithy wiped a meaty arm across his forehead, leaving a streak of soot behind. "But they only stayed a day."

Cailean's gaze narrowed. "Why was that?" He stood in the doorway of the smoky forge. Outside, night was settling over Morae. He'd asked at a few places, and no one had been helpful. Until he'd stopped here.

"Our chieftain refused to throw any of his men into the ring." The blacksmith cast Cailean an assessing look, no doubt taking in the enforcer tattoos that covered his arms and snaked up his neck. "With war looming, he doesn't want to waste resources."

Cailean nodded. That made sense. Even so, frustration pounded like a fist against his ribs. He was still one step behind Eilig.

"Do you know where they went?"

"They took the highway west … heading to Cannich presumably. My wife passed them on the road. A ragged group they were too."

Cailean took this in with interest. Once, Eilig mac Frang had led the most successful fighting band in Albia. No wonder his former master had been so difficult to find. His fights no longer drew crowds.

At first light tomorrow, he'd make for Cannich.

In many ways, The Upland capital was the best place for him to face Eilig again. It was big enough for him to move about without drawing too much attention to himself, and the sort of place where his former master would linger a few days. He'd be getting desperate to earn some coin now.

However, there was another reason why Cannich suited him.

The overking would have druids working for him—and at least one sacrificer among them. The following evening would be a full moon. Gateway was upon them. The fight with the hill-tribe warriors had drained Cailean, he could feel exhaustion starting to pull at his bones, a sign he needed to take part in a blood-letting.

It would be best if he was at full strength when he took on Eilig.

The fight master would be aging now, and by all accounts was lame these days. It had been twenty years since he'd seen him last. Nonetheless, he wouldn't make the mistake of underestimating him.

Bree was sitting a few yards back from the fire, wrapped in a drying sheet, when the wattle door creaked open and Cailean ducked inside.

However, upon seeing her half-clad state, he halted abruptly, his gaze raking over her. "I thought you'd be dressed." His tone was almost accusing.

"I washed some of my clothes earlier," she replied, gesturing to the garments hanging on the wall next to the fire. "They're almost dry." Pausing, her gaze settled upon his face. "Did you find out what happened to Eilig?"

"Aye." His eyes glinted then.

"And where are they?"

"They've headed for Cannich. And by tomorrow evening, we'll be there too. The prick's days are numbered." He unslung a cloth bag from over his shoulder and set it down on the table. "Here ... I bought you a couple of things"

Bree stilled. "You did?"

"Aye." He pulled out a long-sleeve woolen tunic. "I thought you'd need a new one of these."

Bree's throat tightened. "Thank you," she murmured, taking the tunic.

His gaze dipped to the bandaged cut on her arm then, his brow furrowing. Returning to the bag, he fished out a stoppered clay jar and a roll of linen. "The crannog's healer has dried whin flowers ... so, I asked her to mix up a paste for you."

Warmth washed over her. His unexpected kindness was disarming. A moment later, the backs of her eyes started to prickle. Ancestors give her strength, she couldn't humiliate herself by weeping.

"That's ... thoughtful," she replied, wishing her voice didn't sound so hoarse.

He made an embarrassed noise in the back of his throat. "Aye, well, let's dress your arm and find ourselves an ale-hall," he said gruffly. "I don't know about you, but I'm hungry."

17: ASKING FOR TROUBLE

TELL HER IT ends here.

Seated at the end of a long table inside the ale-hall, Cailean fought the urge to frown at the glamored Shee female opposite. Bree had just speared a piece of garlic sausage on the end of the small steel eating knife she carried with her. She then sniffed it experimentally.

Cailean's fingers clenched around his own eating knife. He then stabbed it into the sausage on his trencher.

He didn't know what he'd been thinking, agreeing to let her travel with him to Morae. He didn't need her assistance with Eilig. She'd caught him at a weak moment maybe. But ever since he'd agreed, regret had been brewing inside him like a storm.

He was a lone wolf, and that was how he liked it.

His wife had nearly brought him to his knees during the summer; he couldn't risk her weakening him again. He couldn't let Bree in—and allowing her to travel with him was just asking for trouble.

The man next to him, who reeked like boiled cabbage, let out a braying laugh at something his wife had just said. In response, the woman started to cackle. The couple were both red-faced from a surfeit of ale, the remains of a huge supper of sausage, braised onions, and coarse oaten bread scattered between them.

Swallowing his mouthful of sausage, Cailean ignored the pair. He was used to being crammed in amongst other customers in ale-halls. Like most, this one was long, windowless, and narrow, with hearths at each end. A fug of smoke hung under the low rafters, and the cacophony of voices was deafening.

However, the noise gave them privacy, even in a crowd.

Steeling himself, Cailean focused on Bree once more. For once, she wasn't interrogating him. She seemed content just to be in his company, something that unsettled him.

He couldn't allow her to get comfortable, to think this would last.

She needed to know that tomorrow he'd ride for Cannich, and she wouldn't be coming with him.

"How is your arm?" he asked, reaching for his cup of ale. He then took a large gulp, anger spiking through him. The Reaper take him, why did he keep fussing over her?

Bree glanced up from her supper. "Better … the whin should heal it quickly."

"We use whin tonic just for sore throats and coughs … I didn't realize it had such powerful healing properties."

She smiled. "It probably doesn't … for you that is."

Cailean stabbed another piece of sausage. Enough with skirting around the subject. He needed to stop blathering on about whin tonic and get to the Gods-damned point. "It was a bold move … to walk away from Sheehallion."

Bree's expression sobered. "Aye," she murmured. "But an easier choice than I'd expected." She paused then. "Once I realized I had to find you."

Tension coiled in Cailean's gut. She wasn't making this easy. "Does the queen know you're here?" The question was asked tersely, and only Bree would have heard him. But he marked her flinch, nonetheless.

She nodded. "Mor has eyes everywhere … she'll know I've crossed into Albia."

"And are you forbidden from crossing back?"

"No," she replied, a groove etching between her brows. "Except that she's highly suspicious of me now." She halted then, her hazel eyes narrowing. "Why? Are you suggesting I do?"

"It might be for the best."

They stared at each other a long moment, and Cailean marked the way her jaw tightened. Frowning, he braced himself to be argued with. He'd known she wouldn't let this go easily.

But to his irritation, she didn't even answer him. Instead, Bree glanced right, her body stiffening.

Something—or someone—had caught her eye.

Do I know him?

The man was playing 'Liar' with a woman a few yards away—each taking turns to shake two dice in a cup and then guess if their opponent was lying to them about the result.

He looked to be of middling age, although he carried his years well, and had umber-colored skin and black hair that curled tightly against his scalp. Leathers covered his lean frame, and when he smiled at the pale-skinned woman with greying tawny hair who sat opposite, he revealed straight, even teeth.

Bree's pulse quickened. The woman was a stranger to her, yet the man definitely reminded her of someone.

Moments passed, and sensing her looking at him, the man glanced Bree's way. Their gazes met, and his dark eyes narrowed.

Bree shifted her attention back to her trencher, her heart pounding.

Iron bite her, she *did* recognize him.

"What is it?"

Bree looked up, meeting Cailean's veiled blue eyes once more.

Her belly clenched then. He wanted rid of her. The garlic sausage and bread she'd eaten churned, nausea following. She'd known this conversation was looming.

Swallowing, she did her best to ignore the sense of impending doom. They'd have to finish their talk later. Right now, she had to speak to someone else.

Without another word to her husband, Bree picked up her cup of ale once more and rose from the table. Then, ignoring his scowl, she moved across to where the couple were now laughing together and slid onto the bench seat next to the woman.

"Sorry for the intrusion."

Their laughter cut off, and the woman's moss-green eyes narrowed. "Can we help you?"

"I hope so."

Bree flashed the woman an apologetic smile before fixing the man with a level look. "It's been a long while … Flynn."

The man stiffened. His reaction was subtle, and he hurriedly masked it, but it was enough.

Aye, it was him.

"You're looking well," she murmured. "Living amongst the Marav clearly suits you."

"You've mistaken me for someone else," he replied coldly, his brows knitting together. "My name's Lycan."

Holding his gaze, Bree shifted her glamor, just a little, so that her face altered. For a heartbeat or two, she let him see her real features and her golden eyes with their slitted pupils.

Alarm rippled across Flynn's face. "Iron," he whispered as Bree let her Marav glamor settle once more.

Aye, he'd recognized her too.

"I knew Mor would catch up with me one day." His throat bobbed then, while beside Bree, his female companion had gone still. "How long have you been hunting me?"

18: AN OUTSIDER

"FEAR NOT," BREE replied, deciding it was best not to make Mor's brother shit his breeches. "I'm not here for you."

Flynn's brow furrowed, even as his fingers tightened around the grip of his eating knife.

"I've left Sheehallion too," she admitted then, "although not through the stones." This wasn't the time or place to regale him with the tale of her past six moons.

Over two hundred and fifty years ago, when they'd been younglings, Bree and Gil had been friends with Mor's younger brothers, Grae and Flynn.

But time had changed many things.

She shifted her attention to the woman next to her. High spots of color had risen to her pale cheeks, her green eyes shadowed with fear. "You must be Ava," she murmured.

The woman swallowed. "I haven't gone by that name in a long time."

"No," Bree answered, her voice lowering. "Not since you were wed to Talorc mac Brude. You did a fine job of making him believe the Shee stole you away. He's persecuted my people ever since." She glanced Flynn's way once more. "And Mor hasn't forgiven you either … although she knows the truth."

Aye, that her brother had passed through The Ring of Caith and given up his long life. For a Marav.

"I don't expect her to understand," he replied, his tone still wintry. "Or you."

Bree stiffened at the scorn that now laced his voice. Naked suspicion hardened his face.

She was aware of Cailean's gaze upon her then, stabbing into her like twin blades.

A warning.

She ignored his stare. Let him fume. She'd return to their table when she was ready. After all, he'd just made his feelings clear.

"She must be special," Bree said then, trying to ignore the ache in her chest. "To give up your long life for."

Flynn stared back at her, and as the moments passed, his gaze softened just a little. "She is," he murmured.

"But you're aging now," Bree said with a shake of her head. Indeed, crow's feet radiated out from his eyes, and lines furrowed his brow and either side of his nose. Silver threaded his once jet-black curls. Lowering her voice again, lest anyone overhear, she continued, "You could have lived for many centuries more, and seen the rise and fall of countless High Kings of Albia, yet you've given it all up … for her. Why?"

Her gaze flicked back to Ava, whose mouth had now pursed. "Sorry," she said, favoring her with an apologetic smile. "But I'm just trying to understand."

"Do you even have to ask, Bree?" Flynn replied, drawing her attention once more. "Or are you so lacking in empathy that you fail to see the obvious?" His dark eyes gleamed. "I gave everything up for *love* … and I'd do it all again in a heartbeat."

Heat swept over Bree. She wanted to tell Mor's haughty brother that she knew what love was. Nonetheless, envy tightened her throat as the moments drew out. Flynn was now part of *this* world, yet she'd always be an outsider looking in.

"I do sometimes think about Sheehallion," Flynn admitted softly, "and those I left behind." He leaned toward her. "How are my kin? Has Mor exiled Grae yet, or have they finally buried their differences?"

Bree went still.

The heat drained from her, a deep chill replacing it. For the first time since rising from the table opposite, she regretted approaching Flynn. Of course, he had no idea what had transpired in Sheehallion in the years since he left.

"They never reconciled," she admitted, her voice roughening.

Flynn's gaze narrowed. "No?"

Bree shook her head. "In the end, Grae tried to overthrow your sister … and in response, she put a price on his head." Flynn's lean body went rigid, but she pushed herself to continue. "I killed him."

"That woman was Queen Ava?" Cailean came to an abrupt halt. Turning to Bree, he then reached out and pulled her around to face him.

They'd left the ale-hall and had been walking back to their lodgings. And along the way, Bree revealed the identity of the man and woman she'd spoken to. And as she'd done so, her manner was stiff, unusually formal.

Dusk was settling, and lads were out lighting the torches and braziers that would illuminate the crannog once night fell. The air was raw, and their breathing steamed in clouds before them, a sign there would be a frost the following morning.

But Cailean barely noticed the cold. Instead, he stared down at his wife's taut face, marking the shadows in her hazel eyes. "Aye," she whispered.

"I thought she was dead."

"No … just in hiding."

Cailean's gaze searched her glamored features. There was a distance between them now, one he wagered had little to do with her conversation with the Raven Queen's brother, and everything to do with him. He should have been relieved, but to his surprise, he wasn't.

All the same, he took care to remove his hand from her arm.

"Your reunion didn't end well," he said after a brief pause. Indeed, he'd seen the fury that had rippled across the man's face, the way his hand had clenched hard around his eating knife. "I thought he was going to stab you through the throat."

She snorted. "I'd just admitted I killed his brother … it was my last job before I departed for Duncrag in the spring."

Cailean cocked an eyebrow. "That'll do it."

"We were friends once," she admitted then, reaching up and pushing a strand of oaken-colored hair from her cheek. "When we were younglings. But over the years, things changed."

Cailean's gaze roamed across her face, taking in her pale skin and the scattering of freckles across the bridge of her nose. They were just an illusion though, and his druid eyes allowed him to see the shimmer that now surrounded her.

"Aye, well … there are some relationships that can never be mended," he replied. Misgiving stole over him as he thought of Enya. He'd let his sister down all those years ago. Had she hated him in the end?

Shaking himself free of regrets about a past he couldn't change, Cailean stepped back from Bree then, and they continued walking toward their lodgings. Above them, the first of the stars twinkled in the clear night sky. The moon was rising, just a night away from being full.

Entering the lean-to, he found a jug of bramble wine sitting on the table near the door and two wooden cups. Their hosts had stopped by while they were out.

"Wine?" Cailean asked as he shrugged off his cloak and hung it by the door. Bree's strange mood was starting to get to him. They both needed to relax a little, especially before he brought up the subject she'd so abruptly terminated earlier.

"Very well," Bree replied, her voice dull.

The instant they were indoors, she'd let the glamor fall, and a golden Shee woman stood before him once more. However, her lovely face was strained, those tawny eyes veiled. There was a brittleness to her he'd never seen before.

Hanging up her cloak, she moved over to the stool she'd placed back from the iron pot over the fire earlier. Cailean put on a log, and she watched as the hungry flames devoured it. Her expression turned distant.

Suddenly, she seemed far away.

19: RISE FROM THE ASHES

CAILEAN POURED THEM both generous cups of wine and handed Bree hers. Their fingers brushed as she took it, and a familiar heat rippled up his arm.

The feline pupils of her eyes dilated, her gaze snapping back to the present. She'd felt it too, the awareness that shivered between them.

Shit. This isn't helping. Doing his best to ignore the tingling in his fingers, Cailean took his wine over to one of the sleeping nooks, heeled off his boots, and climbed in, moving the furs so that they provided a pillow for his back against the rough stone wall.

Then, cradling the cup of wine in his hands, he leaned into the nest he'd created.

Meanwhile, Bree didn't move from her stool.

Now that he'd left her side, her attention returned to the flames. The fire burned bright, hungrily devouring the lump of pine he'd just added. Sipping her wine, she continued to stare at the fire, its light making her eyes glow like two candle flames.

Cailean couldn't help it, he drank the sight of her in.

Sitting like that, her expression solemn, kissed by firelight, he'd never seen anything more beautiful—or otherworldly.

There would be no mistaking her for a Marav woman now.

Look away, you fool.

It was dangerous to gaze at Bree like this, especially after his decision to continue to Cannich without her. But he couldn't help it. As both Marav and Shee, she ensnared him.

Silence swelled in the lean-to, broken only by the crackling of the fire. And as Cailean drained the last of his wine, he couldn't bear it any longer. "Sometimes it helps to share heavy thoughts."

Bree blinked and glanced his way. Her lips then curved into a tight smile. "Trust me, you don't want to hear these. They're just full of self-loathing and defeatism."

He snorted. "That doesn't sound like you."

She cut her gaze away. "No," she replied, her voice catching slightly. "I admit, I don't feel like myself tonight."

He raised an eyebrow. "Did meeting Flynn again rattle you that much?" He really shouldn't be asking so many questions. However, he couldn't help himself.

"Maybe." Her gaze fixed upon the dancing flames once more. "He was a reminder … that it doesn't matter how far or fast I flee, I can't outrun myself … or the life I've led."

"Is that what you're doing … running?"

She swallowed. "Maybe." Silence fell, and then Bree lifted her chin, her gaze settling upon him. "You're right. I shouldn't have come looking for you." The pain in her eyes made his chest involuntarily tighten. "I'm not usually someone to linger where I'm not wanted."

He stared back at her. He couldn't deny her words, especially after what he'd said to her earlier. Suddenly though, he wished he hadn't been so blunt about it. He could be a callous prick at times.

Bree dragged a hand down her face, exhaustion rippling over her features. "I left Sheehallion, following a mad impulse … believing that I could make a fresh start," she admitted softly. "But I can't."

"Why not?" he asked cautiously. They were straying into dangerous waters now, yet he couldn't help but push things further.

"Because some people don't deserve a second chance."

He frowned. The fatalism in her voice unnerved him. "Do you really believe that?"

She nodded. "I've slain so many. Each mark was just a job to me. The first few turned my stomach, although it didn't take long before I felt nothing."

He nodded. "It was like that for me too. When I began serving the High King and was bidden to hunt and kill those who'd never done me any wrong, I thought I wouldn't get used to it … but I did."

Their gazes held then before Bree grimaced. "And that's the problem, isn't it? When death leaves you unmoved. You should always feel *something* when you take a life."

He didn't reply, even if uneasiness shifted deep in his chest. This wasn't a subject he enjoyed discussing, especially since thoughts of reckoning dogged his every waking moment these days.

"You're no longer the Raven Queen's assassin," he said after a heavy pause. "You can be whoever you choose now."

"Can I?" Pulling a face, she turned back to the fire, avoiding his eye. She paused then and lifted the cup she still clutched to her lips, draining it. "That need not concern you though … I shall let you go on your way tomorrow. I've pushed myself on you long enough."

Cailean stiffened, a chill washing over him, even as he kicked himself. Wasn't this what he wanted? "Where will you go?"

"It doesn't matter."

His pulse quickened. Aye, it did. Rolling out of his sleeping nook, he set his empty cup aside and approached the hearth, pulling the second stool around and lowering himself onto it so he was facing Bree.

Surprised by his move, she straightened, her expression wary.

"You can't just give up," he said firmly. "It isn't in your nature."

Her lips lifted at the corners, although her golden eyes remained bleak. "I'm not like you, Cailean. You've got a purpose … even if it's a blood-thirsty one."

"Well, *find* yourself a reason to live then," he countered, trying to ignore the ache in his throat. The Hag's nails, he couldn't stand seeing her like this. He wanted to grab her by the shoulders and shake her until fire ignited in her eyes once more. "You've burned your old life to the ground … rise from the ashes, for fuck's sake."

Her gaze snapped wide at his vehemence, and her breathing grew shallow.

They stared at each other for a few heartbeats, and then something inside Cailean gave way.

He leaned in, captured her face in his hands, and kissed her.

Bree gasped, her lips parting under his, and his tongue swept in, devouring her.

A groan rumbled in his throat. She tasted of wine and woman, like she belonged to him. The faint scent of rose wrapped itself around him as he slid a hand to the back of her head and deepened the kiss. While she'd been a Marav woman, he'd associated the sharp scent of lavender with his wife, not rose. In the past, when he'd hunted the Shee, rose had been a warning. He'd found the perfume cloying. But not any longer.

Instead, it awoke a primal urge inside him. One he was tired of fighting.

Bree kissed him back hungrily now, her tongue sliding against his, her hands splaying across his chest, and her fingertips digging through the leather into his flesh.

Cailean hauled her off the stool and onto his lap so she sat astride him. She was taller as a Shee and so bent her head as she gently bit his lower lip and raised her hands to cup his face. The gesture was both tender and possessive.

And then their mouths savaged each other's, need quickening like a flame on dry tinder.

Gods, he'd tried to forget what she tasted like, how good her body felt pressed against his. But he couldn't. And when she ground herself against him, and a groan tore from her throat to find him rock-hard for her, heat swept over him, incinerating any coherent thought.

He was supposed to agree with her—to confirm they'd go their separate ways the following day. Instead, something had shattered inside him.

He wanted her naked. Now.

Reaching up, he started untying her leathers, stripping them off her, while she tore at his vest and breeches too.

Panting, they wriggled out of their clothing, and when—at last—firelight played on her long limbs and smooth skin, Cailean pulled her back astride him on his lap. He then slid his hands down the long arch of her spine before he ran his fingertips up the smooth skin of her arms, to the delicate sweep of her collarbone and swan-like neck.

"Am I still pleasing to you?" she asked huskily, her eyes glowing as she watched him. "Even like this."

"Aye," he murmured, as his fingertips traced the underside of her small, high breasts. He then dragged his thumb over a hard nipple, heat coiling in his belly when she gasped. He couldn't believe she'd worry about such things, yet he'd happily reassure her. "You're beautiful."

Her golden eyes grew limpid at these words. He meant them too. Leaning in, he trailed his lips up her neck to the shell of her ear.

"Hold tight," he whispered, his belly clenching as she shuddered against him. "Let's move somewhere more comfortable."

In response, Bree wrapped her arms and legs around him, clinging to Cailean as he rose to his feet and carried her to a sleeping nook. Then, laying her down upon the furs, he crawled over her, his mouth capturing Bree's once more for a long, hot kiss.

She writhed against him, her hands sliding against his skin.

He drew their kisses out, until they were both panting, before moving down to her breasts. Pushing them together, he feasted upon their swollen tips. His groin throbbed with each hoarse moan she made, every whispered plea.

How many times over the past moons had he recalled her husky voice urging him on, begging him to take her? How many times had he taken himself in hand, giving himself the release he needed yet never feeling fully satisfied? Too many, and he'd cursed himself after each *incident*.

But he wasn't cursing himself tonight.

Instead, he let his bitterness and regret go. He let himself have what he craved.

20: STAY WITH ME

HIS MOUTH ON her breasts, the way he drew each nipple deep and sucked until she whimpered, turned Bree's body molten.

Sprawled upon the furs underneath Cailean, her senses reeled.

How had this happened?

One moment, her gut had been twisted in misery as she faced the reality of her situation. And the next, he'd risen from his sleeping nook and taken a stool opposite, staring fiercely into her eyes.

It surprised her that Cailean didn't want her to give up. He'd seemed vexed at her despair. She thought that he wanted her gone.

But, instead, he'd kissed her.

Bree hadn't been trying to manipulate him. The misery that clutched at her breast wasn't feigned. Her encounter with Flynn had left her shaken. After learning that she'd hunted and killed his brother like prey, he'd looked at her as if she were a monster. Unworthy of redemption.

The revulsion in his eyes had haunted her ever since.

But Cailean had challenged her; he wouldn't let her give up.

And now, she couldn't think about anything else except that they were both naked, firelight bathing their sweat-damp bodies, and that she ached for him.

He was taking his time though, sucking her sensitive nipples with agonizing sensuality. And all the while, an aching, melting sensation pulsed between her thighs.

Reaching down, she raked her fingers through his short hair and hooked a leg over his thigh, tugging him closer. "Please, Cailean," she gasped. "More."

Releasing the nipple he'd just been lathing with his tongue, he favored Bree with a smoldering look that made her belly clench and moved sideways, onto his back upon the furs. Then, he drew her up onto her knees. "Turn around."

Trembling now, Bree complied, allowing him to slide underneath her, parting her legs wide as he did so. She now knelt over his face, looking directly at where his swollen shaft reared proudly toward her.

Bree's breathing quickened at the sight of it, the crown glistening with his arousal. Sighing, she leaned forward, one hand wrapping around the base of his rod. Her lips parted then, and she greedily took him deep into her mouth. A moan escaped her as she did.

Breathing a curse, Cailean gripped her hips and lowered her down so that his breath whispered over the aching flesh between her thighs.

And then, an instant later, he was devouring her.

Hunger twisted in the cradle of her hips, and she sank against him, giving herself up to sensation.

Stroking his bollocks with one hand and gripping the base of his rod with the other, she sucked him, taking him in as deep as she could. The tip of him hit the back of her throat, and her eyes watered, but she didn't stop.

She was as ravenous for him as he was for her—and the deep groans that rumbled through his chest now merely drove her wild.

This act was intense, so much so that it wasn't long before she shattered against his wicked mouth, hot pleasure throbbing and rippling through her loins.

She gave a choked cry, even as she brought his rod deeper still.

And then, Cailean's hips arched up to meet her mouth, a strangled sound ripping from his throat as he spilled.

She drank him deep before, still shuddering from her release, she licked the long, glistening length of him.

Panting, Cailean lifted her off his face.

She moved around so that he could pull her against him. And there they lay for a while, their bodies glistening with sweat, both breathing hard as the hearth popped and crackled.

They fit perfectly. Throat constricting, Bree traced her fingertips over his damp skin, following the inked swirls and designs, and the infinity serpent that coiled around a bicep.

New beginnings. She swallowed hard. *If only it were that easy.*

There was no getting away from it. She'd spilled too much blood, taken too many lives, to deserve a happy ending.

Cailean had tried to convince her that wasn't the case, but the heaviness in her chest said otherwise. This encounter had been thrilling, and unexpected, but it changed nothing.

"Stay with me." The words, softly spoken, drew her out of her thoughts.

Bree raised her head, meeting his eye. "What?"

His woad-blue eyes were dark in the firelight. "I was an arse earlier … and I'm sorry," he said, his voice roughening. "But forget what I said. Don't leave me tomorrow. Come with me to Cannich. Help me find Eilig." His gaze grew limpid as it fused with hers. "Let's start again."

Bree's lips parted, her heart slamming against her breastbone. "You don't—"

"I do," he cut her off, anticipating her protest. "I'm no good at this, Bree … but for you, I shall try." He reached up then, his thumb skimming down her jaw and across the swell of her lower lip. She shivered under his touch.

Ancestors, she wanted him still. A needy ache now built deep in her womb.

"You're not the only one with regrets," he went on, his voice lowering once more. "I just don't let myself dwell on them." He brushed the back of his knuckles down Bree's cheek. Her breathing grew shallow at the emotion that now glistened in his eyes. "But despite all my snarling and grumbling, I don't regret *you*."

Bree's mouth tugged into a half-smile. "Even though I've brought you no end of trouble?"

He laughed, and his sudden mirth took years off his face. A moment later, his expression grew serious, his gaze softening. "You have," he replied huskily. "My wild, willful wife."

They stared at each other for a long moment then, while Bree's pulse fluttered.

The despair that had choked her earlier, that had turned the world the color of smoke, lifted, and suddenly hope ignited deep in her chest.

"You were sent to test me," Cailean continued, his fingers trailing down her neck to her collarbone. "To torment me."

Bree wanted to answer him, yet she was finding it difficult to concentrate, especially now that his hand slid down to the swell of her breast. And when his thumb brushed the sensitized nipple, she gasped. A moment later, something hot and hard pushed against her hip.

Glancing down, her gaze met his shaft, ready for her once more.

The ache in the cradle of her hips started to throb.

"Ride me, Bree."

Heat flushed across her chest. Her breathing coming in shallow bursts, she pushed herself up and climbed astride him.

"Fuck me," he growled, his chest rising and falling sharply too. His erection now thrust up between them, jerking in eagerness.

Sweat beaded upon Bree's skin once more. Nodding, she wrapped a hand around his girth and rose up onto her knees, positioning the tip of him at her entrance.

And then, she slowly lowered herself down upon him, a deep groan escaping her.

He was big, and this position was intense, for she took him deep. She stretched around him, and when she eventually settled herself upon his rod fully, the ache in her womb brushed the edges of pain.

Bree stilled, letting herself adjust to him—and all the while, her gaze never left his.

The expression on Cailean's face was fierce, raw, and her heart started to thump hard, emotion swamping her.

She'd never felt this *vulnerable* during coupling, and the new sensation scared her a little. For the first time ever, she let a lover see beyond the shield she'd always presented to the world.

Reaching between her slick thighs, Cailean slid the pad of his thumb over the sensitive bud of flesh that he'd licked and sucked earlier, circling gently. A melting sensation flowed through Bree's loins, and a groan escaped her. The discomfort deep inside her eased, and then she gave her hips a slow roll.

Cailean hissed a curse through his teeth, and she did it again, enjoying the way his cheekbones flushed and his eyes glittered.

And then, she rose up, sliding herself along the long, thick length of him before bearing down sharply upon him once more.

Their guttural cries echoed through the lean-to then. Pleasure gathered in her loins, as heavy and sweet as honey, and she circled her pelvis again, sucking in a sharp breath at the delicious sensations that now rippled through her lower belly.

"Fuck!" Cailean panted. "Bree … I—"

His voice cut off as she rode him now, her body shuddering with each long slide.

And as they coupled, she watched his face. Shades, how she loved seeing ecstasy ripple over his features, hearing the groans that tore from his throat, and watching his hard-won self-restraint unravel before her eyes.

But at the same time, she was struggling to hold herself together. Each time she bore down upon him, he stroked a place deep inside that turned her liquid. It wasn't long before she was writhing upon his rod, wild pleasure pulsing and shuddering through her.

Bree cried out, clutching at him as she peaked.

Cailean took control then, gripping her by the hips and drawing her up and down the heft of his shaft, deep and hard now.

His face was taut, the tendons in his neck corded as he arched up into her with each thrust, his skin glistening with sweat.

And then, as Bree choked out his name—her body quivering like a sapling in the wind—he too shattered, a shout tearing from his throat.

21: A MEETING ON THE ROAD

"WILL YOU KILL him tonight?"

Cailean's broad back tensed against Bree at her direct question.

"Probably not … I should take part in a blood-letting first." He paused then. "Once we arrive in Cannich, I won't waste any time finding myself a sacrificer."

"You haven't participated in the ceremony since partnering with me?" Her pulse fluttered then as she remembered the intensity of the blood-letting, how it had felt to have earth magic surging through her veins.

The tattoo of Feannag's large hooves on the road echoed through the still morning. Skaal loped alongside, silent and watchful. They'd left Morae at first light, and if they rode swiftly, they'd reach The Upland capital by dusk.

"No … I haven't had the opportunity." Cailean's left hand, which had been resting on his thigh while his right held the reins, moved to her arm, his fingers sliding down to her wrist. "But there's a full moon out tonight … and I will make the most of it."

In response, Bree laced her fingers with his. Arms clasped loosely around Cailean's waist, the warmth of the sun on her face, she felt almost at peace with the world. The eve before had been an upheaval, a sundering of sorts, but what had begun in despair ended in joy. She'd been ready to walk away from Cailean—and then he'd surprised her.

It also was a relief not to be in pain any longer. Ever since applying the whin ointment to her arm, the wound no longer burned. Shee healed fast once whin counteracted the iron; the cut would be scabbed over by the evening.

"I could tell that the Druthin warriors drained you," she admitted then.

"Aye … more than I care to admit," he replied with a sigh. "There's a fatigue dragging at me now, one no amount of sleep can cure."

"Not even a few more vigorous tumbles with your wife will help?" she teased, her mouth curving.

Cailean laughed, his fingers tightening around hers. "Do you *want* to wear me out?"

Bree snorted, heat kindling in her lower belly as she recalled the wild night they'd just spent. It was no surprise Cailean was tired. She was too. They'd had little sleep in the end.

"I hope this band of fighters is still in Cannich," she said, turning the conversation back to more serious matters.

"They will be," he replied. She heard the edge to his voice, the urgency that simmered just beneath. "Gateway is upon us, and Eilig won't want to be on the road when The Slew come out to play."

A pause followed before Bree cleared her throat. "Can I partner with you again … tonight?" Her pulse quickened then. The ritual was an intense, if unnerving, experience. Yet the blood-letting bonded them, and she was eager to share that closeness with him again.

Cailean squeezed her hand. "You can't, Bree … not now you've returned to your Shee form."

She stiffened against him. "Why not?"

"Because the sacrificer would see through your glamor, and even if they didn't, the moment the ritual began, you'd be unmasked."

"Of course." She kicked herself for not grasping the obvious. "Sorry … I wasn't thinking."

A hollow sensation settled in her belly then. She was Shee and he Marav, and there were some things they could never share.

Sensing her shift in mood, Cailean tightened his grip on her hand once more. "I wish it were different … but taking part in a blood-letting with you would be too dangerous. It might not even work … Shee blood and earth magic have never mixed well."

"You're right," she answered, cursing the sudden huskiness in her voice. "I don't know why I suggested it."

A strained silence fell then, and Bree was struggling to think of something to ease it, when specks in the distance caught her eye. Her gaze narrowed. "We've got company."

Cailean released her hand and leaned forward. "I can't make them out," he muttered. "What do you see?"

Her keen eyesight scanned the dark shapes on the horizon. They were riding through a wide glen, sculpted peaks dusted with emerald-green rising up on either side. "Rows of men upon heavyset horses." She saw them clearly now, their spears bristling against the washed-out blue of the sky. "Warriors."

Cailean growled a curse. "Great, that's the last thing we need."

Bree tensed. "They aren't looking for you?"

"No … but I'm supposed to be dead, remember?"

"Aye." Bree cut Skaal a sidelong glance. The fae hound still ran at their side, and as the glen they rode through was bare of vegetation, there was nowhere for her to hide. "How could I forget?"

All too soon, the warriors approached, the Cannich banners—a bloodied ax against a field of charcoal-black—visible now. However, when the lead riders spied Cailean, they brought their horses to a halt, waiting for him to reach them.

Before they did, Bree hastily glamored herself, even as her pulse quickened to a canter. She had to be ready, in case things went ill.

The rider nearest, an angular man with hawkish features and long red hair tied back at the nape, viewed Cailean with interest before his attention shifted to Skaal. The fae hound had halted at Feannag's side.

The man who had the bearing of this group's captain turned his attention to Cailean once more, raking his gaze over him. "I've heard the High King's chief-enforcer travels with a fae hound." His gravelly voice carried in the still morning air. "But I didn't expect to meet either of you today."

Bree's racing pulse slowed, relief washing over her. Clearly, word hadn't reached Cannich of Cailean mac Brochan's demise.

"Aye, well … you have," Cailean drawled back, and it struck Bree how easily he slipped back into his old role. It fitted him so well. Did he miss the power he'd wielded, the awe and respect he inspired among the Marav?

"And what brings you to the far north, mac Brochan?"

"The High King's business."

The captain raised ruddy eyebrows. "Aye?"

"Aye."

An awkward silence followed, swelling until the captain's brow furrowed. "I suppose that's to be expected," he grumbled. "Since he's traveling north too."

Bree's breath caught at this news, while Cailean's broad back tensed against her. However, he recovered swiftly. "The High King is expecting me to meet him at Cannich. Do you know how far away from the fort he is?"

"I'm not sure," the captain replied. "Although his armies had reached Dulross around five days ago."

Bree's heart kicked. She hadn't expected Talorc mac Brude to leave the safety of Duncrag, especially now—and the discovery that he was bringing an army into The Uplands made her uneasy. What was the bastard up to?

"I will wait for him at Cannich then," Cailean replied, his tone offhand now.

The captain cast him another probing look. "The overking will be pleased to see you, mac Brochan. He has many questions about the High King's plans."

Cailean gave a non-committal grunt, making it clear that he'd only share what mac Brude had permitted him to.

The captain scowled at the chief-enforcer's rude response.

Another silence fell, and Bree started to sweat. They reminded her of a pair of stags in rutting season: staring each other down, deciding whether it was worth locking horns.

Moments passed, and the captain urged his horse on, raising his hand to let his company know they were on the move again.

As he passed Cailean, the two men eyeballed each other. The captain then took a good look at Bree. Her skin prickled under his inspection. It was likely none of these warriors knew that the High King's chief-enforcer had taken a wife. But even if they had, they'd be wondering why he was traveling with her, alone, in the northern reaches of The Uplands.

"You enjoyed that, didn't you?" she muttered as Cailean urged Feannag into a canter, and they left the company of warriors behind.

Cailean snorted. "Aye … until I learned that the High King is on his way."

"That was a surprise," Bree admitted. "What's he planning?"

"No idea." He paused a moment, tension rippling through his big body once more. "You said there was an army rallying at the gates of Duncrag nearly a moon ago?"

"Aye … a sea of wolf, stag, and shield banners was camped there," she replied. "Although I thought they'd gathered to *defend* the capital."

"They might have been," he answered, his voice hardening. "But clearly … something has changed."

22: DO WHAT YOU MUST

CAILEAN GAZED UP at Cannich's heavily defended walls, warmth suffusing his chest.

Returning here was a homecoming of sorts. Despite that he'd spent most of the last decade based at Duncrag, he'd often traveled to the northern capital. The overking could be trying, yet even he couldn't ruin the fort for him.

He was an Uplander by birth, after all.

Cailean knew Cannich's labyrinthine wynds well and appreciated its remote setting, perched upon the large flat summit of a rock cliff, ringed by high stone walls. The fort resembled a solid grey crown upon a giant's weatherbeaten head.

However, even from this distance, he marked the pikes thrusting up like hedgehog spines against the darkening sky. The Whistle, which blew in from the northwest on this late afternoon, carried with it the scent of woodsmoke blended with the tang of iron.

The capital of The Uplands was preparing itself for war.

Cailean's mouth compressed as he considered what lay ahead for Albia. There had been no great battle in his lifetime, but that was about to change. In the turns of the moon ahead, many Marav would likely die for their High King. And to what end? So that Talorc mac Brude could say the score had been settled.

Would the man ever find the vindication he craved?

Would *he*? Cailean pulled himself up sharply then, uneasiness stirring in his gut. That was the first time he'd ever compared himself to the High King—a man so driven by his need for vengeance it had become a sickness. No, he wasn't like him.

Once he took Eilig's life, he'd leave the past behind him.

Weariness pressed down upon him then, heavy hands upon his shoulders. Aye, he needed the blood-letting. His body ached this afternoon, and he felt overly warm—a sign he needed earth magic.

"You'd better make yourself scarce, lass." He glanced down at where Skaal loped beside his stallion. It felt odd, knowing she understood him, and he didn't like leaving the fae hound behind every time he entered a fort. However, she drew far too much attention. "This shouldn't take longer than a couple of days."

Skaal cast him a glance, her golden eyes glinting in the lowering sun, before she shifted her attention to Bree. It was clear they'd just touched minds. The fae hound then veered off the road and disappeared into the trees.

"What did she say?" he asked.

"She told me to look out for you."

He gave a soft snort. "Overprotective beast."

They approached Cannich on the East Road, one of the three highways that cut through a carpet of ancient woodland; twisted oak, elm, and pine covered the rolling valley beneath the fort.

Ahead, a high wall circled the base of the massive chunk of rock, where ten-foot-tall iron gates blocked the way through.

"You can tell it's Gateway," Bree noted then. "There's a watchfulness in the air."

Cailean frowned. Indeed, the darkening sky already held an ominous look. "Aye, The Slew are waking up."

A shiver rippled down his spine then. There was a fate worse than being sent to the Underworld after death, and that was to join the ranks of the 'unforgiven'. The spirits of the damned were caught between the Otherworld and the Underworld and left in Albia to feast on the spirits of mortals.

Ahead, the guards were starting to draw the gates closed. Cailean urged his stallion into a fast canter, calling out to the men to wait.

They did, their gazes tracking him as he approached.

"You're shutting up early?" Cailean greeted the warriors.

"Aye, we always do at Gateway." One of the guards, a lanky man with an eyepatch, flashed him a smile. "It's been a while, mac Brochan."

Cailean grunted, even as his lips lifted at the corners. Aye, he'd have preferred not to be recognized, but this man's robust welcome made him feel as if he'd just stepped back into his old life for a moment. He'd always enjoyed the camaraderie, the banter, he shared with the warriors here. Uplanders were tough and more plain-spoken than Southerners, yet he'd always admired their grit. "I've been busy," he replied.

"Where's your hound?" The second guard asked, even as his gaze flicked to where Bree sat silently behind Cailean. His eyes were bright with curiosity.

"Hunting, most likely."

"Shall we send word ahead, to let King Ailean know you're here?" the warrior with the eyepatch asked.

"No need … my wife and I will find lodgings elsewhere tonight," Cailean replied firmly. "I'll see him in the morning."

The guards nodded, heeding him.

"Aye, well … make sure you're indoors by nightfall," the one-eyed warrior warned, stepping back to let them pass.

Cailean offered the man a grunt of thanks and urged Feannag through the gap.

In the lower ward beyond, they rode along a path, past a row of barracks, where warriors clad in leather and fur cooked their suppers over hearths outdoors. It looked as if the entire lower ward—the narrow space between the walls and the base of the rock—was crammed with Cannich's garrison.

Bree's arms, which looped around his waist, tightened then, warning him that the proximity of iron—for steam billowed from the entrance to a forge they now passed—was bothering her.

Reaching up, he wrapped a steadying hand around her wrist. He wanted her to know he understood, and that he'd help, where he could. His throat tightened then. What had happened to him? For years, he'd told himself life was easier when you didn't let others in. Wasn't he happier on his own? He'd tried hardening his heart, to send his wife away, yet Bree's sorrow had torn through his defenses. He couldn't keep lying to himself. He cared for her. Deeply. There was no denying it now.

The night before had changed everything, and he was still reeling from it.

"King Ailean *has* been busy," Cailean noted, reining in the sensations that scared him a little. He guided Feannag toward the road that wound its way up to the summit of the rock. "None of this was here when I visited in the summer."

"He's clearly eager to please his High King," Bree replied.

Cailean snorted. "King Ailean is rarely 'eager to please' … it's fear of mac Brude's wrath that keeps him in line, little else."

The road up to the fort was narrow and perilous, just wide enough to travel up single-file, and with a few passing places dug into the rock. However, the views were spectacular, and Cailean couldn't help but cast looks out across the blanket of wintry woodland—skeleton trees interspersed with dark-green conifers—where Skaal and Tivesheh would be waiting.

Reaching the top of the rock, they passed through another set of iron gates, with high stone walls rearing up either side, and into the fort proper.

The roar of cheering voices reached them then, and Cailean's attention cut to a space ringed by spiked wooden palings. A banner hung over the entrance, showing two half-naked fighters locked in mortal combat.

A moment later, another roar went up, and then voices started to chant as if urging someone on.

Cailean drew Feannag to a halt. His pulse quickened as he listened to the fight taking place just yards away.

Bree's hold around his waist tightened. "That's the band of fighters you're looking for, isn't it?"

"Aye." His belly clenched then, violence igniting in his veins. He couldn't believe it. Finally, Eilig was just a few yards away. "I should deal with him now." Gods, he itched to ram his blade through the fight master's throat.

"Cailean." Bree put a hand over his, drawing him out of murderous thoughts. "You need the blood-letting first, remember?"

Tension rippled through him.

Curse it, he hated being so reliant on earth magic for his strength. This was the price he'd willingly paid to become an enforcer. But there were times when he resented it. Now was one such occasion.

"Aye," he ground out, leashing the urge to leap off Feannag, draw his sword, and wade into that enclosure. "I do."

Eilig would have to wait, as planned, until tomorrow. He'd be ready then.

Dragging his gaze from the entrance to the enclosure, he urged Feannag across the wide space, the stallion's hooves clip-clopping over dirt and stones. There was an ale-hall nearby where they'd find lodgings for the night.

The wynds—narrow lanes—of the fort were emptying out as daylight faded. Wisely, the inhabitants of Cannich had hurried indoors. They'd be sprinkling salt around the hearths and across thresholds tonight and donning iron protection charms, to keep the dead at bay. Already, the locals were setting up braziers and lamps outside doorways—for firelight warded off malevolent spirits—and women laid out trays of freshly baked cakes and pies as offerings.

As hoped, the ale-hall had space for them. It had two wings out back connected by a yard, where the proprietor hired out accommodation. It was expensive, for Cailean had to pay to have his horse stabled as well, and he handed over the three silver pennies to the proprietor's daughter with gritted teeth. His coin reserves were seriously dwindling these days, especially after the items he'd bought for Bree in Morae.

Impatience thrummed through him then. The day was waning. He had to seek out a sacrificer before nightfall. He needed to refill the well, so he could focus on dealing with Eilig.

Pocketing the coins, the lass watched him with interest, ignoring Bree, who waited behind him. Pretending not to notice the flirtatious smile she gave him, Cailean met her eye. "I require a favor."

"Oh, aye?" she replied, inclining her head.

Bree made a warning sound in the back of her throat.

Resisting the urge to look his wife's way—maybe he should have warned her he'd need to do this first—Cailean nodded. "A partner for blood-letting."

The ale-hall keeper's daughter's eyes widened before she tossed her long walnut-colored hair over her shoulder. Of course, it was an honor for any woman to be asked to partner with an enforcer for the ceremony. "This evening?" she breathed.

"Aye … now."

Casting Bree a veiled look—her gaze full of questions—the young woman nodded. "Let me fetch my cloak."

Outside in the yard, between the accommodation wings, while they waited, Cailean turned to his wife. Her expression was veiled, yet the hurt look in her eyes made his chest tighten. "You know why I couldn't ask you, Bree," he reminded her softly. "I can't delay this."

Indeed, as if sensing the rising of the full moon, his entire body had started to ache. He was also sweating now, despite that it was a cool evening.

She nodded, a muscle in her jaw feathering. "Of course. Do what you must."

Cailean sighed. That wasn't the response he'd hoped for, and he was about to reply, to attempt to reassure her, when a thin shriek cut through the air. Skin prickling, he glanced up at the sky, where the last rays of light were fading. Dark clouds boiled overhead. The Whistle gusted across the fort, making the flames of the brazier that burned a few yards away gutter.

But that noise wasn't the wind. It sounded as if The Slew had already taken wing.

The lass emerged from the ale-hall then, wrapped in a fur-lined cloak, her cheeks flushed with excitement.

Stepping back from him, Bree murmured an oath under her breath. She then gestured to the ominous sky. "Go on. And I'd hurry before the night is crawling with things you won't wish to meet."

23: IRON AND STEEL

NODDING TO THE red-robed sacrificer, Cailean rose to his feet. As he did so, he noted that the strength had returned to his limbs. He was himself again.

He helped Evina, the serving lass from the ale-hall who'd partnered him, up as well. Above, the full moon played hide-and-seek with dark clouds, yet the blood-letting had been successful. The silvery glow of Cailean's tattoos faded now, as did the rush of elation that the ritual brought.

They stood upon a grassy mound on the eastern edge of the fort, where a circular stone had been embedded into the earth. The sacrificer, a woman Cailean's age, her auburn hair woven into intricate braids, had been much easier to deal with than Gregor mac Hume. Back at Duncrag, the chief-sacrificer had never missed an opportunity to undermine his rival.

Ever since the early days of their training back on the Isle of Arryn, they'd rubbed each other the wrong way. It was a relief to have this ritual led by someone who didn't take vindictive pleasure in slicing Cailean as deeply as possible across the palm. The wound she'd made on both their palms had already healed, although he could still feel it tingling.

Earth magic now burned fiercely in his veins once more.

Evina's gaze was slightly glazed as she steadied herself against him.

"Time to get indoors," the sacrificer warned, casting a frown at the sky. "I'd walk home fast, if I were you, mac Brochan."

Aye, just like the guards at the gate, this sacrificer knew who he was. Tomorrow, the overking would likely send for him; there would be no getting around it. All the same, he had important *personal* business to attend to first—and he wouldn't be waylaid.

"We will," Cailean assured her.

The sacrificer turned then, robes billowing, and gestured to the two other druids who'd stood behind her during the ritual, chanting. All three of them hurried away down the slope to the turf-roofed cottage where Cailean had found them earlier.

"Come." Cailean set off, drawing Evina with him. "Let's get you home."

A torpor filtered over him then, a familiar tiredness dragging at his limbs. It was different from the exhaustion that warned him his earth magic was fading though. As always, after bloodletting, all he wished to do was sleep.

"That was … surprising," Evina said dreamily, cutting him a coy look under long lashes. "So …" Her voice trailed off there as she struggled to find the right word to describe the experience.

"Intense?"

"Aye."

"I appreciate you joining me," Cailean said, injecting a brisk note into his voice. The lass had flirted with him all the way to the sacred mound. He didn't want to encourage her further.

"That woman you were with earlier," Evina said then. "Why couldn't *she* partner you this eve?"

"She wished to," he answered, his tone cooling. "But … it isn't possible."

Evina waited for him to elaborate.

He didn't. Truth was, he'd hated choosing someone else besides Bree to partner him. His gut clenched then. They'd never be able to share this again.

Leaving the druidic compound behind, Cailean led Evina through a network of wynds in-between tightly packed cottages, byres, and walled gardens where vines crept over lichen-encrusted stone. Upon the southern edge of the fort, the beehive-shaped broch rose up above the turf roofs beneath it. King Ailean resided there, and on previous visits, he'd hosted Cailean, putting on a feast to welcome the High King's chief-enforcer.

Not tonight though. Gateway provided a welcome distraction.

A wooly sensation clouded his mind then, a response to blood-letting that only rest could take away. He'd be himself by morning though—and ready to take on Eilig.

They made their way through the deserted wynds as The Whistle whined in their ears and tugged at their cloaks. Above, the dark sky looked as if it were boiling now, and when Cailean glanced up, he spied black shapes fluttering across the face of the moon.

The fine hair on the back of his neck prickled.

Over the past few years, Gateway had grown increasingly dangerous for the Marav. As a child, he'd known it was best to keep indoors on the night that the dead came out to dance, but of late, stories of attacks, disappearances, and killings, had become more common.

It was as if The Slew, and the other restless spirits that stalked the night when autumn slid into winter, grew bold, hungry.

Cailean cast a glance at Evina, reassured to see that she still wore a serene expression. Indeed, he'd been relieved she'd agreed to join him, for most folk preferred not to stray from their hearths tonight. Nevertheless, the ale-hall keeper's daughter appeared confident that she'd be safe in an enforcer's company—that and she was attracted to him.

Aye, he wasn't oblivious to such things.

He paid little attention to the looks she kept stealing him though. Instead, the air tonight put him on edge, and he'd be relieved when he safely delivered the lass home.

They turned the final corner before the ale-hall, and Cailean quickened his step. The shrieks in the sky above were getting louder. After his brush with The Slew in the summer, he had no wish to face them this evening, not when they were ravenous.

However, when he fixed his gaze once more upon his destination, he spied a small bent figure crouched upon the dirt-packed lane, feasting upon the tray of honeyed seedcakes that had been left outside a doorway.

Cailean drew to a sharp halt, bringing Evina with him. Her shocked inhale warned him that she'd seen it too.

The creature hadn't noticed them yet, for it was too busy stuffing a large cake into its mouth.

"The Hag's tits," Evina muttered. "A trow."

Cailean's mouth compressed. *Shit.* He was bone-weary and his head felt as if it were filled with porridge. All he wanted to do was crawl into the furs. All the same, a lone trow shouldn't be too difficult to deal with.

He hadn't seen many of them over the years. Nonetheless, the wiry imp, which stood around just over four-foot in height, was the sort to take advantage of the cakes left outdoors at Gateway. The Uplands were said to be full of trows. Troublemakers—only coming out at night, for daylight turned them to stone—they dwelt in the hills and on the edges of peat bogs. Over the years, during his many campaigns to the north, Cailean had made a point of choosing his campsites carefully, looking out for the tell-tale *knowes*—earthen mounds—where trows lived. It was odd to see one here, so far from its burrow.

Pushing Evina behind him, he drew the dagger at his hip. "Back up, slowly," he ordered. "I'll deal with it."

Then, stepping forward, he cleared his throat.

The trow dropped another cake it was about to sink its teeth into and turned.

A sagging face, covered in warts, dominated by a huge hooked nose regarded him. The creature's deep-set eyes glinted in the light of the brazier burning by the wall of the ale-hall as they regarded each other.

"Move away now," Cailean greeted the trow, raising his iron blade. "We don't want any trouble."

Like most faery creatures, trows were leery of iron, and it drew back its lips, revealing a set of yellowed stumpy teeth. However, instead of backing away, as he'd expected, the trow withdrew a stone-bladed hand ax from its belt, which it then hurled at him.

The imp's aim was deadly, and only his enforcer reflexes saved him. Jerking sideways, he felt the brush of stone just a whisper away from his right ear. Pushing its advantage, the trow then whipped out a long-bladed knife. It gleamed in the firelight, and Cailean frowned.

Sheehallion steel.

What was a trow doing with such a fine Shee weapon?

With a whoop, the imp launched itself at him.

Cailean met it, the clash of iron and steel reverberating down the empty wynd. Gods, the wee bastard was fast, and it kept trying to drive its blade into his lower legs. Fighting something much smaller than him had its challenges.

Muttering a curse, his temper rising now, he drew one of his fighting knives from across his chest with his free hand and slashed at the trow. It danced back, easily dodging him, its beady eyes glittering with savage joy.

A shape moved past Cailean then, catching him by surprise.

Evina darted forward and, snarling a curse, threw a handful of salt into the creature's eyes.

The trow shrieked, the sound slicing through the air, dropped its fine dagger, and clutched at its face. It then turned and fled, howling, down the wynd.

Cailean watched it go before casting Evina an incredulous look. The young woman no longer wore a dreamy expression. Instead, she stood, hands on hips, her gaze fierce.

Meeting his eye, and seeing his reaction, she arched an eyebrow and patted the leather pouch upon her belt. "We Cannich lasses never go anywhere without our salt. It's the best way to send imps running."

Stepping inside the room he'd taken behind the inn, Cailean found Bree still awake. His wife sat upon the pile of furs, knees drawn up under her chin.

She'd been staring into the mid-distance, her golden eyes shadowed, but upon his entrance, her gaze cut his way. "It's done?"

"Aye." Cailean pushed the door closed behind him and dropped the wooden bar to secure it.

"And is your companion safely indoors?" There was no mistaking the pointed edge to her voice.

He nodded, thinking it best not to mention that he'd had to peel Evina off him moments earlier. The Slew and the prowling creatures outdoors weren't the only ones to be wary of tonight—and the lass hadn't been pleased when he'd refused a tumble.

Her gaze roamed his face. "It went well?"

"Aye … until we met a trow just outside the ale-hall." He approached her then, lifting the dagger he'd retrieved from the street outside. "And it attacked me with this."

Bree took the weapon, examining its hilt and blade in the glow of the candle burning next to the sleeping nook. "You realize it's a Shee weapon?"

"Aye," he replied, lowering himself to sit on the edge of the furs next to her. "A fine one too."

"You're right about that." She glanced his way then, a groove etching between her eyebrows. "The dagger has a moonstone pommel and a folded steel blade … it was made in the forges of Caisteal Gealaich."

Cailean inclined his head. "How does a trow get its hands on such a fine blade?"

Bree glanced back down at the dagger. "I'm wondering the same thing." She paused then, her features tensing. "When a faery creature of Albia wields Sheehallion steel, it makes them stronger." She raised her chin, her gaze fusing with his. "A trow can fight in daylight if it grips one of these … without the fear of turning to stone."

24: KILLING DISTANCE

BREE WATCHED CAILEAN butter an oatcake. His movements were deft and hurried. His brow was furrowed as if the oatcake had done him a personal injustice. Ever since awakening, he'd been on edge, taciturn.

They sat at a small table in a corner of the room they'd taken, knees brushing as they broke their fast. It was a companionable moment, one Bree would have usually enjoyed—if Cailean hadn't been so tense.

Nonetheless, his face was far more rested. They'd curled up together in the furs the night before, wrapped around each other. He'd fallen asleep within moments—slipping into a deep, exhausted slumber—although Bree had lain for a long while, listening to the steady beat of his heart against her ear.

She hadn't questioned him further about the blood-letting. In truth, she was still sore about it. No, it wasn't jealousy that chafed at her now—for she'd been impressed to hear about Evina throwing salt in the trow's eyes—but the knowledge that this would be repeated, many times, if she and Cailean remained together.

She'd *never* be part of the blood-letting with her own husband.

"Can I join you today … when you face Eilig?" she asked finally.

Cailean glanced up, his frown sliding into a scowl.

Seeing his reaction, Bree's jaw tightened. "I won't interfere."

Her husband quirked a dark eyebrow. "Can I trust you to keep your blade sheathed … even if things don't go my way?"

The oatcake she'd just eaten churned in her stomach at these words. "Of course, things will go your way," she scoffed. "You're the best warrior in Albia."

"*One* of the best," he corrected her. "Eilig was once an enforcer too. He served mac Brude's father but decided the life wasn't for him. He never liked taking orders from anyone but himself."

Bree pulled a face. Her husband didn't need to worry though—she wouldn't intervene. This was his reckoning, and she'd let him have it.

"Will he still call on earth magic?" she asked after a pause.

He nodded. "Even if an enforcer leaves the service of an overking, or the High King, he remains a warrior-druid," Cailean replied. "We are bound to earth magic … which was why I had to undergo the blood-letting last night." He paused then, his blue eyes shadowing. "There's no getting rid of it."

Apprehension fluttered up in the cage of Bree's chest. "Aye, well, you're younger than him," she replied. "And I swear I will stand back."

Their gazes fused, the moment drawing out before Cailean replied, "Very well."

"Why did it have to take him? My boy!"

The woman hunched, sobbing in the doorway, weeping. A man comforted her, stroking her back.

Halting before them, Cailean met the man's eye. "What happened?"

Heavy clouds hung overhead when Bree and Cailean left the ale-hall and made their way down to the fighting enclosure. Walking at her husband's side, Bree had marked the pale and strained faces of the locals she passed. The atmosphere in the fort this morning was subdued; a strange hush had settled.

"A botach forced its way in last night," the man replied, his voice raw with grief. "It jumped the salt and took our child."

"We shouldn't have been so stingy with the salt," his wife choked out. "It's our fault!"

"I'm sorry," Bree murmured, even as the woman began to sob once more, louder now.

The man nodded, although it was clear he barely heard her.

Glancing at each other, Bree and Cailean moved on, leaving the grieving couple behind them.

Her husband stalked now—purpose in every stride—and she struggled to keep up with him.

"It was an eventful night, by all accounts." Her hand strayed to the new dagger she carried at her waist, under her cloak. That a trow would carry such a weapon was mystifying—and worrying.

"Aye." Cailean glanced her way, blinking as he yanked himself free of his thoughts. "Gateway has grown increasingly dangerous over the years … do you think your people could be responsible?"

Bree frowned, considering his question. "It would be unusual," she replied. "We don't control The Slew. And apart from fae hounds, we have little to do with the faery creatures beyond the veil."

"Are the tales true then … that they were cast from Sheehallion?"

"Aye, although that was a long time ago."

Cailean swung his attention away, focusing on the wide space up ahead before the gates of the fort. Warriors were sparring here, their grunts and curses rising into the damp air.

Ignoring them, he strode around the edge of the area, his shoulders set, to the archway that led to the fighting enclosure.

Bree slowed her pace slightly, allowing him to draw ahead. He was preparing himself now—for a long overdue reckoning.

Within the enclosure, she stepped into a sawdust-covered arena marred with large dark spots: blood from the previous evening's fight. Bench seating, where the spectators watched, ringed the arena. There, she halted a few steps behind Cailean, surveying the scene within.

A big man with chiseled features, a thin scar across one cheek, and close-cropped grey hair, his bare arms blue with tattoos, was taking four fighters through drills.

The iron collars each of the warriors wore gleamed dully in the pale daylight. They were all heavily-muscled, scarred individuals, with grim faces and dead eyes. Slaves.

Although it wasn't them that Cailean was focusing on, but the fight master who snarled instructions, as they fought each other with bound blades.

"Move your arses!" he roared. "I've seen cripples move faster than you lot!"

At that moment, the fight master noticed they had an audience. Scowling, he turned from his still dueling slaves. "The next show's tonight," he barked. "Fuck off until then."

"I'm not here for that" —Cailean stepped forward, his hands flexing at his sides— "but for you."

His pulse thumped in his ears now.

Gods, he couldn't believe it, Eilig mac Frang was standing in front of him, within killing distance. How many times had he lain awake after he'd begun his training upon the Isle of Arryn, imagining this moment? Of course, as the moons slid into years, he'd stopped himself from thinking about taking revenge against his former master—but once he'd dredged the old hate up, it wouldn't let him go.

The older man's grey brows drew together, confusion flickering across his face. The scar Cailean had given him on the day he'd learned the fight master was bedding Enya was silvered with age now.

Heat stirred in Cailean's gut. "Don't you recognize me, Eilig?"

The fight master's pale-grey eyes widened. "Cailean?"

"That's right."

Eilig dragged his gaze over him, a smirk tugging at his mouth. "I've followed your career over the years," he drawled. "Your sister is so proud."

Is. Cailean's heart kicked against his ribs. "Enya's alive?"

The fight master's smile widened, malice flickering in his eyes. "Aye ... she's borne me three sons."

Cailean's blood started to roar in his ears. The Reaper take him, he wanted to draw his broadsword and cut Eilig's head off right now. The fire that smoldered in his belly flared hot. Aye, he wanted reckoning for every beating. Every humiliation. For his mother, father, and sister. For the innocence Eilig had stolen. For the family he'd ruined.

"Draw your sword, Eilig."

The fight master gave an incredulous laugh, the abrasive sound drifting over the arena. Meanwhile, the four slaves had stopped sparring. Gazes sharp, they were now watching the two men who stood around five yards apart.

The fight master's attention strayed over Cailean's shoulder, to where Bree was standing, glamored as a Marav woman. "Who's this pretty thing?" he murmured, licking his lips.

Cailean didn't reply. Moments passed, and when it was clear that he wouldn't be making introductions, Eilig shook his head mockingly. "It's a bit late for retribution, *lad*." The fight master drew the sword strapped to his back in one smooth, easy movement.

Cailean's lip curled. Suddenly, the years fell away, and he was thirteen, dripping blood into the dirt as Eilig loomed over him, fists raised, daring him to rise. "It's never too late," he said softly.

He then drew his own blade and lunged.

25: WELL ALONE

ARMS STILL FOLDED across her chest—to prevent herself from grabbing one of the knives under her cloak and flinging it straight into the fight master's throat—Bree watched the two men face off.

The slaves moved back to look on from the spectator benches, while Bree remained by the gate, forcing her feet to grow roots. Underneath her apparent calm, she itched to join the fight.

She'd seen the look Eilig had flashed her, and she still seethed. A blade to the gullet would wipe the insolent grin off his face.

Bree ground her teeth in frustration. *You promised Cailean you wouldn't interfere.*

And she wouldn't. Not yet.

Eilig still wore a smirk though, even as he swung his blade to block his opponent's first strike. Bree had to hand it to him, the man's arrogance was impressive. Most people wouldn't look so confident with Cailean mac Brochan bearing down upon them.

Her husband moved with fluid grace—in contrast to the fight master, who favored his left leg badly.

Both warrior-druids fought with heavy broadswords, a blade that had to be wielded two-handed. Despite that Eilig was hampered by his sore leg, he was brutal and precise, expending no more energy than necessary. It became evident early on that they were evenly matched.

Bree's gaze narrowed. Indeed, their fighting styles were eerily similar. It made sense, for Eilig had taught Cailean to fight. All the same, the realization put her on edge.

They moved around the arena, each giving ground reluctantly.

Fighting with broadswords wasn't a dance like it was with a longsword. The blade that hung at Bree's hip would be wielded differently. There was more play, more parrying and feinting. But the two warriors swung their blades like clubs, the clang of iron splitting the air every time they collided.

Bree's heart started to pound as she watched the duel unfold.

He favors his left, so make use of it.

Don't give any ground.

Make another downward cut.

Shades, she had to bite her tongue. It wasn't like her to stand on the sidelines. She liked to be in the thick of things.

And yet, she'd given Cailean her word.

Meanwhile, the fight drew out. It wasn't long before sweat gleamed on both men's faces. Cailean's black cloak billowed out around him as he moved, sawdust kicking up beneath his boots.

And gradually, the smirk slipped from Eilig's face.

"Not bad, *lad*," he panted, swinging his blade at Cailean's gut, only to meet his opponent's blade yet again. "You've improved."

Cailean merely grunted in response. Clearly, he wasn't about to let his former master distract him.

"Your sister was inconsolable after you left, you know?" Eilig goaded, trying another tactic. "She was so sure you'd come back for her … but I told her you wouldn't. And I was right."

"I'm here now," Cailean replied through gritted teeth as he deflected a vicious thrust.

"Aye." Eilig's mouth twisted. "Too late."

Bree thought Cailean might have snapped up the bait, might have lunged at his former master, but instead, he kept his temper leashed. And as the fight continued, a deep groove etched between Eilig's brows. His lameness was worsening too, and he was starting to lumber.

"Slowing down, eh?" Cailean taunted him.

"Fucking horse kicked me in the knee a moon ago," he wheezed, bleeding now upon his right arm where Cailean's blade had scored him. "Fighting me won't change a thing, you know? Your parents are still dead. Your sister is my woman … and you're still the brat who abandoned her." His handsome face twisted into a sneer. "Face it, you and I aren't so different. We put ourselves first … and there's nothing wrong with that."

Snarling a curse, Cailean slashed at him, driving the older man back across the arena. They both dripped blood, from shallow gashes to their arms, but barely appeared to notice.

Eilig's tattoos flared silver then, as he drew on earth magic to defend himself, but Cailean didn't let up. His own tattoos started to glow, and the air became heavy with the resinous scent of pine and the acrid odor of campfire ash.

Bree's breathing grew shallow, and it took all her will not to shift back, toward the archway. She dropped her hands to her sides then, flexing them. "Finish him, Cailean!" she shouted, unable to hold in her frustration any longer.

The two men fought on. And then, Cailean struck hard—hard enough to make Eilig stumble. It was the moment he'd been waiting for, and he swung again, his blade slicing deep into the fight master's side.

Eilig roared and staggered sideways, his knee giving way as he slashed his blade once more.

But now that Cailean had the advantage, he pressed it.

Bree's skin prickled as she observed him. Her husband's skill was breathtaking to watch. Pride swelled in her breast. He was good.

Injured, Eilig was much slower, and although his tattoos still pulsed as if moonlight rippled through them, he couldn't defend himself against the flurry of hammer blows that rained down on him. Each one drove him back, until, finally, he was on his knees.

His broadsword slipped from blood-slick fingers, thudding onto the sawdust. Clutching his injured side, Eilig glared defiantly up at Cailean. "Dog-humping turd," he ground out. "You should have left well alone."

"I think not," Cailean replied coldly. "I've waited too long for this. Say a prayer to The Reaper, for you're about to meet him."

In response, Eilig spat on the ground between them.

A heartbeat followed, and then Cailean swung his sword, cleaving the fight master's head cleanly from his shoulders.

The head rolled onto the ground, while blood pumped from his severed neck.

Eilig's body stayed upright for a moment longer before his tattoos faded and he toppled sideways.

Bree's pulse thumped in her ears as relief flooded through her. "Finally," she gasped before releasing the breath she hadn't realized she'd been holding. "You drew that out, didn't you?"

Panting, Cailean tore his gaze from where his former master's head sat in the sawdust—his features still contorted—and flashed her a grin. "Eilig isn't the only one who knows how to please a crowd."

"Does it feel as sweet as you expected?" she asked, deliberately challenging him. Gaining revenge wasn't as straightforward as most people believed. She recalled then the way Mor's eyes had shadowed when she'd brought her Grae's severed head—but then, he'd been her brother, while Eilig had only ever been Cailean's enemy.

"Sweeter," he replied, his gaze glinting. "My only regret is that the shit-eater's death was swift."

Sheathing his sword, he turned then to face the enslaved warriors who looked on from the benches.

One of them, a heavily scarred man with piercing dark eyes, nodded at him. "Well fought."

Cailean inclined his head, acknowledging the compliment. "My sister, Enya ... where is she?"

The scarred slave gestured left. "Next door ... at the fight master's lodgings."

He nodded before turning on his heel and heading toward where Bree waited.

"Wait!" One of the other slaves—a short, broad man with a lumpy nose that looked as if it had been broken countless times—stepped forward then. "So, we belong to you now, do we?" There was no mistaking the belligerence, the bitterness, in his voice.

Cailean halted and glanced over his shoulder, his gaze shifting between the faces of the men before him. "You're all free now," he told them tersely. "Find yourselves a smith and remove those collars."

Enya stared at Cailean, her face draining of blood. "You *killed* him?"

"Aye," he replied, waiting to see relief and vindication illuminate his sister's eyes. It was slow arriving. "I cut off his head."

Standing within the fight master's lodgings—a cottage tucked in behind the fighting enclosure—he wondered if he should have delivered the news that he'd just beheaded Eilig with a little less bluntness.

Enya was blinking at him as if he'd been speaking another tongue. Meanwhile, her three sons, the eldest of which looked around eighteen, stood behind her. The lads were all big for their ages and muscular like their father. And like their mother, they all now wore stunned expressions.

For his part, Cailean was still reeling from the discovery that his sister was still alive, still Eilig's woman. He didn't want to dwell on what she'd been through over the past two decades. The thought made his gut ache.

They stood in the main living space of the cottage. It was a simple yet comfortable dwelling, with sheepskins covering the dirt-packed floor, and faded wall hangings obscuring the stacked-stone walls.

Behind Cailean, Bree shifted slightly. Before they'd entered the fight master's lodgings, she'd warned him that his sister might not be pleased to see him, and as such, he'd braced himself for a cool welcome. Nonetheless, he'd been initially encouraged when joy had flared in his sister's gaze after he'd stepped through the threshold.

Moments passed, and then high spots of color rose to Enya's cheeks, and her blue eyes—the hue of woad like his—glittered. Time had been kinder to his sister than he'd expected. Life as Eilig's slave hadn't worn her out. Her black hair, long and lustrous, fell in a curtain over her shoulders, and she held herself tall and proud.

And as their stare drew out, he realized that it wasn't jubilation that brightened Enya's eyes and brought color to her cheeks, but grief … and rage.

His breathing grew shallow as realization dawned. Unlike years earlier, Enya didn't wear an iron slave collar. The long sleeveless midnight-blue tunic she wore was of decent cloth, and upon her right bicep gleamed two bronze arm rings.

Gods … no. Dizziness swept over Cailean.

All these years, he'd imagined his sister enslaved, brutalized. Dead. But here she was, looking like a … wife.

Bile shot up, stinging the back of his throat.

"You *bastard*," Enya finally rasped, her hands fisting at her sides. "You *fucking* bastard."

"He had it coming," Cailean bit out the words, even as he started to sweat. This was all wrong. Why wasn't his sister congratulating him for beheading the fight master? What had Eilig done to make her so compliant? Bree stepped up next to him then, placing a restraining hand on his arm. However, he wouldn't be silenced. "That sack of shit destroyed our family. I did this for us … for *you*."

Enya's hand shot out, her palm catching him across the cheek. The blow left a burn in its wake. "Liar!" she shouted in his face. "It was for *you*." Breathing hard, she shoved him in the chest. "It's been twenty years, Cailean. *Twenty. Years.* Did you really think nothing would change?"

He stared back at her, stunned.

"Eilig gave me my freedom years ago." She spat the words out at him now, while her sons shifted backward, as if cowed by their mother's venom. "We made a family together … but now you come wading back into my life and destroy it."

"Enya," he rasped. "Don't tell me you *loved* him?"

"Aye!" she shrieked, trembling with fury now. Her hands clenched and unclenched at her sides as if she was trying to stop herself from clawing his eyes out.

His chest constricted. *What a bloody mess. You fucking clod-head.*

"It's your turn to bleed now, uncle." The eldest son moved forward once more. This time, he gripped a carving knife—one he'd swiped from the large scrubbed table behind him. His light-grey eyes glittered.

"Put that knife away, fool," Bree spoke up then, her voice sharp. "Before you cut yourself."

The youth ignored her. Encouraged by their brother's balls, Cailean's other nephews grabbed knives of their own. All three of them now advanced on him.

He watched them, his gaze narrowing incredulously. These three idiots had more courage than sense.

"Lads," Enya rasped, glancing over her shoulder at her sons. "Don't—"

"Move aside, Ma," the eldest ordered. "Let us deal with him."

Clenching his jaw, Cailean reluctantly drew two of the knives from the belt slung across his chest. An instant later, the scrape of metal against leather warned him that Bree had also drawn a weapon.

"Listen to your mother," His gaze swept over his nephews' rigid faces. "Or this won't end well for you."

26: SUMMONED

THE MOMENT THEY stepped onto the wynd outside the dwelling, Bree turned to her husband.

"Cailean," she said softly, reaching out and placing a hand on his arm. Instinctively, she knew she had to be gentle with him, for she sensed his brittleness, like a sheet of hide left out too long in the sun.

"Aye," he replied hoarsely. He blinked then as if he was having trouble focusing on her.

Bree swallowed. She didn't know what to say. Words couldn't fix what was broken. Nothing could. "The Gods played a cruel trick on you today," she whispered.

The weak mid-morning sun gleamed on the sweat that still slicked his face and bare arms after his fight. His chest rose and fell sharply, revealing that he was in the grip of strong emotion. She wasn't surprised. The scene she'd just borne witness to was harrowing indeed.

She'd thought blood would be shed in the end, for the glint in those lads' eyes had been murderous. However, the sight of their uncle's blades, and her own, had checked them. And when their mother had started to weep—deep, harrowing sobs—they'd lowered their weapons.

Cailean and Bree had left the cottage without another word.

But now, Cailean had halted in the middle of the lane and stood there, as if his feet had just grown roots.

"The Gods aren't to blame," he replied hoarsely. Lifting a hand, he dragged it down his face. "I brought this on myself." He broke off then, cursing. "I can't believe she'd fall for Eilig … after everything that prick did."

"Time changes people, Cailean," she whispered.

A nerve flickered under his right eye. "Aye … some more than others."

Silence fell between them before she gently squeezed his arm. "What now?" They needed to continue this discussion, for the pain inside her husband had to be lanced or it would poison him. Nonetheless, this wasn't the time or place.

He heaved a deep, ragged breath. "Now, we leave … let's get back to the ale-hall and collect Feannag."

"Mac Brochan." A gravelly male voice intruded then, making them both turn. A group of leather-clad warriors, domed iron helmets jammed onto their heads, stood behind them.

Bree's stomach clenched. Releasing her husband's arm, she stepped back from him. Shades, was the Fort Guard going to arrest Cailean for killing the fight master?

"What?" Cailean snapped.

"King Ailean wants to see you," said one of them, a tall, rangy warrior with a leathery face.

"Now?"

"Aye. You've been summoned."

Bree fought a frown. So, they weren't going to question him about Eilig?

Cailean didn't reply immediately, and Bree wondered if he'd refuse the order—not a wise idea since they were outnumbered and surrounded by high stone walls. Getting out of Cannich wouldn't be easy.

All the same, she readied herself to act, her pulse quickening. If her husband decided to slash his way out of this fort, she'd fight at his side.

Moments passed, and eventually, Cailean muttered a curse under his breath. He then turned to Bree, his gaze meeting hers. "Wait for me at the ale-hall … this shouldn't take long." He stepped in close then, lowering his voice as he added. "Perhaps the overking has learned why mac Brude marches north."

Stepping inside the smoky hall of the overking of Cannich's broch, Cailean choked down his churning irritation.

Ailean mac Nairn was vexing at the best of times. Even so, there was a part of Cailean that was curious to hear what he had to say. As the High King's chief-enforcer, he'd once been the first to know when something was afoot. But now, he was in the dark—and it frustrated him.

Focusing on the looming conflict also helped distract him from the self-loathing that had dug its teeth into him like a rat and wouldn't let go.

Watch yourself with mac Nairn, he warned himself as he crunched across the dirty rushes toward where the king awaited him on the high seat. *He can be a tricky bastard.*

The Upland king had always reminded him of a spider. He was a swarthy man with a short, thick body and long gangly limbs. A shock of black hair crowned a large head, and deep-set brown eyes tracked Cailean as he approached. Beside him sat Queen Dalria, a pretty, if petulant-faced, woman who wore her golden hair in two long braids.

"Mac Brochan," the king greeted him sourly. "Since when do you arrive in Cannich and not announce yourself?"

"Apologies, sire," Cailean replied. "But I was on leave and am here visiting kin."

King Ailean pursed his lips at this response, his dark brows knitting together. "With the High King's imminent arrival here, I imagined he'd sent you ahead."

Cailean didn't reply to this grumble. He merely halted a few yards back from the high seat and waited for the king's questions. Of course, he wouldn't be able to answer any of them.

Impatience thumped in his chest as the moments slid by, and his belly started to ache. *You have made a Gods-damned mess of things, mac Brochan.* He knew how lust for revenge blinded people yet had thought he was different. He wasn't.

He really was the same as his High King.

The overking's wolfhound, a lean dog with a wiry coat that sat beside its master, began scratching itself then. Scowling, mac Nairn kicked it. The hound yelped, stopped scratching, and slunk away.

"Our High King is being secretive," the overking muttered, tapping his long fingers upon the carven armrest of his chair. "And I don't like it. He tells me to ready my army … to recruit as many hill-tribe warriors as I can get my hands on … but refuses to tell me why."

Cailean shared the overking's confusion. However, he couldn't admit such to him.

Mac Nairn heaved himself forward then, his gaze spearing Cailean's. "Why is he marching north? Does he know something I do not? Do the Shee plan to attack us?"

"I cannot say, sire."

"Cannot … or *will* not?"

Cailean remained silent. Curse mac Nairn, he had nothing useful to offer, after all. His gut cramped then, as the memory of the look on his sister's face moments before he left the cottage intruded. Her anguish. Her grief. Striking off Eilig's head had been satisfying indeed, but in killing the fight master, he'd ruined Enya and her sons' lives.

Gods, he wished he could claw back time and change what he'd done.

Retribution had initially tasted so sweet, but now it was bitter enough to choke him.

"Why would he bring the armies of Duncrag, Braewall, and Baldeen north?" the overking went on, oblivious to the fact that Cailean was barely listening to him. "Unless he has gotten wind of something." He paused then, resentment smoldering in his peat-colored eyes. "I tire of being the last to know, whenever there is something afoot. I'm an overking, not some rabble-rousing chieftain."

"Our High King will be in Cannich soon," Cailean replied, unable to prevent his voice from hardening. "You'll be able to take your grievances up with him then."

Mac Nairn scowled at this response, a muscle bunching in his jaw.

Cailean wasn't entirely unsympathetic.

The truth was that the High King didn't treat Cannich's ruler well. He didn't like the power that the overking held, for The Uplands bred the strongest warriors in all of Albia and governed the various chiefdoms in the north.

In the past, before mac Brude's time, The Upland overkings had risen against their High King a few times, and bloody wars marked Albia's history. As such, mac Brude was wary of mac Nairn and had deliberately excluded him from meetings he held with his other two overkings.

"In his last missive, he said that he's bringing his family north with him," Queen Dalria spoke up then, her already high-pitched voice shrill with disapproval. "Does he expect us to provide accommodation for them?"

Cailean drew in a slow, deep breath, praying to the Gods for patience. Did he look like a courier? "I cannot say, Your Highness," he replied coldly.

A tense silence fell in the hall. It was a large circular space dominated by one enormous hearth in the center. Servants and slaves moved quietly around the fringes, leery of disturbing, or vexing, their liege.

"And how far away is the High King?" the overking ground out eventually, his voice rough with anger now. "Surely, you can tell me that, mac Brochan?"

"Two days at most." It was a guess, although, after his conversation with the warriors bound east the day before, it seemed probable. Like the overking, he was mystified by the High King's behavior—although mac Nairn's incessant questioning was starting to vex him. All the same, a sage voice whispered to Cailean to keep his temper in check. He couldn't let his inner turmoil turn him reckless—not if he wanted to walk out of here without a fight. The overking's warriors lined the hall, watching them. He could take them on, yet he'd done enough damage today. "As soon as he makes camp outside Cannich, mac Brude shall call upon you."

King Ailean scowled. "I'm sure he will."

Pacing the yard behind the ale-hall, Bree glanced up at the darkening sky. Dusk was settling. Where was Cailean?

When he'd assured her that his meeting with the overking wouldn't take long, she'd thought him overly optimistic. Even so, she'd expected him earlier than this. And as the day drew out, and her husband didn't appear, she started to worry.

Maybe mac Nairn *had* arrested Cailean for beheading the fight master.

Perhaps word had reached them that the High King's chief-enforcer was supposed to be dead.

Bree swiveled on her heel and stalked another circuit of the yard.

A strong wind had whipped up from the northwest. The Sweeper, which scattered the straw that littered the yard and tugged at the lumps of turf on the surrounding roofs, just added to her disquiet this afternoon. Gateway was over now, yet there was a different kind of tension in the air.

If Cailean didn't appear soon, she'd go looking for him.

"Bree."

Whipping around, she found her husband striding into the yard. His face, which had softened after their night together in

Morae, had regained its former hardness. His jaw was set, his brow furrowed, and his blue eyes steely.

Bree's stomach tensed. She'd hoped the afternoon might have allowed him to cool down. But remembering the scene with his sister and nephews that morning, she wasn't surprised he looked so forbidding.

Even so, she ached to reach for him. She hadn't ever been overly tactile; she'd been brought up in an emotionally distant household and wasn't comfortable with displays of affection. But despite that, the urge to step into him, to wrap her arms around his torso and bury her face against his neck, was almost overwhelming.

She prevented herself though. Now wasn't the time.

Cailean halted before her. "King Ailean is a burr up my arse," he growled, raking a hand through his short dark hair. "The bastard kept pelting me with questions I couldn't answer."

Bree cocked an eyebrow. "You didn't learn anything useful from him then?"

He shook his head and pulled a face.

"You held your tongue, I hope?"

"I wouldn't have returned to you if I hadn't." He glanced around then before muttering a curse. "I wanted to get out of this fort … but the king insisted I remain for the noon meal … followed by an afternoon meeting with his warriors."

"What's another night?" Stepping close, she reached out then and caught his hand in hers. Actually, she'd have preferred to move on from Cannich—for them to get away from this brewing conflict—but it was too late in the day to move on; dusk was almost upon them. "Right now, neither of us has anywhere we need to be."

27: LOOKING FOR REDEMPTION

PUTTING DOWN HER wooden spoon, Bree regarded her husband. Seated opposite her—they'd taken their supper in their room rather than join the noisy crowd in the ale-hall itself—Cailean had barely touched his stew.

Instead, his gaze had turned inward as he silently ruminated.

Watching him stare down at the cup of ale he gripped, discomfort shifted in the pit of Bree's belly.

He was retreating to a place where he felt safe, where self-loathing could bloom—a place she wouldn't be able to reach him. She couldn't let him go there.

"Do you want to talk about it?" Bree asked finally.

Cailean glanced up, a groove appearing between his eyebrows. "No."

"It might help."

"Would it?"

Their gazes held, yet she didn't flinch away from the hardness on his face. "It's not your fault."

He shook his head, a muscle bunching in his jaw. "Aye, it is. Eilig was right. I'm selfish."

"You're no different from most of us then." She flashed him a thin smile. "It's how we survive."

His eyes guttered. "Aye, and my sister pays the price."

"You weren't to know she was in love with Eilig," she shot back.

"Maybe not … but if I'd made this about Enya and not about me, I might have acted differently." His face twisted. "Instead, I had to get my revenge. I didn't care about anything else."

Bree made a frustrated sound in the back of her throat. "Self-pity doesn't look good on you."

He jolted at that. His eyes narrowed then.

She stared back at him, unflinching. Fortunately, his gimlet stare had never cowed her. She had to get through to him, even if that meant he turned the rage that was eating him up inside on her.

She could weather it.

"Aye, you've made mistakes … I have too," she said after a long pause. "Back in Morae, I'd lost hope … but you gave it back to me. Now, I'll return the favor by telling you that *neither* of us is a lost cause." Her pulse quickened as his gaze glinted. "The truth is that Eilig mac Frang had it coming. Is it your fault that Enya has poor taste in men?"

"You talk as if my sister had a choice," he countered roughly. His fingers now held the cup in a death grip. "She didn't."

"Neither did you." She leaned forward then, her fingers gripping the edge of the table. "You both did the best with the fate the Gods dealt you." They stared at each other across the table, the air drawing tight between them. "But you're wrong. This has never been just about vengeance, Cailean … you might not realize it, but you were looking for redemption as well."

He snorted, the firelight playing across his taut face. "Don't make me sound noble," he ground out. "I'm not … and after everything I've done over the years, I don't deserve salvation."

"I refuse to believe that," she shot back. "There's *much* about you that's good. You're loyal, steadfast … protective."

Anger darkened his face, and he shoved himself up from the table. "I'm not listening to this horseshit."

Undaunted, Bree rose swiftly to her feet and moved around to face him. Ancestors, he was tall. Even though she was an athletic Shee female, she still had to raise her chin a little to hold his eye.

"Aye, you will." She shoved him in the chest, deliberately provoking him. "You looked out for Mirren and dealt out justice after she was raped, even though you angered the High King. You sent me back through the stones when you could have thrown me to the wolves. Shades … you even earned the love of a fae hound." Tears stung her eyes then. She couldn't help it. The emotion gathering in her chest was overwhelming. "And if you want to make things right with your sister, we'll stay here at Cannich until you do. But don't you dare give up!"

Moments passed, and she watched the anger drain from his eyes. "It won't work." His voice was thin now, raw. "She'll never forgive me."

"Aye, she will." Bree broke off, her heart pounding. "But first, you need to forgive yourself. Let this self-loathing go. Let. Me. Help. You."

Cailean stared down at her, his expression anguished. "You deserve better than me, Bree."

"No." She shook her head, vehement now. "We were meant for each other," she whispered as a tear slid down her cheek. "Alone, we'd never have broken free of the past. Together, we're stronger. Better."

His lips parted, and something like wonder darkened his eyes. Lifting a hand, he brushed the back of his knuckles across her cheek.

Bree couldn't help it; she shivered.

"My stubborn, fiery wife," he said huskily. "You won't let this go, will you?"

She huffed a shaky laugh. "Never."

His gaze turned limpid, his thumb skimming lightly over her mouth and down her jaw to her neck. It then settled in the hollow between her collarbones, where her pulse fluttered.

A wave of dizziness swept over her.

Reaching up, she steadied herself by placing her hands against his chest. And under her right palm, she felt the thunder of his pulse. "Cailean," she breathed, as longing twisted deep in her chest.

"It's terrifying," he whispered back. "The power you have over me"

"And you … over me. You could crush my heart, you know?"

"But I won't." He slid his other hand up and cupped the back of her head. "Instead, I will guard it." He bent his head, his lips brushing her cheek. It was difficult to concentrate then, for the tip of his tongue circled the shell of her ear.

A deep sigh shuddered out of Bree, and her fingers splayed wide against the wall of his chest. Her body was melting now, their surroundings fading. The crackle of the fire in the nearby hearth, the wail of The Whistle against the walls—all of it disappeared as Cailean walked her backward.

And there, pressed up against the stacked-stone wall, he cupped her face with his hands and kissed her deeply, tenderly.

Bree kissed him back with the same gentleness. In the past, their embraces had been fevered, wild. But the emotion of this moment couldn't be denied. After their fraught exchange, they both needed this.

Her hands slid up to his face too, her palms cupping his cheeks, where stubble rasped across her skin. Their lips parted, their tongues entwining. The masculine scent of him invaded her senses, and the heat of his mouth drew her in.

She linked her arms around his neck now, craving more.

Cailean answered by pressing the full length of his body against hers.

Groaning against his mouth, she parted her legs, wrapping them around his hips. The kiss was still tender, still exquisitely slow, yet desire clenched in her gut.

Ancestors, how she wanted him. She would never stop wanting him. Not until the long years of her life faded to mist and shadow.

She felt his arousal then—a thick, hard column against her belly—and ground herself against it. She did so slowly though, matching the unhurried exploration of their mouths. Bree didn't want to rush this.

Eventually, as Cailean continued to kiss her, his hands moved down, unlacing her leather vest. He then slid it off her before drawing up the woolen tunic he'd bought her in Morae.

Murmuring an endearment, her husband bent his head. An instant later, his hot mouth drew one of her nipples in, sucking and pulling at it with languorous, sensual intent that made her whimper.

She watched then as he sucked her other breast while stroking the naked skin of her torso. Bree started to tremble. His hands, big and calloused, were so gentle tonight, so warm. And every caress of his palms against her skin felt as if he was claiming her.

Sighing, she reached for the laces of his breeches. A moment later, she drew the scalding hot length of his erection free, sliding her fingertips over the satiny skin. The crown was leaking, and she gently rubbed her palm over its slickness.

Cailean's low groan rumbled in his throat.

Meanwhile, Bree heeled off her boots and let him undo the close-fitting leather leggings she wore. He slid them down over the swell of her hips. She then kicked them off. She now leaned against the cold wall, naked, while Cailean was still clothed.

His gaze raked over her bare skin, burning into her. He then stepped back and divested himself of his vest, breeches, and boots. Gloriously nude, the firelight playing across the bulges of his biceps and the sculpted muscles of his chest, he stepped into Bree once more, gathering her against him.

Their mouths found each other again, still tender, yet with more urgency now.

"Bree," he groaned as he slid his hands over the dips and curves of her body. "Mine."

"Aye," she whispered against his lips. "Yours."

He nudged her thighs apart with his knee then, a hand slipping between them. His thumb circled and stroked her slickness—the pad grazing her most sensitive spot—and suddenly, Bree was trembling. Her legs could barely support her now. Heat washed over her, sweat beading upon her skin. His touch was devastating. The pressure in her chest tightened further, for the emotion building there was too powerful to be contained.

Cailean's eyes gleamed in the firelight, unnaturally bright. His hands traveled down the long curve of her spine then, cupping her arse possessively. He lifted her up, and she spread her legs wide to receive him. An instant later, he slid into Bree with aching slowness, filling her inch by delicious inch, until he was buried fully inside her.

Letting out a low, breathy moan, she wrapped her legs around his hips and rolled her own against him, bringing him even deeper.

He gasped—the sound thrilling her, a shudder passing through his strong body—and she repeated the move.

"Wife," he ground out, gripping her hips as he slowly drew back, letting her feel his thick hard length. "Do that again and this will be over far too soon."

Bree huffed a breathless laugh. However, she heeded him.

She wanted to savor this coupling, to draw the pleasure out. And Cailean clearly felt the same. Gripping her hips tightly, he withdrew, almost to the tip, before inching back into her. And then, he repeated it, again and again.

All the while, they stared into each other's eyes. The intensity of the moment—and what it meant to them both—made an ache rise under her breastbone.

Both their bodies were slick with sweat as Bree clung to Cailean, shudders rippling through her, aching pleasure coiling in her womb. She could feel his tension building too, the vibration of it in his arms, for she gripped his biceps, bracing herself against him as he took her. She was gloriously wet now, heat flooding her loins with every long, sensual slide.

He kept his self-control leashed, plowing her slowly, until she came apart, her hips kicking against his. She writhed on him.

Shades, it was too much. Too good.

She screamed then, intense pleasure rippling and pulsing through her. It turned her inside out, and she clutched at him.

Cursing, Cailean finally let himself go. He plunged into her now in deep, hard, claiming thrusts.

She bucked against him, savage joy blooming in her breast when he bellowed her name, the heat of his release pulsing into her.

28: FIGHT OR FLEE

GRADUALLY, THE WORLD came back into focus.

Cailean was aware that he was leaning heavily upon Bree and was likely squashing her against the rough wall. However, his legs had gone weak in the aftermath of his climax. He wasn't sure how much longer he could remain standing. And so, still breathing hard, he pushed himself off his wife, scooped her up, and carried her over to the waiting nest of furs.

Stretching out next to her, he propped himself up onto an elbow and gazed down at Bree.

She stared up at him, her face soft, her golden, cat-like eyes glowing.

Cailean's throat tightened. He wasn't used to the vulnerability she roused in him. He'd once dismissed his reaction to her as weakness, but not any longer. She told him things he didn't want to hear, made him face things he'd rather turn away from. She gave him strength and soothed his bruised soul.

He'd suffer for this woman, and he'd do it willingly. He wasn't a man who did anything in half-measures. Perhaps he'd always known this about himself, known that once the walls came down, he'd be done for.

None of that mattered now though. She'd spoken the truth. If he wanted to make things right with his sister, he couldn't just slink away with his tail between his legs, defeated and despising himself.

Instead, he had to fight.

Bree's cheeks glistened in the firelight. He lifted a hand, smoothing the tears away with his fingertips. But as the silence drew out between them, the ache in his throat became unbearable, as did the burn behind his eyes. And when Bree raised her own hand—which trembled slightly—and caressed his cheek, he realized that she wasn't the only one overcome by this moment.

"The Hag's teeth," he muttered, his voice catching. "What's wrong with me?"

Her sensual mouth curved into a smile that made his breathing catch in his chest. "Nothing," she whispered.

A shriek ripped Bree from a deep, peaceful sleep.

Jolting upright, she lunged for one of her blades, only to realize that she was naked and her fighting knives and longsword were out of arm's reach.

Likewise, the noise had yanked her husband awake.

Cailean rolled off her and grabbed his breeches, hauling them on.

"The Slew shouldn't be out tonight," she gasped, leaping out of the furs and hurriedly dressing. Lacing her vest over her woolen tunic with fumbling fingers, she glanced over at where Cailean was strapping on his knife vest.

"No." Her husband's face was grim, his blue eyes steely. "But something else is."

Bree yanked on her boots, collecting her weapons as she followed Cailean to the door. "What time is it?"

"Early."

They stepped out of their lodgings, into the yard between the two accommodation wings—and froze. The sky was ablaze, acrid smoke choking the air. Screams punctured the night. And then a bright, piercing sound drifted through the air.

Bree's breathing caught, even as Cailean cursed.

They both knew that noise. It wasn't the thunderous rumble of a Marav battle horn, but the commanding cry of a Sheehallion trumpet.

Bree's blood started to roar in her ears.

Her people were besieging Cannich.

Whipping around, she faced Cailean. "We have to get out of this fort."

Stubbornness settled over his features. "Not without my sister."

Bree nodded, checking her panic. Aye, he was right. They couldn't leave Enya and her sons to the mercy of the Shee. "Right," she said, flicking her fingers by her sides to glamor herself. She then drew her longsword. "Let's go find her then."

Beyond the ale-hall, panicked locals packed Cannich's twisting wynds, while off-duty warriors hurriedly buckled on their weapons and armor as they rushed by. Cailean caught one of them by the arm, pulling the woman up short. "Are they inside the walls?" he demanded.

"Not yet," the warrior replied, her voice hoarse from the smoke. "Although, the Shee have ladders up against the gatehouse. They're hurling buckets of flaming pitch over the walls. It won't be long until they're inside." The woman's armored chest heaved. "Watch yourselves … powries and trow are inside the fort."

She wrenched herself out of his grip then and hurried on, pushing her way through the panicked throng that gathered nearby.

"Get inside," Cailean bellowed, elbowing his way into the crowd. "Lock your doors and shutter your windows. Rouse your hearths, scatter salt, and gather what iron you can!"

They heeded him, scurrying away as he strode through their midst. The cottage his sister resided in was tucked into a wynd behind the fighting enclosure, not far from the entrance to the fort. When the Shee surged their way inside, Enya and her sons would be trapped.

Bree followed her husband. Above her, the smoke from the blazing dwellings the burning pitch had set alight cleared for a moment, and she saw that the sky had turned from black to a deep indigo. Night would soon give way to dawn.

The wynds grew thick with warriors now, all surging toward the gates and the ladders leading up onto the walls. A dull boom reverberated through the night then, followed by another.

Bree's heart lurched. *Shit.* They were using a battering ram on the gates.

Reaching the cottage, Cailean hammered at the door with his fist. "Enya!" he shouted. "It's me, Cailean!" He paused then, waiting for her to answer, yet she didn't. "Gods-damn it, sister." He slammed his fist against the door thrice more. "Let me in!"

No one answered. And eventually, with a snarled curse, he kicked the door in. Darkness yawned before him, indicating that no hearth burned within. Grabbing a burning torch off the wall outside, and drawing his dagger, he stepped indoors.

Bree entered at his heel. Halting in the living area, where they'd met Enya earlier in the day, she glanced around. The interior of the cottage was tidy, the dirt-packed floor swept clean. The curtain that divided the living and sleeping spaces had been tied back.

The cottage was empty.

"The Reaper's turds," Cailean ground out. "Where are they?"

"It looks as if your sister and nephews are no longer living here," Bree replied, noting that the hearth had been neatly laid, yet not lit.

"Come to scavenge, have you?" A rough voice intruded. "At the first sign of trouble, the crows circle!"

Bree swiveled on her heel and came face-to-face with a stocky man with heavy features and thinning white hair. He bore a heavy iron poker, and she clenched her jaw as he waved it in her face.

"We aren't looters," she replied brusquely. "We're looking for someone."

"Enya and her sons," Cailean cut in, bearing down on the man. "Where are they?"

The man's heavy brow furrowed, even as the hands gripping the poker trembled slightly. Nevertheless, he held his ground. "The fight master's wife and her lads left yesterday," he growled.

Bree's breath gusted out of her. "They're no longer in Cannich?"

"No. They loaded mac Frang's body onto a cart and departed around noon."

Bree cast a look in Cailean's direction, to see his gaze had shadowed. Aye, he'd be relieved Enya was safe. But unless he hunted his sister down, he'd never make things right with her.

And to do that, they needed to get out of this fort.

"Come on," she said, edging around the poker-wielding man. "Time to go."

Bree left the cottage first, and had just stepped out onto the wynd beyond, when a stone hurtled through the air, slamming into her side.

Cursing, she lurched sideways, drawing her knives as she righted herself. She twisted then to find three powries stalking her. Their red eyes glowed in the dim light, their blood-stained caps bobbing as they moved. Meaty fingers, tipped in blade-like nails, wrapped around the hilt of gleaming daggers.

More Sheehallion steel.

"Thieves," Bree snarled. "Where did you get those knives?"

Something was very wrong. Powries never left the ruins they inhabited, and just like trows, didn't carry Shee weapons but pikes fashioned from ash.

The powries didn't reply. Instead, they rushed, howling, at her.

An instant later, Cailean was at Bree's side, his broadsword glinting dully in the torchlight as he swung it toward the first of her attackers. Together they cut the three imps down. Flames bloomed brightly in the lane as each powrie fell, their fine weapons clattering to the ground.

A roar went up then, the sounds of rending iron and splintering wood filling the air.

Breathing hard, Bree whipped around, her gaze traveling down the wynd to where a crowd of leather-clad warriors surged. Smoke billowed, and then shouting rang through the air.

Cailean cursed. "They're inside."

She cut him a look, witnessing the hard expression that had settled over his face. "What now?" she asked as her heart thundered in her chest. "Fight or flee?"

Their gazes fused. "How big is the Raven Queen's army?"

She swallowed. "Last time I saw it, it was a thousand strong … at least."

"To get up here, they've already defeated an army of three hundred at the base of the rock," he replied. "Cannich's garrison is half that number. They can't hold the fort on their own … not without the High King's help." A muscle feathered in his jaw. "Whatever we do, this fort is going to fall." He stepped close then, his gaze never leaving hers. "I'm not throwing our lives away. We flee."

Her heart kicked against her ribs. "But how?" She gestured toward the gates, where screaming had begun. "That's the only way out."

A thin smile curved her husband's lips, his gaze glinting. "Aye … but I have an idea."

29: KEEP YOUR DISTANCE

"YOUR IDEA IS shit." Bree folded her arms before her and lifted her chin. "Try coming up with a new one."

Cailean shook his head, a groove etching between his eyebrows. "It's the best … the *only* … chance we have."

"It's madness."

They'd returned to the ale-hall—pushing their way through smoky streets, and dealing with more powries and trow too, before reaching their destination. They were standing inside the stables, next to where Feannag snorted and pawed at the straw in his stall. The chaos raging close by, the clang of metal and screams, had put the stallion on edge.

In response, Cailean lifted the loop of rope he'd just taken down off the wall. "Only if we don't put on a convincing show." He stepped close then, challenge gleaming in his eyes. "Come on, Bree. Show me your courage."

Heat swept over her. "I'm not afraid for me," she whispered. "I can lie my way out of this if need be." She broke off then, swallowing. "But the High King's chief-enforcer is a prize, indeed. You don't want Mor getting her hands on you."

"She won't. Not if we play this right."

Her pulse leaped into a gallop. "You want me to take you prisoner?"

"Aye." He thrust the coil of rope out to her. "Go on." Impatience crept into his voice, his brow furrowing once more. "We don't have time to stand here arguing. This must happen now … or not all."

Growling a curse, Bree took the rope, her fingers tightening around it. She then raked her gaze over him, taking in the array of iron weapons strapped to his body. "You realize that you're going to have to take all of that off?" she pointed out, her voice hardening. She had to make him understand what he was asking—just how vulnerable he'd be soon.

But Cailean didn't hesitate. Instead, he nodded and started unbuckling the knife belt across his chest.

"Stand aside!" Bree yelled, her voice cutting through the din. "I've got the High King's chief-enforcer!"

Yanking hard on the rope, she urged Feannag forward. She didn't glance over her shoulder to see how Cailean was faring. She didn't dare.

The only way this would work was if she pretended to be an assassin with a prize for her queen.

Her shout drew stares from the Shee warriors she approached. They were a fell sight: faces and silver scale armor smeared with grime and blood, their long hair rippling down their backs. The warriors wielded longswords, daggers, and longbows, but Bree faced them down.

And they watched as she rode straight for them, their eyes widening in surprise.

"The chief-enforcer!"

"By the Great Raven … what's he doing here?"

"The queen's assassin has him."

It didn't take long for word to spread, rippling down the wynd like a stone thrown into a still loch.

"Keep your distance," Bree warned them. "Even without his iron blades, he's dangerous."

A Shee warrior—a tall, rangy male with cold eyes and oaken hair—pushed forward, drawing the slender dagger at his side. "Time for this Marav butcher to taste steel," he snarled.

"Get back!" Bree snapped, blocking him with her sword. "This prize isn't for you, but for our queen." She cast a warning look around her, even as she urged Feannag on once more. *Keep moving, lad.* "Mor will have the guts of any of you foolish enough to touch him." Her lip curled then. "She has plans for this shitbag."

Scowling, the warrior drew back.

The stallion plowed forward, and the crowd gave way.

Dawn was breaking, a blaze of gold that gilded Cannich. The fort was overrun now. The Shee had broken through the gates and bested the garrison. The fighting had moved to the broch itself, where the overking and his warriors and druids were making their last stand.

The clang of iron against steel and hoarse shouting echoed behind them, mingling with the sobbing of those who'd been captured by the Shee. Nearby, a woman started to keen, no doubt weeping over the death of a loved one.

Jaw clenched, Bree rode on.

She'd betrayed her people before, but not like this. The old Bree would have answered her queen's call, would have helped her take Cannich—without hesitation, or pity for those who lived here.

But she'd changed.

She followed the Raven Queen no longer. Instead, the man she towed behind her had her loyalty. She didn't care about this war. Let the Shee and Marav kill each other; she wanted no part in it. All she wanted was to get her and Cailean out of Cannich alive—then they could start afresh and put all of this behind them.

As they crossed to the gates, which now hung off their hinges, walking over the bodies of those who'd fallen, she glanced over her shoulder at Cailean.

Hands bound before him, the rope tied around his neck, her husband wore a fierce look. Meeting her eye, he snarled at her—and in response she gave another, hard, jerk of the rope, nearly bringing him to his knees.

There were many eyes still upon them; she had to make this convincing. She bared her teeth at him then. "Keep moving, scum!"

"Vicious Shee bitch." He spat on the ground.

"Dog-humping Marav." Bree hauled on the rope once more and was rewarded by a choking sound.

"Fuck," he wheezed. "You're enjoying this, aren't you?"

"Not at all," she muttered.

Moments later, Feannag passed between the gates, and they began the descent down the road that wound its way to the bottom of the rock. However, a steady stream of foot soldiers climbed to the fort, to assist those already inside. The way was narrow, and those traveling up had to pull into passing places to let them by.

"Keep back!" Bree shouted once more, waving her sword before her. "I've caught the High King's chief-enforcer … and I'm bringing him to our queen."

And they heeded her, even if Bree's throat was raw by the time she reached the lower ward at the base of the rock. It was a mess down here. Her people had razed the camp, leaving it a smoking ruin. The ramparts were smoke-blackened. Bodies littered the ground amongst tattered Cannich banners, many of them bristling with raven feather-fletched arrows.

Angling Feannag through the gap that had once been the gates into the lower ward, Bree's heart started to hammer against her ribs.

This was where things got dicey—the part of Cailean's plan she'd balked at the most. Somehow, amongst the excitement and chaos of a successful siege, she had to slip away.

Sheathing her sword, she stopped announcing her presence now. Instead, she rode south, through the swirling press of Shee astride stags and elks. Amongst them, she spied trow and powries perched upon the backs of rams and mountain goats—blades of Sheehallion steel clutched in their clawed hands. To her shock, there were also tattooed warriors, their bare limbs smeared with woad, upon sure-footed garrons.

Iron, she'd never thought she'd see the day Marav sided with fae against a common enemy. She knew that the hill-tribe warriors hated Talorc mac Brude that much, but what had Mor promised them?

And amongst the army stalked huge fae hounds, their hackles raised, golden gazes hungry.

Bree's breathing grew shallow. She'd thought the Shee army large before—but with Mor's new allies, it was vast. Her blood chilled then as realization dawned. This was a force meant for more than taking one fort. It was one designed to conquer.

Just a short while earlier, she'd told herself that this conflict between Shee and Marav didn't matter to her, yet now she wasn't so sure. If Mor was planning something huge, there wouldn't be a soul, on either side of the veil, who wouldn't be touched by it.

Bree's stomach twisted. And if that happened, it wouldn't matter how far or fast she and Cailean ran, this war would affect them.

Keep moving, Feannag. The stallion had slowed his stride, snorting nervously as a trow seated upon a large black ram with curling horns leered at him. *Don't let them cow you.*

"Where are you heading with him?"

A commanding voice pulled her up short. Spine straightening, Bree shot an imperious look at the Shee warrior, one of Mor's captains judging by the fine silver cape that rippled from his shoulders, who strode toward her.

"I'm taking this prisoner to the Raven Queen," she answered, her voice clipped.

The male's tawny gaze narrowed as it settled on Cailean. "Shades, isn't that—"

"Aye. It's the chief-enforcer himself," she cut him off haughtily. "Now, if you'll excuse me, I must—"

"You're going the wrong way, Fellshadow," the captain growled, making it clear that although she didn't know his face, he recognized hers. He then jerked his head left, toward where the crowd was at its thickest, where raven banners snapped in the morning breeze. "Mor is over there." His eyes glinted. "I shall escort you."

It was hard to keep her nerve then.

Iron smite her, this was what she'd feared. Her mind scrabbled, looking for an excuse, a way out. But there wasn't any.

Nodding, she reined Feannag left, falling in next to the captain. She didn't dare look over her shoulder, to try to catch her husband's eye.

"Clear the way!" The captain shouted. "We must see the queen."

The crowd parted, allowing them through, and up ahead, Bree caught the gleam of sunlight on obsidian. Mor's crown. The Raven Queen was there, at the heart of her army, astride a great white elk, a fine cloak of crow feathers rippling down her back. Eagal hunched upon her shoulder.

Gavyn was there too. Tall and proud, resplendent in black like his queen, the Captain of The Ravens rode a leggy elk.

Neither of them had spied Bree yet. But any moment they would—and when they did, it was over for Cailean. And her.

Panic slammed into her chest. Shades, she couldn't give him to them. She had to do something. Her fingers clenched upon the reins, sweat sliding down her back now.

Eyes fluttering shut, she silently asked forgiveness from the Ancestors, for she was about to draw a blade against her own people. Aye, she'd killed Shee before, at Mor's instruction. But this was different.

Her breathing quickened and grew shallow.

Aye, she could fight like a cornered fae hound, but she was surrounded. At least this way, neither of them would be taken prisoner.

They'd die as they'd lived—as warriors.

A horn's loud wail ripped through the morning then, causing the cold, smoky air to shiver.

Bree's eyes snapped open. That wasn't a Sheehallion trumpet.

Her gaze swept over the sea of silver armor around her. They were on higher ground here. She could see across the bulk of the Shee army. It spread out upon the grassy meadows around the foot of Cannich's rock, to the edge of the woodland to the south—and the highway.

And there, a dark line of iron helmets and standards—spears bristling against the pale sky—approached. And as the army marched toward them and the ground shook under its weight, the morning sun illuminated a fluttering wolf's head banner.

30: ONE TERRIBLE, VIOLENT SONG

"FORM THE LINES!" A call went up. Around Bree, the army shifted, the warriors and their mounts moving to obey.

The captain who'd been escorting Bree to Mor cast her a distracted glance. "Stay back … our queen will deal with the chief-enforcer later." The male then strode away, no doubt in search of the elk or stag he'd ride into battle.

"The High King is here!" The news traveled swiftly, excitement rippling over the army waiting before Cannich. The Shee warriors' eyes gleamed, while trow and powries chattered and whooped, and the hill-tribe warriors shared eager glances and violent grins.

Bree watched the captain go, her heart lurching into her throat.

Just like that, they'd been given a reprieve.

It must be now.

They wouldn't get another chance. Whipping out a knife, Bree twisted in the saddle to find that Cailean had anticipated her. He was standing close, bound wrists upraised. Their gazes glanced off each other as she freed his hands and sliced away the rope from around his neck. An instant later, he'd vaulted up behind her.

Wordlessly, she passed him her hunting dagger and one of her fighting knives.

"Go!" he growled in her ear.

Bree didn't need to be told twice. Drawing her longsword once more, she angled Feannag right, plunging into the lines.

Getting through wasn't easy, for the crowd was dense. But Bree angled the stallion toward the nearest edge of the press of warriors, which ended around twenty yards from the woods.

Steel swiped at her as some of the Shee warriors realized she was trying to flee. A few tried to stop her, but Feannag was already charging past, weaving his way through the ranks of elks, stags, rams, mountain goats, and fae hounds.

Eventually, Bree had to slash her way out. She felt Cailean's body shift and twist behind her as he wielded the blades she'd given him. The sharp tang of pine and campfire filled her nostrils then. He'd summoned his earth magic. Usually, the smell would have made her pulse lurch, but she was too distracted to care.

A powrie sprang forward, steel blade slashing. It stabbed at Feannag, aiming for his chest. *Jump!* Bree touched the stallion's mind just in time, and he leaped high, clearing the imp and the goat it sat upon.

And then they were through and galloping toward the tree line.

Crouched over Feannag's neck, Bree cut her gaze left, back toward the South Road, where the High King's army gathered speed now. A roar went up, crashing over the meadows.

And the Shee force thundered forward to meet their foe.

The collision of both sides—bodies, shields, and blades— rang in Bree's ears as Feannag reached the trees.

"They're following," Cailean grunted.

"How many?"

"Around half a dozen. All Shee."

A flash of white appeared to her left then. Tivesheh.

Bree's heart lurched. *Come closer!* The stag obeyed, and an instant later, he was running alongside Feannag, shoulder-to-shoulder. Nimbly, Bree swung a leg over the stallion's withers and flung herself onto her stag's back. She and Cailean would be able to fight more easily on their own mounts.

They flew through the trees, Feannag and Tivesheh's hooves churning up the bed of rotten fallen leaves. The land rose, climbing to a hill. And when they reached the top, the trees drew back.

"We can't outrun them!" Bree shouted to Cailean.

"Then we'll make our stand here." Cailean pulled Feannag up, the tattoos that covered his arms flaring silver in the morning light. He gripped both the blades she'd given him, controlling his stallion with his thighs. Feannag swiveled on his powerful hind legs, rearing as the first of the Shee burst from the trees upon a brown stag.

The warrior had drawn his longsword, a feral light gleaming in his obsidian eyes. Five more Shee streamed onto the hilltop after him.

They met them in a clash of steel that rang through the trees.

However, shortly after they engaged their pursuers, Cailean leaped down from Feannag's back, continuing the fight on foot. Bree followed moments later, and soon they fought back-to-back as the Shee formed a ring around them.

Sweat slid down Bree's spine as she struck, parried, and feinted. Curse it, these six were good.

A vicious snarl announced Skaal's arrival. Bree hadn't seen the fae hound as they'd fled through the woods, but like Tiv, she'd been watching and waiting. All the same, Skaal's attack surprised Bree. Fae hounds were protectors of Shee barrows. Her people had always had their loyalty. But not this hound.

And with Skaal's help, they turned the tide against their attackers.

A short while later, the twitching bodies of the Shee who'd pursued them were scattered around the clearing.

Breathing hard, Bree and Cailean's gazes fused. Her ears strained, trying to pick up the sound of anyone approaching from the north. But she caught nothing except for the roar of the unfolding battle that rolled over her. Even from this distance, it was overwhelming.

Straightening up, she looked through the gap between the trees where Cannich and the land beneath it were visible.

Black smoke billowed from within its high stone walls. The Uplands capital was aflame.

Cailean stepped up next to his wife and watched the battle unfold. The splintering of wooden shields, the scream of iron against steel—and of iron against iron too, for the hill-tribe warriors had turned on their own people—and the roars of fury and agony assaulted his ears.

It all blended into one terrible, violent song.

Cailean's already pounding heart lurched.

Moons earlier, he'd have been in the thick of things, slashing his broadsword through the press of Shee and their allies. He'd have defended the High King with his dying breath.

But that man had died, and another had been born. One that was no longer Talorc mac Brude's dog. Just as Bree had turned her back on Mor.

They were both down there amongst the melee—the Raven Queen and the High King—and they'd likely face each other in the end.

He tore his gaze from where silver and black surged against each other, like two seas meeting, and looked back at the smoking fort. His gut twisted then. He couldn't believe Cannich had fallen to the Shee. The 'Jewel of the North' was being destroyed, and there was nothing he could do about it.

At least Enya got out.

Aye, she had, although his sister was the least of his worries right now. His skin prickled as he continued to watch the fort burn. With Cannich taken, the northern Uplands would belong to the Shee.

Talorc mac Brude had to win this battle. If he didn't, the delicate balance of power between their races would shatter, and they'd all be up to their necks in shit. And where would his allegiance lie then?

There's much about you that's good.

The night before, he'd hated himself, but his wife had pulled him free of the mire. Gods, he wanted to be the man Bree saw— wanted to make his life mean something half-decent. She thought he was loyal, steadfast, and protective, yet so far, he'd left nothing but a legacy of violence and death.

"What now?" Bree asked then.

Cutting his attention away from Cannich, he raked his gaze over her, checking for injuries. However, despite a shallow scratch to her cheek, she was unharmed.

His fierce Shee wife stared back at him, her eyes glowing. There was no mistaking the challenge in her stare—and Cailean would answer it.

"Yesterday, I discovered that the High King has brought his family north with him," he replied. "They'll be following the main host, traveling with the baggage train and rearguard most likely."

A nerve flickered in Bree's cheek. "Lara and Mirren are here?" she whispered.

"Aye, and the queen consort too." He paused then, as screams from the battle below rent the air. "The High King has spent years amassing his armies, but I'm not sure it'll be enough to defeat the might Mor has rallied … not with her new allies. We need to warn the rearguard and get the High King's family to safety." He paused then, his gaze fusing with his wife's. "I care what happens to Lara too," he said softly. Indeed, he'd always respected her, and after she'd partnered him at blood-letting, a bond of sorts had formed between them. "I'll not see the princess, or anyone with her, come to harm."

Bree nodded, her jaw setting in a determined expression he knew only too well. She stepped back then and moved toward where Tivesheh waited with Skaal and Feannag. "Let's go and find them."

31: IN FOR THE KILL

TIVESHEH SPRINTED SOUTH. Trees passed by in a blur, branches whipping against Bree's face. Crouched low over his withers, she was dimly aware of Skaal racing beside her. The fae hound was fleet, little more than flashes of moss-green through the dark of the trees. Behind her, the thunder of Feannag's hooves warned Bree that Cailean was doing his best to keep up.

They cut through the woodland to rejoin the highway.

However, as Bree crested the last hill before a steep slope that angled down to where the road snaked through a pine-clad glen, she caught sight of a host of Shee warriors—at least two dozen of them—racing south on elks.

Drawing Tiv up, she leaned forward, her sharp eyesight scanning the group. Clad in black leather armor, their pitch-colored cloaks billowing behind them, the figures were distinctive. And just as distinctive was the swarm of stocky imps—with bobbing red caps upon their heads—crouched on the backs of mountain goats behind them.

"Iron," she breathed, as her heart lurched into her throat. Even from this distance, she caught a flash of pale hair.

Gavyn Frostshard was leading them.

"Who are they?" Cailean pulled Feannag up next to her.

"Mor's Ravens," Bree replied. "Her personal bodyguard … the deadliest of all Shee fighters. And they've got over fifty powries with them."

Cailean ground out a curse. "They're going to reach the rearguard before us."

"Aye." Bree cut him a sidelong glance, seeing her own frustration mirrored on his face. "But not by much."

Tivesheh ran as fast as The Sweeper, and yet he wasn't fast enough to catch The Ravens.

Galloping on the road now, Bree caught sight of the camp ahead. Supply wagons—large wooden carts with hide awnings over them—had been parked in a wide circle around a carpet of tents. Riderless elks and mountain goats stalked outside the camp, waiting for the call of their masters.

The Ravens and their allies were already inside the camp.

Shouting, followed by terrified screams, cut through the damp air, and Bree's stomach clenched.

Lara and Mirren were trapped in there. She had to get to them.

Stop here, she instructed Tivesheh. The stag skidded to a halt just yards before the wagons, and an instant later, Bree leaped nimbly off his back, drawing her blades as she went.

She sprinted toward the perimeter and had almost reached the nearest wagon, when she heard Cailean pull up behind her, and the thud of his boots hitting the ground. Feannag had made a valiant effort to keep pace with Tivesheh yet had eventually fallen behind.

Climbing the wagon with ease, Bree scaled the top and dropped onto the ground inside the encampment.

Her nostrils flared at the reek of iron in here. The Marav warriors defending this camp were heavily armed. She resisted the stench and tried to ignore her twitching muscles. She'd wade through a forest of iron to get to her friends. She'd lied to Lara and Mirren—deceived them as she had Cailean—but she'd make it up to her friends now.

She'd prove to them that they could count on her.

Cailean landed next to her then. He too had scaled the wagon easily, moving with a fluidity she'd come to recognize in him. The tattoos on his neck and arms glowed silver now, the smell of pine and ash catching in her throat.

Skaal leaped down next to Cailean, her hackles raised.

They'd jumped into the thick of things, for a few yards away, Marav warriors, clad in boiled leather armor and wearing domed iron helmets, were facing off against a cluster of powries.

Bree skirted around the skirmish, noting that the warriors were holding their own. She wouldn't interfere. Instead, she and Cailean needed to get to Lara and the queen—before The Ravens found them.

Side-by-side, they wove through the press of tents, and in the meantime, the screams grew louder.

Bree's breathing quickened.

Shit. She hoped she wasn't too late.

Cailean scooped up a sword from a fallen Marav warrior and helped himself to the man's fighting dagger as well.

Bree didn't like having iron nearby, but he needed those blades.

They were getting closer to the heart of the camp now, where the bodies of the men and women who'd tried to fight off the Shee and powries sprawled, their blood seeping into the peaty ground.

Summoning his earth magic, he stalked forward, cutting his way through the swarm of powries descending upon him. They rushed at him and Bree fearlessly though, steel knives flashing.

Cailean met them with a snarl. These murderous imps wouldn't stop him from getting to the queen and her daughter. All those years ago, he'd sworn fealty to the High King, but today, he'd show where his loyalty truly lay. To Queen Teva and Princess Lara: two women who'd been dragged into this war by a man who cared about nothing but his hatred for the Shee.

He was almost through the fray when a piercing scream drew his attention. He whirled right to see a lean, black-clad figure advancing on a woman he'd bailed up against the side of a tent. Three youths lay around the woman, all bleeding and clutching their wounds. However, their mother defended them still, gripping a fighting dagger.

Cailean's heart bucked.

Enya. Her sons had tried to protect her and failed—and now she stood alone.

The Raven went in for the kill then, the slender blade he wielded flashing bright in the sunlight.

But suddenly, Cailean was there, his iron blade blocking the lethal swing. The Shee's yellow eyes snapped wide, for Cailean's speed had taken him by surprise. Not waiting for the Raven to rally, he kicked him hard in the knee, sending him reeling. An instant later, the Shee was on his back with an iron blade driving through his throat.

Yanking his sword free, Cailean whirled to face his sister.

Enya, pale and trembling, stared back at him.

"Cailean!" Bree shouted from up ahead. The ring of weapons colliding and Skaal's snarls followed. His companions had moved on and needed his help. Nodding to his sister, he whirled away and plunged after his wife and the fae hound.

Together, the three of them cut their way forward, and a short while later, they emerged in the heart of the camp. Here, the Ravens had engaged the ring of Marav defending the royal pavilion—a large tent where a wolf banner hung from a pole.

However, when Cailean's gaze settled upon the rip in the side of the tent, his breathing caught. The Hag's curse. They'd already forced their way inside.

He cut Bree a look. Aye, she too had spied the gap. A nerve flickered in her cheek, her tawny eyes shadowing. "Shit," she rasped.

Their gazes fused, and Cailean flashed her a hard smile. "We'll save them. Ready?"

Bree's eyes glinted, her jaw firming as she nodded.

With Skaal snapping and snarling behind them, they slashed their way through the Ravens, catching many of the Shee by surprise.

Moments later, they leaped inside the pavilion.

The bodies of guards littered the floor, their blood soaking into sheepskins. Slaves and servants cowered in the shadows. However, Mirren, wild-eyed and clutching a bleeding arm, crouched a few yards from where two Shee warriors—both tall and lean, one fair-haired the other dark—held blades to Queen Teva and Princess Lara's throats.

Despite the grunts, cries, and clang of blades outside the pavilion, a heavy silence had settled within.

The magic in Cailean's blood called to him, yet he leashed it a moment, his fingers flexing on the grip of the broadsword he held before him. *I'll kill these two whoresons.*

And he would. But first, he had to ensure the queen and the princess were out of danger. The Raven Queen's retribution against the High King had been vicious indeed. She'd taken Cannich and raised a terrifying army to take on the Marav. Cailean couldn't stop what she'd started, but he could stop the Shee from murdering these women.

Teva was weeping, tears running down her pale cheeks, while Lara's face was taut, fury burning in her eyes. Fortunately, though, the princess minded the blade that the fair-haired Raven held at her throat.

But at that moment, Lara's attention seized upon Cailean, shock igniting in her gaze.

Aye, he was back from the dead.

Meanwhile, the Shee who held her captive wasn't paying the princess, or Cailean, any mind. Instead, he stared at Bree. A muscle feathered in his jaw, disbelief flickering in his slitted eyes.

Bree returned his glare. "What's this, Gavyn?" she demanded roughly.

His lip curled. "I don't answer to you, turncoat."

"He's taking them hostage," Mirren replied, her voice husky with pain.

Bree flashed the lass a quick, concerned look. The maid stared back, gaze glittering. There was no recognition in her eyes though. She didn't know her friend in her Shee form.

Meanwhile, the blond warrior, Gavyn, edged backward, toward a second hole they'd ripped in the tent. "Time to go, princess." All the while, he kept the flat of his steel blade against his captive's throat. Green eyes wide, her defiance wavering now, Lara moved with him.

Queen Teva started to sob then, a keening sound that cut to the bone. Heat started to pulse in Cailean's gut. Teva was a gentle soul who'd spent a sheltered life within the safety of Duncrag's high walls. This was too much for her. A moment later, the queen's captor slapped a rough hand over her mouth, gagging her. "That's enough. Shut up."

Cailean stepped forward, earth magic rising in a burning tide inside him. A silvery glow lit up the tent then. "You're not taking them."

Both Ravens' faces tightened, their nostrils flaring.

Druidic magic swirled through the pavilion, the air pungent with resin and campfire.

The dark-haired Raven's step faltered, his lean face draining of color. But that didn't stop him. Still gripping the queen close, the Shee drew nearer to the hole in the tent.

Cailean ground his teeth. He wanted to unleash himself on them, yet if he did so, the queen and princess would likely die. These two pricks might have been instructed to take the High King's wife and daughter captive rather than kill them, but Teva and Lara were still in danger. The dark-haired Raven had a glint in his eye now that warned Cailean and Bree not to make any sudden moves.

Even so, every passing moment galled him. He wanted to act, to cut these two Ravens down.

Gavyn's companion snarled a curse then.

Queen Teva had somehow managed to bite his hand. Fear had turned her savage.

Cailean's stomach swooped. It was a brave if reckless move.

"Bitch!" An instant later, the warrior sliced his blade deep across the queen's pale neck, steel flashing.

Blood spurted, and Lara's scream pierced the air.

Cailean snarled a curse and leaped forward. However, the Raven thrust the choking woman at him, and Cailean had to drop his weapon to catch her.

The Shee warrior then pivoted nimbly on his heel and dove for the gap in the tent.

32: SAVE HER

HE NEVER REACHED safety.

Thud. A knife drove between the fleeing warrior's shoulder blades.

He gave a wheezing cry and staggered, falling against the side of the tent. Deep shudders wracked his body as he twisted and clawed, trying to reach the embedded knife, to pull it free.

Lowering Teva to the ground, Cailean slammed his hand over the queen's sliced-open throat. However, he couldn't stem the blood that pulsed between his fingers. Teva's eyes were wide, terrified, as she flailed under him.

He cut his gaze right then, to where Mirren had risen to her feet. The iron blade she'd just hurled had sunk deep.

His attention didn't linger on her though, for at that moment, Gavyn hauled Lara through the gap.

Bree dove after him.

Jaw clenched, Cailean let the queen sink back onto the sheepskins. He'd removed his hand from her throat now, and their gazes locked. Teva's eyes glistened. They both knew there wasn't anything he could do. His gut twisted in response. "I'm sorry," he whispered.

"Go," she mouthed, blood dribbling down her chin. "Save her."

Mirren moved to the queen's side then; the lass would stay with Teva while she died—but Cailean couldn't linger here any longer.

He launched himself to his feet, scooping up his sword as he went. He then drove his broadsword through the chest of the Shee who thrashed on the ground. *For Teva, you shitweasel.*

Yanking the blade free, he plunged outside.

Smoke and heat slammed into his face as he emerged from the pavilion.

He glanced around him, panic rising. Where was Bree? The attackers had set the camp on fire. Tents blazed around him, while powries streaked past, flaming torches in their clawed hands.

One lunged for him, and he skewered it on his blade. The powrie screeched before disappearing in a flash of light, its torch rolling onto crushed grass.

Moments later, Cailean waded into the battle that raged just yards away. Marav warriors converged on their attackers, driving them back from the royal pavilion. The Ravens and their imps had done a lot of damage, yet the tide was turning against them. And now that they had the princess, the attackers were retreating, heading toward the perimeter.

And in the midst of it all, Bree stalked Gavyn. Her long braid flying as she pivoted, ducked, and slashed, his wife fought her way through the press. Each step brought her closer to her quarry.

Cailean's heart lurched at the sight of her. She was magnificent. A warrior to the core. But she was also surrounded.

Gavyn was dragging Lara backward, while his warriors closed in, forming a protective ring around him. An elk emerged through the wreathing smoke then, between two crumpled tents. The beast, a leggy male with vast pronged antlers, snorted, pawing the ground, awaiting its master.

Cailean's heart started to kick violently against his ribs as he began slashing his way through the fray.

No, the whoreson wasn't going to abduct Lara and carry her back to the Raven Queen. Gods knew what Mor would do to her.

"Give it up, Gavyn!" Bree shouted as she cut down the last Raven who stood between them. "You'll never get the princess onto that elk's back. The moment your knife slips. I'll have you."

"Fuck off, traitor!" he snarled back. However, Cailean spied desperation in his silvery eyes. He knew Bree was right.

Sensing that the tide was turning, Lara's tear-stained face twisted. She started to struggle then, heedless of the blade still at her throat. It pierced her skin, blood trickling down her neck, yet she fought on.

Cailean cut his way toward Bree and Lara, scattering powries as they tried to bring him down. Just a few yards separated them now, but it suddenly seemed vast.

The Shee and powries were still withdrawing, but not fast enough.

He was aware then that a handful of Marav warriors had also managed to fight their way in next to him. The High King had left a decent force behind with the baggage train, and although they'd initially been caught off guard, they rallied now, tightening the noose.

Meanwhile, blood continued to slide down Lara's throat, staining the neckline of her tunic.

Gavyn snarled curses at her, but she was beyond listening. Beyond caring. She'd just seen her mother slain and faced being carried away. He wouldn't take her alive.

Cailean admired her spirit. But by the Warrior's bloody blade, if Lara didn't cease fighting, she'd shortly follow her mother to the Otherworld.

The elk stood behind them now, tossing its head and warning the Marav away with its antlers. However, Gavyn would never get Lara onto its back without making himself vulnerable.

And when he did, Bree would be on him.

Realizing that the game was up, Gavyn yanked his blade away from the princess's throat. He used Lara as a shield then, thrusting her at Bree while he leaped nimbly onto his elk's back. "Ravens, fall back!" he bellowed.

Bree pushed Lara behind her and leaped forward, her blade slashing.

Gavyn and his mount were too quick. They bounded away through the smoke, followed by a wave of screeching powries. Some of the Ravens also followed, although the stragglers were forced to turn and fight.

The princess was in the middle of it all, undefended.

Cailean cursed, pushing forward to put himself between her and danger.

Cringing as blades clashed around her, Lara dropped to her knees, covering her head with her hands.

Meanwhile, Bree had joined the fight against the remaining Ravens, who now backed toward the perimeter. Freedom wasn't far off—a gap between the wagons where the others had fled.

The thunder of elk hooves departing on the road beyond shook the smoky air.

Bree fought on, her long steel blade flashing. Arrows flew now, for some of the Ravens had drawn longbows. But she held fast, heedless of the danger.

And as a Raven drew back an arrow, aimed directly at Bree's chest, dread washed over Cailean. She hadn't seen it, her attention riveted upon the warrior she was currently fighting.

He was at the princess's side now, yet he had a choice. Lara or his wife. He couldn't protect them both.

Cailean didn't think. The decision was instinctual.

His tattoos flared white-hot as he leaped forward, closing the gap with unnatural speed, and flung himself between the archer and Bree.

Thud.

The loosed arrow hit his flank. The force of the impact knocked him sideways, straight into Bree, and the pair of them tumbled to the ground.

The roar of angry shouts assaulted his ears then, just as searing pain bloomed down his left flank. Grunting a curse, he pushed himself off Bree to see a flood of Marav warriors rush past them, descending upon the Ravens.

"Cailean!" His wife was staring at where the yew arrow, fletched in raven feathers, protruded from his side. Bree's eyes were wide, alarmed, and following her gaze, he saw why.

He gritted his teeth as the burn in his side grew hotter. *Shit.* It had gone deep.

Heat swept over him then, and a strange tingling began in his limbs.

"I'm fine," he muttered, even as his speech slurred. His mouth felt as if it were stuffed with wool. Suddenly, he couldn't speak at all, couldn't think.

Fuck. The arrow must have been poisoned.

His mouth worked as he tried to tell Bree. However, she was nothing but a blur, and the words she gasped made no sense at all.

Agony punched into him then, and darkness dropped like a veil.

"Is he alive?"

Breathing hard, Bree looked up to find Lara standing over her and Cailean.

Blood still trickled down the princess's throat, although she paid it no mind.

Frankly, Bree couldn't believe Lara still breathed. She'd been sure Gavyn would slit her throat, as his companion had done with Teva. Instead, he'd spared her. Aye, he was a vicious bastard—and had killed without compunction before—but something had stilled his hand this time.

The reason didn't matter, she supposed—what did, was Lara had survived. Her gaze was currently riveted upon Cailean. He lay on his back, passed out cold.

Bree's heart lurched. This was her doing. She'd been so caught up in the battle that it had consumed her. Hunting Gavyn had turned her feral. Yet the bastard had escaped. In the meantime, she'd left Lara undefended and put herself in harm's way.

And as a result, Cailean had taken an arrow that was meant for her.

"The arrow's poisoned," she replied, a chill washing over her. Shee poison, Nightbane especially, was lethal.

Lara breathed a curse. She shifted her attention to Bree, gaze narrowing.

"Your neck?" Bree asked, trying to ignore the burgeoning hostility in the princess's eyes. "Is the cut deep?"

Lara raised a trembling hand to her throat. "I don't think so," she replied huskily, even as her fingers came away red. She was shaken by her ordeal, although impressively calm. Bree wasn't surprised; she'd always sensed Lara was strong.

Mirren approached then, moving to the princess's side. The lass's face was ashen, her hands blood-stained.

Both women now stared at Bree, clearly trying to decide who and what she was.

Exhaling sharply, she drew in a deep breath. "You don't recognize me, do you?"

Lara's eyes widened, while next to her, Mirren murmured an oath. "Fia?"

"My real name's Bree." She paused then before adding. "I'm a Shee assassin who was sent to spy on the High King."

Both women blinked, confusion shadowing their eyes.

"I will tell you *everything* later," Bree assured them when neither Tara nor Mirren answered. "But first" —she nodded to the arrow that protruded from Cailean's side— "he needs a healer."

Lara's face tightened, yet she nodded. "Aye … we must seek out Eldra … if she's still alive."

A horn blew then, a deep, mournful sound that shook the air.

Lara gasped, relief flaring in her green eyes. "Father."

Bree's heart lurched into a gallop. Iron smite her. The last thing she needed was to face Talorc mac Brude right now. She might be able to convince Lara she was a friend, but the High King wouldn't see past the fact she was Shee.

However, with Cailean lying on the ground next to her, she wasn't going anywhere.

And so, as the first standards appeared through the clearing smoke, she steeled herself for what was to come.

Figures appeared on horseback, a smaller group than she'd expected. A man, tall and lanky with short fair hair, clad in enforcer black, led them. Once Cailean's second, Torran mac Rab now led the High King's enforcers. Blood splattered, his handsome features pale and strained, he drew up his horse, surveying the broken tents and churned-up ground littered with bodies.

His gaze widened as it settled upon Cailean's prone body and Bree crouched beside him. Torran's hand strayed to the dagger at his hip, even as his gaze met Lara's. "What happened here, Your Highness?"

"The Shee attacked us." Her voice faltered. "The queen is dead."

Torran's face went rigid. "Your Highness, I—"

"Didn't you meet the fleeing Shee and powries on the road?" She cut him off, taking a step forward, her gaze dragging over the company with the chief-enforcer.

Torran shook his head. Bree counted only three other enforcers and barely more than thirty warriors behind him.

A tremor shivered through Lara, and she wrapped her arms around herself. "What happened?" she whispered. "Where's my father?"

Torran stared back at her, a nerve jumping underneath one eye. "It's over, Your Highness. Our army is beaten. The Shee hold Cannich."

Lara stared back at Torran, swaying slightly on her feet. "The High King?"

"He fell, princess … as did your husband."

Bree stilled at this news. Mor had done it. She'd achieved what no other Shee ruler ever had: she'd taken control of part of Albia. Her belly churned then as the significance of this moment settled deep into her bones.

The conflict between Shee and Marav was only beginning.

33: AMONGST THE STONES

SHARP NEEDLES PRICKED Bree's skin. She coughed, the odor of pine resin and ash catching in her throat. Grey standing stones, their rough sides pitted with age and covered in lichen and moss, surrounded the princess and her entourage.

Shades, this was the last place she wanted to camp for the night. And yet it would be the safest spot for the Marav.

Once Torran and the other survivors joined them earlier, the rearguard had packed up swiftly and set off south. Dragging wagons after them, they couldn't move fast, and Bree found herself constantly looking north, expecting to see a wave of Shee surge into view; but as the day wore on, none did.

And finally, they'd stopped here—at The Ring of Ard.

One of the three stone circles of Albia, these standing stones sat in a narrow glen, shadowed by pine-clad mountains to the north and the east. Ferns and gorse carpeted the valley floor, yet the area around the stone circle was clear, almost as if vegetation couldn't thrive in its proximity.

It was safe enough to make camp within the stones this evening, for they'd passed Gateway, and Mid-Winter Fire was still a turn of the moon away. Even so, every fiber of Bree's being screamed for her to run as they lurched to a halt inside the circle.

Fighting it, she took slow, deep breaths.

Of course, the earth magic was at its thickest at the heart of the ring of stones, so Lara and her protectors would shelter here. The rest of their ragged army put up their tents around the edges.

Climbing from the wagon, Bree flexed her hands at her sides.

The earth magic pushed against her, abrasive and aggressive. Indeed, her usually strong limbs felt weak and shaky inside the circle. The urge to turn on her heel and flee reared up, yet she pushed it down.

She wouldn't leave Cailean.

The day was drawing to a close now, the last rays of sun bathing the pitted surface of the standing stones.

Pulse racing, she cut her gaze from the monoliths, her attention settling upon the prone figure lying upon his back in the wagon. Her husband's face was pale and sweaty. Cailean hadn't awoken since taking that arrow in the side. His skin was hot to touch now, and blood soaked through the heavy bandage that wrapped about his naked chest.

Reaching out, Bree clasped his limp hand in hers. "Fight, mac Brochan," she whispered. "Don't let it beat you."

Her breathing grew shallow then. *This is my fault.*

Cailean's eyelids flickered, and he mumbled something incoherent in reply. Her chest constricted. She hated feeling this powerless. How she wished they had access to Shee healers. Eldra was talented and had extracted the arrow and done her best to make him comfortable before they set off south, but her own people had greater knowledge of the healing arts.

Nightbane killed swiftly. Without the druidic magic that flowed through his veins, Cailean wouldn't have lasted this long.

The healer's assistants appeared then, men and women clad in mauve robes. Wordlessly, eyeing Bree as if they expected her to spring at them, they hauled Cailean off the back of the wagon.

Bree moved to help, but they shrank away.

Jaw clenched, she stepped back, letting them carry her husband toward the healing tent.

Unsurprisingly, she wasn't popular amongst the people here.

Before they'd set out earlier, Bree had explained herself fully, while Lara, Torran, and many others listened. And when she'd finished her tale, she'd braced herself to be taken prisoner. However, Lara hadn't given the order.

All the same, she'd watched Bree warily, and the gazes of the other Marav surrounding her had bordered on hostile. Aye, Bree had tried to save their queen and princess, but she was still one of the enemy.

Indeed, a group of warriors setting up a tent nearby was currently glaring at her.

Bree ignored them. All she cared about right now was saving her husband's life.

Her gaze traveled then to where four black-clad figures were dropping ward stones around the perimeter: Torran and his enforcers. It was a wise precaution, just in case the earth magic that swirled around the stones wasn't enough to keep the Shee at bay.

Bree's pulse fluttered. Hopefully, it would be.

Nonetheless, there was a watchfulness in the air this evening, almost as if the surrounding woodland had eyes.

Turning, she made to follow Eldra's assistants and Cailean into the healing tent. However, a male voice forestalled her. "Bree!"

A man was walking toward her. Tall and lean, his light-brown hair shaved close to his scalp, he sported a black eye and bruising to his face. Tribal tattoos inked his pale skin. The man was clad in a plain grey tunic and leggings and walked barefoot.

An iron collar circled his neck.

Bree's brow furrowed. "Aye?" She didn't recognize the slave—and yet the voice was familiar, as was his stride. Nevertheless, she didn't have time for this. Cailean was inside the healer's tent now, and she had to join him.

The slave's swollen mouth curved into a thin smile. "You don't know me then?"

Bree's breathing hitched.

He had hazel eyes and a scattering of freckles across the bridge of his nose. Even with a battered face, the man reminded her of someone—of her own reflection in the looking glass when she'd been a Marav woman. This slave could have been Fia's brother.

The man halted before her, although the prickling cold of the iron around his neck made her want to take a step back.

Despair clutched her by the throat before she croaked. "Gil?"

"Aye."

Bree stared at him, her heart suddenly pounding so loudly that she could hardly hear herself think. "What are you doing here?"

He swallowed. "Mor has named you a traitor to our people." His gaze guttered. "And I was punished for it."

Her stomach flipped over as she took in his battered face. "What happened?"

Gil's mouth twisted. He then gestured to the tall stones that loomed over them. "She sent me through The Ring of Ard at Gateway ... and her Ravens were waiting. They beat me senseless and left me on the road. The High King's army found me. They took me to be a hill-tribe warrior and slapped a slave collar around my neck."

Bree cursed, viciously.

Gil grimaced, wincing as his split bottom lip started to weep. His gaze roamed her face then. "I was there ... earlier," he said after a pause. "When you burst into the tent with that enforcer. I saw it all."

Bree swallowed, wishing her throat didn't feel as if someone had it in a chokehold. Her legs, already weak from being surrounded by earth magic, trembled now. "And?"

A groove etched between Gil's eyebrows, making him look remarkably like the Shee male she remembered. "I never thought you'd betray our people."

Bree's chest constricted. "Neither did I," she whispered. "But alliances sometimes change." And they had. She'd found something in Albia worth fighting, and dying, for.

Brother and sister stared at each other, and all the while, pressure built under Bree's breastbone.

Gil jerked his head toward the healing tent. "And you did it ... for him?"

"I did." Stepping forward, she put her hand on his arm. "I'm so sorry, Gil." And she was, desperately. Her actions had made her brother an outcast. They both knew she couldn't fix this.

His hazel eyes glittered, his body tensing under her grip. "So, am I."

34: MY WISH IS THE SAME

"HE'S FADING."

ELDRA'S announcement made Bree flinch. Seated at Cailean's side, she'd been wiping the sweat from his skin with a damp cloth.

She was still reeling from seeing Gil—and discovering what Mor had done to him—but she couldn't remain with her brother. Not with her husband so ill.

Beside the sleeping pallet, Skaal stirred. The fae hound sat up and stretched out her neck, nudging Cailean's arm with her wet nose. It had surprised Bree that Skaal ventured inside the stone circle. Such places were repellent to her kind. Just like her, she'd be suffering. And yet, here the fae hound was—at Cailean's side.

But he didn't stir. The flickering light of the nearby brazier illuminated the sickly yellow cast to his skin, and the way his eyes had sunk into the sockets.

Straightening up, Bree turned to look at the healer. The woman's expression was grim, her mouth pinched. "I've used all the cures for poison I know … but nothing is working." She paused then, her brow furrowing as her pale eyes bored into Bree. "It's Nightbane, you say?"

Bree nodded, even as dizziness swept over her. "It's the poison Shee archers most commonly use on their arrowheads."

"I've seen dead warriors with yellow skin after a skirmish with the Shee," Eldra admitted, her frown deepening. "And with badly festered wounds … however, it killed them long before I could be of any help." She paused then. "What comes next?"

"Shortness of breath … until you are left gasping for air." Dread caught in Bree's throat. "Death comes swiftly after that."

"Surely, you must know the cure?" Lara spoke up then. Standing behind the healer, arms folded, her gaze cut into Bree. The princess's eyes were red-rimmed. A bandage wrapped around her throat after her brush with Gavyn's blade.

Bree's pulse accelerated. She'd spent most of the afternoon hunting through her memories for one, but the answer had eluded her. "I'm not like you, Lara," she admitted huskily. Indeed, the princess had spent many mornings with Duncrag's healers, learning how to mix ointments and tend ailments. "My grandmother was a healer … I should have paid more attention to her."

"Think," Lara shot back, her tone steely now. "You're Cailean's only chance."

Sweating, Bree glanced over at where Eldra also watched her, a blend of distaste, fascination, and concern in her gaze. "Surely, your people have many cures to counteract poison's gall?" she asked.

Bree stilled.

Poison's gall.

An old rhyme, one her grandmother had sung to her when she'd been a youngling, surfaced then. She hadn't thought of it for over two centuries.

Breathing fast, she closed her eyes and traveled back through the years to her bower, where an older Shee female with a mane of white hair bounced a youngling upon her knee.

Eyes squeezed shut, her voice faltering slightly, Bree began to sing.

> *"Whin for iron's bite.*
> *Mallow for fever's burn.*
> *Sorrel for the bloody flux.*
> *Yarrow for soured wounds*
> *Wormwood for poison's gall."*

Her eyes snapped open then. That was it. She swiveled back to Eldra. "Wormwood root, pounded to a liquid and poured into the wound."

"Wormwood?" Eldra scowled. "Never heard of it."

Panic fluttered in Bree's chest. "It's a common enough herb."

The healer took a step forward, her tall frame bristling with urgency now. "It'll go by another name here. Describe it to me."

Bree raked a hand through her hair. "It's green and leafy … and appears in large dense growths."

"That describes over a dozen herbs. Be more specific."

"Once a year … in late summer, it has pale yellow flowers."

Eldra's face was still blank.

"The leaves are bitter … but edible." Heart pounding, Bree raked through her mind for any other details of the herb. Iron, how she wished she'd paid more attention to her wise grandmother; she'd reached over five thousand turns of the year before The Great Raven claimed her.

"Can you make the leaves into a tea?" Lara asked then. The princess's heart-shaped face was taut, a nerve flickering in her cheek.

"Aye … it helps stomach ailments."

Eldra made a sound in the back of her throat. "It's *mugwort* you speak of."

Bree's heart lurched, hope flowering. "So, it grows here too?"

"Aye … although as it's no longer in flower; the herb will be hard to find," Lara replied. "Especially since it'll be dark soon."

Bree stood up with a swiftness that made both women take a rapid step back. Even weakened inside the stones, she was fast. The Marav weren't used to the fluidity of Shee movements. "I'll find it."

The warriors guarding the perimeter of the camp, just beyond the ring of stones, stepped aside as Bree stalked past. She carried a flaming torch, for, indeed, the gloaming was deepening. Before long, night would smother the world.

Her stomach was in knots now, even as determination drove her forward.

She wouldn't give up on Cailean. She couldn't let him die. She had to make this right.

And as soon as she stepped beyond the wards, out of the circle where earth magic hummed like a hive of bees, the pressure on her skin eased and strength returned to her wobbly legs once more.

On her way out, she passed a tall figure robed in scarlet. Gregor mac Hume watched her, his face twisted into a scowl.

She hadn't spoken to the chief-sacrificer since her return, although like everyone, he'd have heard her story. Luckily for mac Hume, he'd remained with the rearguard; unlike the chief-bard and chief-seer, who'd both fallen alongside the High King in battle.

The chief-sacrificer, who'd just finished slitting open a hare and laying its entrails upon a large flat stone beyond the wards, would likely spend the night making sacrifices to the Gods. He'd be calling on their protection.

"Shee slut," he growled as she strode by. "I knew at blood-letting there was something wrong with you."

Bree ignored him, even as she recalled the look on the mac Hume's face the night of the blood-letting moons earlier, once the ceremony had concluded. It was the only instance when she'd seen the chief-sacrificer appear unsure of himself.

Nonetheless, his hard gaze tracked her as she strode across the valley floor toward the line of trees north of The Ring of Ard.

Two sets of glowing eyes watched her from the shadows between the trees.

Bree drew the hunting dagger at her side. Of course, as a Shee, she was safer out here than any Marav. All the same, it was wise to be wary of the faery creatures—especially since some now followed the Raven Queen.

However, as she neared the trees, she saw that the glowing eyes belonged to two wulvers. They watched her from the shadows, shaggy wolf heads on the sinewy bodies of men. Both wulvers wore nothing but tattered breeches, and knife belts across their hairy chests.

Bree's gaze narrowed. She'd seen plenty of wulvers over the years, although none of them had been armed. Despite their frightening appearance, they were usually timid unless provoked. Fortunately, there was no aggression in these wulvers' stances or their gazes now—just curiosity laced with feral cunning. Wulvers had been mistreated by the Marav, especially under the reign of High Kings like Talorc mac Brude, who reviled all faery folk.

But Bree was one of the Shee, and the wulvers let her pass unchallenged.

Striding into the woods, she immediately set about searching for wormwood.

Lara, of course, was right. It was difficult to make out one plant from the next on the woodland floor in the fading light. Fortunately, both sunrise and sunset in Albia were slow, a gradual lengthening of shadows. Bree's keen eyesight made her task easier as well. Moving carefully now, and sweeping her torch before her, she studied every patch of bracken, every growth of nettle and fern—just in case there was something else nestled amongst it.

In Sheehallion, wormwood grew everywhere. Eldra had assured her that mugwort was also relatively common here, yet as she searched, she found none.

Corpse candles flickered around her, seemingly friendly golden lights, beckoning the unwary. They didn't affect Bree, although she'd never seen so many out. The woods glimmered with them.

A shriek cut through the trees then, one that made the fine hair on the back of her neck prickle. Something rustled in the bushes to her right, and she swiveled around, lowering herself into a crouch.

Instinctively, she knew the wulvers hadn't followed her. Something else watched her from the shadows. She felt its malice, its hunger.

Bree flexed her fingers around the pommel of her dagger. "Come out and face me," she growled, inclining her head. "If you dare."

But whatever stalked her remained hidden.

Bree continued her search, although now the skin between her shoulder blades prickled.

On and on she walked through the woods, and as her search drew out and the gloaming deepened, desperation fluttered up.

There was no wormwood to be found.

Eventually, as the last of the light faded from the sky above the treetops, she came across a burn, a narrow stream that cut between moss-covered banks and slippery rocks. The sound of trickling water shattered the dusk's watchful silence.

Bree followed its course for a short while before she halted at the bank and breathed a curse, her voice catching. Time was running out for Cailean. With each moment she wasted out here, looking for this damned herb, he was inching closer to death.

She was about to fail him.

Crouching, she scooped up cold water and drank before splashing her face. The chill sharpened her wits once more, and her pulse started to thump in her ears. No. She wouldn't. She'd circle back now toward the stones and take another route. And this time, she'd find that fucking wormwood.

Decision made, Bree was about to rise to her feet and turn on her heel when a voice, female and thin with age, intruded.

"You never made your wish."

Bree's gaze snapped up, even as she lifted her blade.

A crone knelt a few yards away, upon a swathe of bright-green moss. Wispy white hair framed a hollowed face and milky eyes. Her gnarled hands were in the clear water, washing what looked to be a white shroud.

A chill washed over Bree before she reminded herself that she wasn't wearing white.

The Washerwoman wasn't washing *her* clothes.

"What shall it be then?" the Ben Neeya spoke once more, revealing yellowed protruding teeth. "Choose carefully this time mind … for I won't seek you out again."

Bree wet her lips, allowing her pulse to settle. Her belly twisted then. She'd never thought the Ben Neeya would give her another chance. After the crone had denied her that wish—to spare Cailean mac Brochan's life—when they'd met in the woods near The Ring of Caith on the eve of Mid-Summer, she'd run.

Her breathing grew shallow.

What a bitter irony that the Ben Neeya had found her now, when she was trying to save Cailean's life—again. She couldn't help but think that The Washerwoman was toying with her. The spirits and faery creatures that roamed Albia could be cruel.

"My wish is the same," she rasped. "Spare Cailean mac Brochan's life."

Unlike moons earlier, when her heart had been conflicted—when she'd been torn between two worlds—there was no doubt within her now.

Moments passed, and the Ben Neeya threw back her head and gave a wheezing laugh.

Dizziness assailed Bree as she stared back at her.

Aye, the bitch was playing games again. She'd come up with another feeble reason to deny her. Heat washed over Bree then as anger bloomed. Cailean was dying, and she was wasting time bandying words with a vindictive spirit that fed off her desperation. She'd had enough of this game.

Straightening up, she whipped around, intending to stalk away, back toward the camp.

But then, a thick profusion of green caught her eye directly ahead. The plant's tapered leaves gleamed in the light of her torch.

Bree's breathing lodged in her throat, and she halted mid-stride.

A healthy growth of wormwood.

Bree whipped back to face the Ben Neeya. "Thank y—"

The words died on her lips, for The Washerwoman had disappeared. Just a moment earlier, she'd been kneeling there in the fading light, her hideous face twisted in mirth. But no longer. Bree stood alone on the banks of the burn.

Pulse racing, she turned once more and rushed to the wormwood. It was the root Eldra would need, and so she thrust into the damp, peaty soil with her blade, digging around the plant.

And as she worked, Bree gave a shrill whistle.

Another shriek cut through the trees, followed by an unsettling chattering sound. The undergrowth snapped.

Bree started to sweat. Her whistle wasn't for them. She had more stalkers now, and they were closing in. She couldn't linger here any longer.

Working as fast as she dared, for she didn't want to leave any of the root behind, Bree continued digging.

Moments later, she rose to her feet, pulling the entire plant from the soil. To the left, she spied silhouettes. All of them were short, although some were broad and stocky while others were thin and wiry. They gripped steel blades. Eyes glinted in the light of her guttering torch.

Bree's heart lurched. Powries and trow were coming for her—a large band of them. She was a skilled fighter, but a quick glance told her she was greatly outnumbered.

Frantically, she swung around, to see a white shape, ghostly at first, moving toward her through the trees.

As always, her loyal stag had been waiting for her to call on him.

Ready to run faster than the four winds?

Tivesheh tossed his head. *Always.*

Sheathing her dagger, Bree tucked the wormwood under one arm and vaulted up onto the stag's back—just as the powries and trow descended upon her.

They boiled around Tivesheh, weapons thrusting, but the stag was faster.

He leaped high, bounding over them, and took off south.

35: I WILL NEVER FORGET IT

CAILEAN HAD LITTLE time left.

As soon as Bree burst in, holding the plant aloft, Eldra acted swiftly. First, she cleaned the roots, before mashing them up in a pestle and mortar. Lara helped her, the two women working deftly and speaking together in hushed voices.

It reminded Bree of when she'd seen the healer and the princess side-by-side in Eldra's healing chamber back in Duncrag. Those days seemed an age ago now. How different things had been between her and Cailean then—the deception she'd woven shadowing every interaction—but they'd started afresh.

Bree's chest constricted. They had a future waiting for them; she couldn't let Nightbane steal it away.

Mirren was present too, ready to fetch anything the healer needed. And in the corner of the tent stood Torran. Arms, scored by scratches and encrusted with blood, folded across his chest, he watched silently, his face set in severe lines.

Bree barely noticed their presence though. Instead, her gaze roamed over Cailean's sweat-slicked body. The tattoos inked across his chest, arms, and neck were dark against the sallowness of his skin. He still gasped for breath, his eyes sunken deep into their sockets.

Skaal pressed close, her gaze fixed upon Cailean's face. The hound gave a low whine as they waited. *Hurry.*

Once the wormwood root had been prepared, Lara and Eldra carefully poured the precious juice into a narrow vial.

Seated at the healer's side, Bree watched her peel off the bloodied bandages that covered Cailean's wound.

One look at it and Bree's breath hissed through her teeth.

It was swollen and weeping pus. The skin around it had turned a sickly yellow, like the rest of his body. Cailean struggled for breath now, each gasp a shallow, rattling wheeze.

Behind Bree, Lara murmured a curse. "I've never seen anything like it," she muttered.

"No," Bree replied hoarsely. "Nightbane gives a foul death to Shee and Marav alike."

"Hold the wound open," Eldra instructed. "As wide as you can manage."

Leaning forward, Bree did as bid, pulling the ragged lips of the festering arrow wound apart. Holding her breath, she watched then as the healer drizzled the liquid inside.

It took a while, but eventually, she emptied the entire vial. Putting it aside, she then nudged Bree out of the way before she gently pushed the wound closed and massaged the skin around it.

"And now?" Lara asked, her voice strained.

"We wait," Eldra replied softly.

Time drew out, and Cailean held on.

Nonetheless, each breath he drew in was an effort.

Bree didn't leave his side, and nor did Skaal.

She was dimly aware of Eldra and Lara behind her, moving around the tent, speaking in whispers. Mirren brought her a bowl of soup, but she didn't touch it. Torran had pulled up a stool on the opposite side of the pallet, a strong, watchful presence.

Together, with Skaal, they held a silent vigil.

Bree appreciated their company, and that no one tried to converse with her.

She couldn't focus on anything except Cailean as she bathed his fever-racked body and watched for any sign of improvement.

But when his breathing started to deepen and the awful death rattle in his chest eased, Bree's chin kicked up, her gaze fusing with Torran's. "Do you think he's improving?"

Brow furrowing, he gave a hesitant nod.

Eldra moved close then, placing a hand on Cailean's brow. "The fever is drawing back," she confirmed. "It's a relief to learn about this antidote … it may come in useful in the future."

Relief washed over Bree, and her eyes started to smart. Suddenly, her throat was so tight she couldn't speak.

A hand squeezed her shoulder then. Glancing left, she met Lara's gaze. The princess's green eyes glistened, her face gaunt with fatigue and her own sorrows.

"He's turned the corner now," another voice whispered, and Bree looked right to see that Mirren had also moved close.

Torran flashed Bree a tired smile. "Aye, he's tough. Cailean's going to be fine."

Her throat started to ache then. These people had all gathered with her at Cailean's side.

She hadn't expected this. She'd braced herself for them—those she'd befriended during her moons at Duncrag—to despise her now that she'd revealed who she really was and the truth of what she'd done.

But they didn't.

"Mulled wine?"

"Aye … a large one. Thank you."

Lara flashed Bree an arch look before nodding to Mirren, who ladled dark, spiced bramble wine from a pot, filling a wooden cup to the brim. "Pour me one too."

The handmaid did as bid, carrying the wines across to where Bree and Lara sat before a glowing brazier. However, as it was made of iron, Bree had shifted her stool back to a safe distance.

It was late now, and a chill was in the air; outdoors, a crisp frost had settled.

However, despite that her limbs ached with exhaustion, Bree couldn't relax. Cailean was over the worst of it now—Eldra was with him—yet her body still felt coiled, tense.

She wouldn't be able to settle, not while they remained within the stone circle.

She thought about Gil then. She hadn't seen her brother since before dusk, for Cailean's plight had consumed her. She wanted to tell Lara about him, but she suddenly felt awkward. Guilty. Ashamed. Gil was here because of her. If she'd stayed in Sheehallion, Mor would have forgotten about her eventually.

Instead, she'd drawn the Raven Queen's eye, and Mor had lashed out.

No, she wouldn't bring Gil up. Not tonight. To do so might put him in danger. Lara was tolerating her presence here, yet she didn't want to push things. She needed to establish trust first.

Wrapping her fingers around the cup, Bree sipped her wine, sighing as warmth slid down her throat. Her gaze then met Lara's. "I never thought to see you in The Uplands," she admitted. "I can't believe your father brought you and your mother north."

The princess stared back at her, a nerve flickering under one eye. "The foretelling made him overconfident," she replied huskily.

"Foretelling?"

"Aye." Lara took a gulp of wine, her fingers clenching around her cup. "A moon's turn ago, father was about to send hosts of warriors to defend Golval and Deeping barrows. However, his chief-seer told him not to. Instead, he foretold that we would face the Shee before the walls of Cannich just after Gateway … and that father would prevail."

Bree frowned. *That explains it.* "That's a bold prediction."

Lara heaved a sigh. "Aye, well, Allaster mac Coll was given three signs. He dreamed of the Great Mare racing across the night sky above Cannich. Then the following day when he cast the bones, the Great Mare fell next to The Warrior … another sign of victory." Lara paused then, grimacing. "And that evening, a mule in the stables gave birth to a foal … and my father was convinced that victory was his. After that, both the chief-seer and chief-counsellor urged him to travel north. Mac Coll's dream was a portent that the battle would unfold in The Uplands."

Bree fell silent after this admission. The portents the chief-seer had been given were powerful indeed. But they'd been wrong. She wagered that Talorc mac Brude had cursed Allaster mac Coll as he fell.

The coals in the brazier crackled then, sending a shower of sparks shooting up. She watched them, her thoughts turning inward.

"I've never been able to study a Shee so closely before," Lara said finally. "You … glow."

Bree glanced up. "Do I?"

"Aye … as if a candle burns beneath your skin."

Bree's lips quirked. "It's the eyes that usually unnerve your kind."

"Aye … they're …" Lara broke off then as she struggled to find the words.

"Goat-like?" Mirren suggested. The maid had perched on a stool a few yards away and was watching their exchange intently.

Bree snorted, focusing on the lass. "Goat-like?"

Mirren stared back, her blue eyes full of questions. "I always wondered how come you didn't know how to use salt to ward off malevolent spirits," she murmured. "And why you didn't know how to play 'Liar'."

Bree pulled a face. "I was out of my depth, I'll admit." She paused then, inclining her head. "You've developed an impressive knife throw. I don't remember teaching you that?"

Mirren flashed her a tight smile. "You didn't … one of the Fort Guard has been tutoring me." She cleared her throat then—casting Lara a nervous look as if expecting to be reprimanded.

However, the princess was looking at Bree, her pine-green eyes unnervingly sharp.

Taking another sip of wine, she waited for her to speak.

"You were brave today," Lara said eventually. "Recklessly so."

Embarrassment prickled Bree's skin, although she forced herself to hold the princess's gaze. "I couldn't let them take you." She paused then, her chest tightening. "I wish I'd been able to save your mother. I'm sorry I failed."

Lara's eyes glistened. "You did your best," she whispered. "And I will never forget it."

36: THE CHOICE IS YOURS

CAILEAN JOLTED AWAKE. "Fuck!"

Pain speared his left side, a deep, throbbing ache that made him choke off a groan.

"I thought the rough ride might wake you. This cart is a boneshaker."

A husky voice drew his attention, and, blinking, as pale sunlight assaulted his tender eyes, Cailean's gaze settled on the face of a beautiful Shee female. The sky above them was the color of smoke, yet, as always, Bree's skin glowed. Her golden eyes glistened as she stared down at him.

The wagon they were riding in lurched then as it hit a pothole, and pain knifed through Cailean's side once more.

He cursed again, through gritted teeth this time.

Grimacing, Bree picked up a cushion and moved around to his injured side, gently pushing it under him. "Here … this might help." She lowered herself down, sliding her legs under his in the narrow space. "I didn't want to shift you … but we have to keep moving."

Cailean blinked. His memories were foggy, as if he were trying to retrieve them from the bottom of a pond. "What happened?" he croaked.

Bree unstoppered a skin of ale then and held it to his lips, letting him take a few grateful gulps. Afterward, a groove appeared between her eyebrows. "How much do you remember?"

His eyes fluttered shut while he waited for his thick head to clear. The ale tasted like nectar. "Right up until after that arrow hit me," he said after a few moments.

"About that," Bree said, her voice sharpening. "Don't you ever do anything so foolhardy again, mac Brochan."

His eyes snapped open, their gazes fusing. "Just try and stop me," he growled. And he meant it too. When he'd seen that Shee archer draw back his bowstring, his response had been involuntary.

Their stare lengthened until Cailean licked his parched lips. In response, Bree held up the skin of ale so he could take another sip. "Is the princess safe?" he asked, meeting her eye once more.

"Aye."

"And the battle?"

"The Marav were defeated. Talorc mac Brude, his overkings, and most of his host are dead."

Cailean's heart gave a heavy thud at this news—not because he'd grieve for the ruthless High King whose lust for revenge had driven him to his end, but for the scores who'd died with him.

Such a Gods-damned waste.

"How many of us are left?"

"A little over two hundred warriors. Four enforcers survived, Torran among them."

Cailean's chest squeezed at the news his friend was alive. It was a glimmer of light in the darkness. He wanted to talk to him. But there would be time for that later.

Right now, it was difficult to see past the throbbing in his side.

"How long … was I out?" he grunted.

"Two days. The arrow was poisoned … but we found the cure." She paused then, her tawny eyes shadowing. "I nearly lost you."

Something clutched at Cailean's chest, and he reached out a hand, his fingers entwining with hers. "You won't rid yourself so easily of me, woman," he said huskily.

Bree favored him with a wobbly smile. "That's a relief." She blinked then, her eyes filling with tears. A moment later, she cut her gaze away, her expression shadowing.

"What is it?" he asked, concern rippling through him.

"Mor sent my brother through the stones," she whispered. "He's now a Marav slave." She paused then, sighing. "I told you she has eyes everywhere. She was suspicious of me when I returned in the summer … and when she discovered I left Sheehallion, I must have proved her right."

Cailean blinked, his pain-muddled mind trying to make sense of her words. "She did it to punish *you*?"

Bree nodded.

"We can send him home."

She swallowed. "No, like me … his life will be forfeit if he ever returns to the Shee realm."

Cailean scowled. Curse it, he wished his head didn't feel as if it were filled with wool. "Have you spoken to the princess … asked her to free him?"

"Not yet," she whispered, cutting her gaze away. "Lara's been so forgiving … I don't want to push things just yet. What if she turns on him?"

"She won't." Cailean's jaw firmed, his fingers tightening around hers. "Not if we speak to her together."

"You look like shit."

A familiar voice made Cailean glance up. They'd stopped outside the hill fort of Dulross, and around him, what was left of the armies of Albia was making camp for the night. Bree had gone off to assist, leaving Cailean alone in the wagon.

Torran stood in front of him, arms folded across his chest. Cailean's mouth quirked into a relieved grin. "So, do you."

He wasn't exaggerating. Healing scratches and lacerations crisscrossed Torran's bare arms, and a colorful bruise shadowed his jaw.

Skaal pushed herself up from where she'd been lying, on guard, next to the wagon. Plumed tail wagging, she rubbed her head against the enforcer then, nearly knocking him over. "Oof … careful, lass." Torran reached down and ruffled the fae hound's furry ears. "Skaal's been looking after you then?"

"It seems so."

"She hasn't left your side since you fell," Torran replied, an eyebrow lifting. "And neither has Bree. I swear, if you'd died, she'd have chased you into the Otherworld and dragged you back."

Warmth washed over Cailean, although he covered his embarrassment up with a shrug. Eldra had told him how Bree had gone out hunting for mugwort and brought it back just in time to save him.

Clearing his throat, he met his friend's eye once more. "How is everyone treating her?" he asked then, shifting to make himself more comfortable. The healer had given him something for the pain, but the throbbing was still there, a constant, like the beating of his heart. "If I hear anyone's disrespected my wife, I'll have their balls."

Torran snorted. "Don't worry … the men are all too scared of Bree to bother her." He inclined his head then. "So, she's coming back to Duncrag with us?"

"Aye," he replied brusquely, even as tension coiled in his gut. Injured or not, he'd take on anyone who criticized Bree. "Have you got a problem with that, mac Rab?"

Torran merely smiled, folding his arms once more. "I suppose you want your old job back?"

Cailean stilled. In truth, he hadn't given the future much thought. He hadn't even spoken with Lara yet. "Would it bother you, if I did?" Indeed, Torran was the chief-enforcer these days; he might not want to give the role up. In his position, Cailean would have fought to keep it. He realized then how much he'd missed his life in Duncrag, his camaraderie with Torran.

To his surprise, his friend's smile widened, his grey eyes glinting. "I'd take offense if you didn't."

"Cailean."

A woman's soft, hesitant voice intruded upon their exchange. Torran moved aside then, turning. Both men's gazes settled upon the newcomer.

A tall woman with long dark hair and woad-blue eyes stood before them.

Cailean's pulse quickened, his belly tensing. With everything that had happened, he'd almost forgotten that she was with the camp. "Enya." He tried to push himself up and then thought better of it. "How are the lads?"

Her throat bobbed. "Bruised and bloodied … but they'll all live."

His stomach unclenched. "Good."

Enya eyed him, tension vibrating off her. "I heard you'd been injured."

"Aye." His gaze roamed over her face, noting how strained her proud features were. "But I'll be fine."

She swallowed once more before nodding. Her hands flexed at her sides. "I wanted to thank you," she whispered. "For saving us."

Cailean stared back at her, and his throat started to ache. "It won't make up for everything," he said huskily. "But it's a start."

Her eyes glistened. "Aye," she whispered. "It is."

"I'm sorry," he said then, the apology tearing from his throat. "My behavior was callous … selfish. I cared more about revenge than you, and I'll never forgive myself for it."

Enya stared back at him, her face softening. She knew what those words had cost him. Aye, Cailean wasn't a man easily humbled, yet he'd swallow his pride now. "If *I* can let it go, then you should too," she replied. "It's time to let the past lie."

Torran cleared his throat then. The enforcer was eyeing them, his face a picture of confusion. "Are you going to introduce us?"

Cailean huffed. "This nosy bastard is Torran … one of the few people I'd trust with my life," he said, his mouth curving into a wry smile. "Torran, meet Enya … my long-lost sister."

"Take his collar off."

"Aye, Your Highness."

The burly smith turned to Gil, favoring him with a brusque nod. "Kneel."

Slowly, his expression still strained—even after Princess Lara's command—Gil obeyed. Wielding a pair of iron pliers, the smith cut his way through the collar. Moments later, it fell away, thudding onto the sheepskins Gil knelt upon.

Without another word, the smith picked up the collar, gave a bow to the princess, cast Bree a glower, and left the pavilion.

Bree, Cailean, Torran, and Gil were alone with the princess once more. Lara had dismissed her servants, save Mirren, from the tent. Once they'd finished making camp at Dulross, the princess had called for them all.

Bree cut her husband a sidelong look. Leaning heavily on a stick, Cailean's face was drawn with pain, yet his expression was determined. While she'd been helping make camp, he'd been busy setting up a meeting.

Lara watched as Gil rose to his feet. He then raised his hand, massaging his neck, eyeing her all the while. The princess's gaze flicked to Bree. "You should have told me that your brother was here."

She managed a tight smile, even as guilt twisted in her chest. "You had enough to deal with."

Lara's brow furrowed. "Were you worried how I would react?"

"Possibly. You have little reason to trust me."

The princess flashed her an exasperated look. "Don't treat me as if I'm made of eggshell. I'm tougher than I look."

Their gazes held before Bree's mouth quirked once more. Her friend was wounded and grieving, but she wasn't beaten. "I know."

Meanwhile, Gil eyed them both as he stood there, still rubbing the welt on his neck where the iron had chafed.

Lara shifted her attention to Cailean and Torran. "Mac Rab has agreed to step down and take his place as your second again," she informed Cailean, her manner turning brisk as she focused on practical matters. "Will you be my chief-enforcer, mac Brochan?"

He returned her gaze, his blue eyes veiled. Bree understood his caution: no doubt, Talorc mac Brude wouldn't have welcomed him back like this. But Lara wasn't her father. Her face was wan this evening, her throat still bandaged, yet she held herself proudly. Defiantly.

The heir to the Albian throne.

"Aye, Your Highness," Cailean murmured, his voice rougher than usual. He bowed his head. "It would be my honor." He paused then, swallowing. "But I will only accept if my wife will be welcome in Duncrag as well."

Lara raised an eyebrow, glancing back at Bree.

Cailean cleared his throat, and she sensed he was about to plead her case. However, she reached out, her fingers closing around his wrist in warning. She appreciated what he'd done today, but she needed to handle this.

"Would you suffer a Shee living in your broch?" she asked softly.

Lara raked an assessing gaze over her. "I would." Warmth flushed across her chest at these words, but Lara hadn't finished. "Albia requires a strong leader now … but a ruler is only as strong as those at their side." Her eyes glinted then. "Would you consider becoming my personal warder and counselor?"

Bree jerked, her lips parting as her breath gusted out of her. The most she'd hoped for was for Lara to agree for her chief-enforcer to bring his wife home, to allow her to reside in Duncrag. She hadn't expected to be offered a *job*.

Her breathing grew shallow then, her chest constricting as emotion slammed into her—a blend of elation and something more complex. Guilt. If she took on such a role, her betrayal of her people would be absolute. Even so, she reminded herself that she'd long passed the point of no return. Mor had already named her a traitor.

"That's quite an offer," she replied huskily, feeling the gazes of Cailean, Torran, and her brother boring into her. Her eyes stung then, and she blinked furiously. "Are you sure?"

Lara stared back, her mouth lifting into an enigmatic smile. "Aye."

37: GOING HOME

THE SIGHT OF Duncrag's beehive-shaped broch, thrusting against dark skies, made Bree's stomach flutter.

Strange, how it felt as if she were going home.

A rueful smile tugged at her lips then as she remembered the first time she'd set eyes on this fort—the dread that had churned inside her as she considered the mission Mor had given her.

All of that was behind her though. She was making a new start.

However, this time, she was doing so as a lone Shee female, surrounded by Marav. And iron. Already on the journey south, she'd burned herself twice on it. Once, when she'd accidentally picked up an eating knife. The metal had bitten into her palm like a snake. Then, she'd brushed her arm against Cailean's chest when he'd just slung his knife belt across his front. The burn had made her yelp, even through layers of clothing.

She sat behind Cailean now, astride Feannag. Traveling in the wagon had become too uncomfortable for him, every jolt painful. As such, it was easier for him to ride, although Eldra had strapped his chest up first.

Fortunately, he'd tied his broadsword and fighting dagger to the front of the saddle so she didn't touch them.

"I never thought I'd return here." The rumble of Cailean's voice roused her then. "I told myself that chapter of my life was done with … that there are some rivers you can never cross twice."

"I believed the same," she admitted, tightening her hold on his waist. "But the twists of fate can surprise you."

"Indeed, it has brought us back here … together."

Her throat tightened, her eyes suddenly hot and prickly. Shades, she was on the verge of tears. "It feels right too," she said, her gaze traveling over the fort's high stone walls. "There are worse places to live than Duncrag."

"Are you ready for this?" Concern crept into Cailean's voice then. His big hand covered hers, firm and warm. "A Shee female guarding the Marav High Queen will create a stir."

She snorted. "It will … but over the past moons I've realized a few things about myself."

"Such as?"

Bree smiled. She leaned in then, her lips brushing against his ear. "You're a protector … and so am I."

The mood within the fort was somber, especially once word spread that only the High King's daughter, and a sparse army, had returned from the north.

Lara hadn't delayed in announcing the news. She addressed the swelling crowd gathered inside the gates, and when she moved on—making her way up The Thoroughfare toward the broch—the wail of grieving widows had followed her. The haunting lament blended with the shrill sound of The Whistle as a grey afternoon slid into dusk.

Bree escorted Lara into the broch now. Her skin prickled as the iron doors loomed before her, yet she set her jaw and kept moving. Luckily, the guards waiting there pulled the doors open as they approached, even if they stared at the sight of a Shee female at Lara's side.

Once they were indoors, Lara went straight to the hall.

"Are you sure you still want me at your side?" Bree murmured, following her across the reed-covered floor. Although they'd only just arrived back, Lara would be expected to give an audience. Already, men and women were pouring into the hall, the agitated rise and fall of their voices echoing high into the rafters. "This isn't going to be easy."

Lara gave a soft snort and lowered herself onto her father's carven chair upon the high seat. "Nothing will be … from now on."

Cailean joined them then, weaving through the press to take his place behind Lara. However, Bree marked how stiffly he held himself, and how ginger his movements were.

"You should be resting," she murmured, casting him a frown.

Cailean harrumphed, his gaze meeting hers. "There will be plenty of time for that. Right now … I need to be here."

Before them, the circular space filled up. Standing next to Lara, Bree weathered frightened, accusing stares. As expected, she was causing quite a stir. Meanwhile, at the fringes of the crowd, she spied figures robed in red, white, blue, and green—druids. Torran waited there too, with the other remaining enforcers. And near the doors, looking like he wanted to bolt, stood Gil. His mouth was pursed as if the smell in here overpowered him.

Guilt knifed through Bree as she watched her brother. He looked so lost standing there, trapped in a Marav body amongst people he'd always considered enemies. She wanted to make this easier for him, but she couldn't. She was relieved he'd accompanied them to Duncrag though; Bree didn't like the thought of Gil roaming Albia, utterly alone in the world.

Despite everything, they were closer these days than they'd been in a long while. Living in Duncrag together would make settling in Albia easier for them both.

Lara waited until the din of voices, some of them sharp with hysteria, died down. And then, she rose gracefully to her feet, surveying their anguished faces.

"As many of you will have heard … we were defeated in the north," she began, quelling the last of the murmuring. "I confirm that an army of Shee … aided by hill-tribe warriors, and a host of faery creatures from our own realm … laid siege to Cannich, and that my father, and his overkings … including my husband … are dead. The northern Uplands have fallen. Mor, the Raven Queen, now controls the land around Cannich."

Some of those in the crowd cursed under their breaths at these devastating words, while others reached up and grasped the iron protection charms they wore around their necks.

"The enemy also attacked our rearguard and attempted to abduct my mother and me," Lara continued, her voice catching slightly. "Queen Teva was killed in the ensuing struggle." She halted there, raising her hand sharply to still the tide of agitated muttering that now rose around her.

Lara waited for the noise to settle before she gestured to her right. "This is Bree Fellshadow, my personal warder and advisor."

A shocked silence fell then, as all gazes fixed upon Bree. Lara let them stare for a few moments before she spoke once more. "Aye, she's one of the Shee … but she is a *friend*."

Warmth suffused Bree's chest at these words. Lara had no idea what such an admission meant to her.

"You won't recognize her in this form," Lara went on, "but the Raven Queen sent her here last spring. She impersonated the chief-enforcer's bride so that she might learn where and when my father would strike the Shee next."

Gasps and growled oaths followed this admission. Meanwhile, Bree's belly clenched. She'd known that Lara would have to address, and explain, her presence here. Nonetheless, she hadn't expected her to be quite so blunt about it. The glares upon her now felt as if they were stripping her skin away.

"Bree was sent to spy upon us … but she has redeemed herself," Lara said, plowing ahead despite the muttering. "She risked her life to warn the chief-enforcer that the Shee were lying in wait at Mid-Summer Fire … yet failed to prevent the massacre that followed, for the Raven Queen attacked earlier than expected."

These words didn't appease the crowd. If anything, it stirred them up. Many of the warriors amongst them looked ready to grab their weapons and rush at Lara's warder. A rumble of growing ire echoed off the damp stone.

Dragging in a slow breath, Bree flexed her fingers, fighting the urge to reach for her knives. She hoped Lara knew what she was doing, or things were about to get bloody. Her new position would end up a short one indeed.

Iron flay me, maybe taking this job wasn't a wise choice.

"Bree and Cailean mac Brochan saved my life." Lara's voice, more strident now, cut through the muttering. "Together they challenged the Shee warriors who tried to abduct me and my mother." She paused, her chin lifting as the crowd quietened once more. "She has pledged her loyalty to me and shall live amongst us now." A hard edge crept into Lara's tone then. A warning. "And anyone who raises a hand against her will face my wrath."

Following Lara and Gil into the large alcove, Bree halted. Her gaze swept over the mountains of dusty scrolls heaped chaotically upon shelves and benches. A large table dominated the space, with more parchments littering its surface. A map of The Uplands of Albia had been rolled out, pinned down with iron weights at each corner.

Bree observed the chaos around her before murmuring an oath under her breath.

In response, Lara cut her a weary smile. As soon as the audience was over, she'd insisted on bringing Gil here.

However, Bree's brother wore a guarded expression. Like her, he wasn't sure what Lara was up to.

"My father never hired an archivist, even though he needed one," Lara said finally. "Some of the scrolls in here were written by his great, great grandsire. It's a mess ... one that will take years to sort out." She paused then, sympathy shadowing her green eyes. "I know it's not the life you wish for, Gil … but the role is yours."

Gil's gaze jerked to her, surprise lighting in his eyes. "You're offering me a position here?"

Lara smiled. "Aye, if you want it."

He stared back at her, a nerve flickering under one eye. An awkward silence swelled in the alcove then before he swallowed and dropped his gaze. "Very well, I accept," he said gruffly.

Bree flashed Lara an apologetic look for her brother's lack of grace. However, her friend merely shrugged. She then focused on him once more. "We will meet again in a few days … and you can advise me on how you plan to catalog all of this."

Gil nodded. Then, following Bree's swift elbow to the ribs, he remembered his manners. "Thank you … Your Highness."

38: BRIEF AND BEAUTIFUL

"THANK THE GODS, that's all over," Lara sank down into a chair by the hearth and took the cup of wine Mirren handed her. "I was dreading my return to Duncrag … and how everyone would react."

The day was done, and they'd retired to Lara's bower to share some wine. From tomorrow—once she took the throne—she'd be expected to move into her parents' quarters. But she'd spend tonight here in her old bower—a small yet richly furnished space. Furs covered the floor and colorful hangings draped from the walls. The air smelled of lavender and rosemary. When she'd resided at Duncrag, Bree had spent many afternoons in this bower with the princess, chatting to her by the fireside as she attempted to learn how to sew and spin.

"You dealt with everything well," she answered, seating herself opposite Lara. "And if you were nervous, no one noticed."

"Aye, they were too busy staring at *you*," Lara said, eyeing Bree over the rim of her cup. "Having a Shee warrior as my counselor and warder has caused quite a scandal."

Mirren poured another cup of wine and held it out to her. Bree took it with a tired smile. "Are you regretting it?"

"No," Lara replied. "Are you?"

Their gazes met, and the challenge in her friend's pine-green eyes made Bree's smile widen. "Not yet." She wouldn't admit it, but she'd found this afternoon even more draining than she anticipated.

Their gazes held for a few moments before Bree's smile faded and she looked away. "I thought you'd blame me for your brother's death," she admitted softly. "After all, *I* warned the Raven Queen about the Marav ambush."

"I wanted to … initially." Bree glanced up to see a sad smile curving Lara's mouth. "But you did try to stop the Shee attack, and that redeems you in my eyes."

Bree stared back at her, even as a blend of guilt and relief clutched at her chest. Lara's good opinion mattered to her.

"I think Bree was a wise choice, Your Highness," Mirren volunteered then, as she retreated to a stool a few feet back from the hearth. "You wanted someone to protect you … well, the folk here are too wary of your warder to come within a few yards of her. No ruler of Albia has ever been safer."

Bree snorted at this, while Lara arched an eyebrow. "Aye, that's right." Her attention focused on Bree once more. "I watched you fight in the north … I've never seen anything like it."

Warmth stole over Bree then, and she realized she was embarrassed by her friend's earnest praise. "I'm over three hundred years old," she murmured. "I've had time to practice."

Both Lara and Mirren's gazes widened at this admission, and she chuckled. "I'm still very young by Shee standards … my people live into the thousands of years."

Lara took a large gulp of wine before giving her head a rueful shake. "We must seem … like children to you."

"Not at all," she replied honestly. "The opposite." Her gaze held Lara's for a moment before she glanced over at Mirren. "I've learned much from you both."

Mirren's mouth quirked. "What … how to play dice?"

Bree gave a soft snort. "Aye, but so much more besides." She paused then, the warmth in her chest building before she pushed on. She'd be candid with these women—she owed them that. "Before meeting you both, I didn't have any friends. I scorned female company as something that was beneath me … but I never realized how lonely I was until I came to live at Duncrag" —she swallowed then to ease the sudden tightness in her throat— "until you *both* showed me what I'd been missing."

Cailean was sleeping soundly when Bree slipped into the sleeping nook next to him. It had been a long day, and she was relieved to bid Lara and Mirren goodnight and retire.

Snores rumbled through the alcove, although the noise wasn't coming from her husband. Skaal was curled up next to the glowing hearth on the other side of their quarters.

Ignoring the fae hound, Bree propped herself up on an elbow and gazed down at Cailean. Even exhausted, his chest wrapped in bandages, he was beautiful.

And he was hers.

Bree's eyes grew hot and prickly, as they had earlier that day, and she blinked furiously.

She'd once detested this man, yet now, she couldn't imagine life without him.

Cailean stirred then, his dark eyelashes fluttering against his cheeks. An instant later, woad-blue eyes fixed upon her.

"What time is it?" he asked drowsily.

"Late … the day is done now. Lara will be crowned tomorrow."

He groaned. "I've slept the afternoon and evening away."

"Aye, but you needed to." She paused then before reaching out and skimming her fingertips over the bandage that wound about his torso. "How are you feeling?"

"Better."

She nodded. "Even so, Eldra insists you rest for the next few days … Torran will look after things until you're ready."

He harrumphed. "I'll go mad just sitting around."

"No," she replied firmly. "It'll do you good."

Their gazes met then and held before Cailean lifted a hand and caught hers, bringing it to his mouth.

The feel of his lips grazing against her knuckles made Bree's heart kick.

"There's much to be done," he said then. "With the Raven Queen in the north, we must rebuild our armies … our strength. Our people need something to cling to."

Bree nodded, something deep inside her chest tightening. *Our people.* Aye, his people were hers now. She'd chosen a side.

Nonetheless, Duncrag was still reeling. After their arrival in the early afternoon, news of their defeat—of the death of so many, of the loss of the north—had rocked the fort to its foundations. But now that night shrouded the world, the turmoil had settled for a short while.

"I wonder when the Raven Queen plans to push south," Cailean continued, his voice hardening. "And how big her ambitions are."

Tension knotted under her ribcage. "That concerns me too. To the Shee, Albia is a cold and brutal land … but Mor has tasted victory now. She might wish to bring this entire realm to heel."

Cailean snorted before wincing. "This 'cold and brutal land' is now your home."

Bree's lips curved. "Aye … and it has my heart."

Their gazes met once more, and Cailean's grip on her hand tightened.

However, as their gazes drew out, the pressure in her chest continued to build. "I want to truly belong here, Cailean," she said softly.

His brow furrowed, confusion shadowing his blue eyes. "What do you mean?"

"It doesn't matter how long I live in Duncrag, I'll always be an outsider … always wary of iron and druidic magic. I'm weaker in the presence of both … something that might hinder my ability to protect Lara in the future."

Cailean's features tightened. "Don't you think I've considered that too?" he said roughly. "This situation isn't ideal, but we've already discussed ways to—"

"We have … but there are other things to think about," she cut him off gently. "If you're lucky, you'll have another fifty years." Bree pulled a face then. "If battle doesn't take you first, of course. But I'm young for a Shee … I'm destined to go on for thousands of years longer." Reaching up, she stroked his cheek. "I want to live on the same timeline as you."

He stilled. "What are you saying?"

Bree sucked in a deep breath before letting it out slowly. She'd pondered this decision and wanted him to know this wasn't an impulsive choice on her part. "I'm going through the stones at Mid-Winter Fire … to return to you as a Marav woman."

Cailean tried to sit up then, cursing as the abrupt movement pained him. "What?"

"I will go through Golval Barrow and then travel to The Ring of Caith."

"No," he rasped, alarm flaring in the depths of his eyes. "You can't travel through Sheehallion … there's a price on your head. It's too dangerous."

"It's a risk I'm willing to take."

"But the Raven Queen will hunt you … and I won't be there to watch your back."

Bree's mouth curved. *My shield.* "Aye, but she won't catch me. I have Tivesheh. He'll bear me swiftly. Mor won't even know I've crossed the veil."

"She'll know."

"I won't be in Albia long enough for that to matter anyway. It's only a two-day journey from the barrow to the stones."

"But wouldn't it be safer just to go to The Ring of Caith … and for you to pass through into Sheehallion and then back again?" His brow was furrowed now, his eyes shadowed with worry.

"No," she replied softly. "Traveling through the stones exacts its price … even for us Shee. To try to pass through the veil twice in such a short time would likely kill me."

His gaze narrowed. "Are you certain of this?"

She nodded. "Last spring, Gil dug up texts in the archives about the stone circles for me at Caisteal Gealaich … before my mission. They warned of this."

Cailean was looking at her now as if she'd lost her mind. But she hadn't. This decision had been building within her for days—and it had been surprisingly easy to settle upon. Tonight, as she'd climbed the stairs to their quarters, she finally made her choice. And now that she had, the 'rightness' of it settled into her bones.

Ever since meeting Flynn in Morae crannog, she'd thought about what he'd done. At the time, she hadn't understood why he'd given up his long life for a Marav woman. But she did now.

"You don't need to do this," he said finally. "You know that I love you, whether you're Shee or Marav. It makes no difference."

Bree's throat constricted. He hadn't said those words out loud before. "And I love you," she whispered. Shades, she did, so much that her chest ached.

He swallowed. "But to give up your long life … for me … it's too much."

Her mouth curved. "This isn't just for you," she whispered. "It's for me too." She leaned in once more so that their faces were just inches apart. "I want to grow old with you, Cailean mac Brochan … to let the years carve lines upon my face. In Sheehallion, it's eternal spring, but Albia has seasons … and if I were Marav, my life would be like that too. Aye, it'll be brief, but it'll be *beautiful*."

39: A STORM OF ARROWS

Golval Barrow,
The Realm of Albia

Two days before Mid-Winter Fire ...

BREE DREW TIVESHEH up before the barrow and inhaled a lungful of gelid air. Sliding off her stag's back, she sank up to her ankles in soft snow. Cailean dismounted next to her while Skaal halted, shaking snow off her thick coat.

It was a three-day ride to Golval Barrow from Duncrag, although the snow had made the trip harder going. They'd been wary during the journey, for the Shee were abroad these days. But Golval Barrow was a safe enough spot, for it lay near the border between The Uplands and The Wolds—far from where the Shee were currently gathered.

The barrow rose before her, its rounded surface gleaming white in the weak sunlight. Behind it, the waters of Loch Caith were pale, iced over. There wasn't a whisper of a breeze this evening, and this close to the barrow, there was no sound of birdlife. The world was frozen, dead.

"Are you still sure you want to do this?" Cailean asked, drawing her attention. "You can change your mind, you know?"

Bree turned to him, their gazes meeting. "I'm sure."

And she was.

Moving close to him, she slid her hands under the thick fur mantle he wore, her arms locking around his torso. She sighed then; compared to hers, his body was a furnace. As beautiful as it was, the winter was taking its toll on her. She'd shivered her way through the past moon and a half, since returning to Duncrag. The Marav didn't enjoy the bitter season either, but for a Shee, who was used to living in sunshine and warmth, it was torture.

The cold drilled deep into her bones and never left.

It was another reason why she had to do this—as a Marav, she'd be able to put up with this chill easier. She thought of the Shee that now lived in The Uplands, where winters were bitter indeed. They'd all be suffering by now.

Reaching up, Cailean brushed a lock of hair that had come free of its braid off her cheek. "I still don't like it," he muttered. His breath steamed before him in a cloud. "I don't want you going anywhere near the Raven Queen."

"It's just two days," she reminded him. "Ride to The Ring of Caith and wait for me."

A nerve flickered in his cheek. "And what will I do, if you don't walk through the stones at Mid-Winter's dawn?"

"I will," she replied firmly.

His blue eyes had turned stormy now, and she could tell he wanted to argue with her. But there was no time.

"I'll see you soon," she whispered, leaning in and brushing her lips over his.

Cailean's arms went around her, and he hauled Bree against him for a passionate kiss. He bent her over his arm, his mouth mating with hers, and when they pulled away from each other, they were both out of breath.

"Ride swiftly, Bree." His expression turned fierce as he stepped back, taking the warmth of his body with him. "And don't you dare let them catch you."

A short while later, Bree walked through the barrow, Tivesheh's hooves thudding in the darkness at her back. It was winter, and the wights in here slumbered deeply. She passed through the veil without hearing a whisper from them.

Even so, misgiving feathered through her. Aye, she was confident she could reach The Ring of Caith and pass back through the veil without drawing Mor's eye. But if she didn't reappear at dawn of the winter solstice, her husband might do something reckless.

Something that would cost him his life.

He hadn't said he'd go looking for her if she didn't arrive at the appointed time. But the glint she'd seen in his eye before she'd turned and walked into the barrow warned her that he would.

And if he walked through the stones, he'd die.

Stepping into the warmth of a Sheehallion morning, she sucked the scent of sweet grass and wildflowers into her lungs. A faint longing tugged at her then, for her past life, before she recalled how she'd spent most of her time here.

Hunting and killing for the Raven Queen.

No, the assassin was dead. Instead, she protected the High Queen of Albia. She was softer these days, more given to laughter—and she was no longer alone in the world.

She had people who cared about her, and soon, she'd return to them.

But for now, she had to focus on getting to The Ring of Caith without anyone spotting her. If they ran swiftly through the day, they'd reach the stone circle with time to spare before sunrise on the solstice.

Leaping up onto Tivesheh's back, she leaned forward and stroked his neck. *The next two days will be grueling,* she warned him. *Are you ready to run hard?*

Always. The stag tossed his head. *I will go as fast and as far as you ask me, Bree.*

Her chest constricted. This would be their last ride together. When she went through the stones this time, she wouldn't be coming back. She wasn't looking forward to saying goodbye to Tiv; they'd been through so much together. But just like the Shee female she currently was, her white stag didn't belong in Albia.

Tivesheh sprang into a bounding run, sprinting over rolling meadows as the last rays of the rising sun turned the sky the color of salmon.

Things started to go wrong later that day.

They'd paused to rest for a short while on the banks of a gently flowing burn, and Bree was helping herself to handfuls of sweet raspberries from bushes nearby, when Tiv snorted.

Glancing up, she turned, her gaze traveling north to where a grassy ridge rose against the cerulean sky. A row of figures riding stags was silhouetted there. Even at a distance, she marked the weapons that bristled on their backs, the quivers of arrows. Warriors. She wasn't sure where they were heading. However, she wasn't inclined to find out.

"Right," she muttered, crossing to her stag and vaulting onto his back. "Time to go."

She'd been planning to ride in that direction, but, instead, they'd be taking a detour, which would unfortunately slow them down.

And then, a short while later, as Tivesheh sprinted through a hazelwood, Bree spied a large raven sitting upon a branch.

It watched, unblinking, as they approached, and a chill slithered down her spine.

Eagal. Mor's messenger.

The bird gave a victorious caw, and her heart lurched.

Shit.

They raced by the tree where he perched, although Bree twisted afterward, looking over her shoulder—only to see the raven take wing, heading southeast.

Toward Caisteal Gealaich.

Shit!

We won't be able to rest tonight, Bree warned the stag, crouching low over his withers. *Something tells me, we'll have company soon.*

Then I shall run faster.

And with that, Tiv flattened into a wild gallop.

They traveled through the night, stopping only briefly so that Tivesheh could catch his breath. All the while, Bree's sharp senses strained for any sign of pursuit.

And as the first blush of dawn lightened the eastern sky, she heard it.

The shrill call of a hunting horn.

Her pulse lurched. Twisting in the saddle, she looked south. Her belly dropped like a stone when she spied outlines on the horizon.

Elks with riders crouched low over their withers.

Mor had sent her Ravens after Bree. There were around a dozen of them—too many for her to take on alone.

Run, Tiv. Run!

She hated to push her big-hearted stag any further, for Tivesheh had traveled long and fast. He was tiring now, his speed slackening. But he just had to hold on a short while longer.

Just until they reached The Ring of Caith.

And there it was in the distance, the ancient stones reaching up to the heavens like bent fingers atop a grassy knoll.

And the sun was about to touch them.

She had to get there for when it did.

However, the ground thundered now. Tivesheh was slowing, and the elks were gaining on him.

Thud. Thud.

Yew arrows flew past her, embedding into the ground or skidding along the grass. Only Tiv's evasive gait, in which he zigzagged wildly, prevented one of them from hitting either Bree or her stag.

Panic bloomed then as they dove through a storm of arrows.

She cut another look over her shoulder.

Gavyn was leading the group, pale hair streaming behind him and face savage.

Like his companions, he'd drawn his longbow, and he was now reaching for a fresh arrow.

Bree's heart lurched into her throat. Any moment, one of those deadly shafts would find its mark. She couldn't let her brave stag be injured.

Goodbye, Tiv. Flee fast!

She'd wanted to say farewell to him properly, as he deserved—but suddenly, she'd run out of time.

She launched herself from his back, dropping into a smooth roll across the dew-laden grass.

40: WHERE I BELONG

AN INSTANT AFTER she hit the ground, Bree was up and running, flitting left and right, just as Tiv had—darting from shadow to shadow as she'd learned during warrior training centuries earlier.

But The Ravens knew all her tricks.

An arrow brushed past her left ear, so close the feather fletching tickled her skin. Another grazed her shoulder, scoring the thick leather armor she wore.

She changed her pattern, ducking right and then left, and then left again, faster and faster, until her feet were flying over the ground.

The hill rose before her, and she raced up it. Arrows stung the air like vicious hornets.

Curses ripped through the stillness.

The Ravens knew she was close to escaping them.

Thud. Thud. Thud. Three more arrows sank into the damp earth right in front of her.

Bree leaped them and raced for the gap between the two largest stones.

She could feel the earth magic now, prickling her skin. However, there was no time to let it bother her. She had bigger problems right now.

Her time was up. Any moment, a bolt would bury itself between her shoulder blades.

Desperation exploded in her breast, along with a fierce determination. No, they wouldn't stop her—Cailean was waiting on the other side, and she'd not disappoint him.

And so, she dove like a swallow, tumbling headfirst through the gap in front of her.

Just as an arrow cracked against ancient stone, and another whistled just above her head.

Bellows of rage followed before abruptly cutting off.

She'd left Sheehallion behind and stepped into the no man's land between two realms.

A heartbeat later, Bree rolled to her feet in the midst of the circle. And just like when she'd passed through before, mist enshrouded her. The air was heavy, pushing at her on all sides, and moving forward was like wading through porridge.

Gritting her teeth, she pushed on, putting up her hands to shield her ears as the ringing began.

Iron, it hurt.

The veil between the two realms wasn't easily breached, and it resisted every step.

Hissing curses, she fought it, leaning into the mist, head bowed, as she crossed the gap between the stones, step by step.

It was hard though, the hardest passing so far. As the book they'd found in the archive at Caisteal Gealaich had warned, the stone circle remembered her and was issuing a warning.

Just one last time!

The metallic taste of blood filled her mouth, and she realized she'd bitten her tongue. Her head swam as the air pressed in, as if it wished to crush her to a pulp.

Screaming a curse, she punched at the mist before her, battering her way through it.

Two steps more and then suddenly, the pressure gave way. An instant later, she was falling.

She landed hard on her face.

Icy cold embraced her, and she dragged in a lungful of dank air, sobbing as relief swept up her throat.

She'd done it.

She was through.

Pushing herself up, she peered into the murky Albian dawn, where snowflakes fluttered like apple blossom from a purple sky. She realized then that she was trembling; the strength of her Shee form had deserted her. Her muscles were weaker, her body softer and more ungainly. It would take her a few moments to get used to it.

A cry ripped from her throat. "Cailean!"

"I'm here." Strong hands grasped her under the arms and dragged her forward, from under the shadow of the stones. "I've got you."

An instant later, Cailean scooped her up, crushing her against the wall of his chest, and carried her down the hill, away from The Ring of Caith.

Still shaking, Bree clung to him.

The scent of leather, smoke, and clove wrapped itself around her—and the tension that had knotted tight under her ribs slowly released.

At the bottom of the knoll, he set her down. Feannag and Skaal were waiting for them under the bare, snow-encrusted branches of a hazel tree that grew on its own, a few yards back from the woods.

Cailean gently took hold of her chin and raised it so their gazes met. Her husband looked frozen to the marrow. The tips of his nose and ears were red, and his breath steamed in the gelid air.

"You're bleeding," he said, his thumb sweeping below her lower lip, and coming away red.

"It's nothing," she gasped. "I bit my tongue on the way through, that's all."

Cailean's gaze dipped right then, his eyes narrowing as his hand lowered to her shoulder guard. Bree stiffened, knowing that he'd seen where the arrow had scored the boiled leather. "Were you attacked?"

"Aye." She swallowed. "Mor's raven spotted me yesterday … and she sent her bodyguards after me … the same ones who tried to abduct Lara." She shuddered then as the realization of how close she'd come to being captured hit her. "They nearly had me."

Cailean breathed a curse. He cupped her face then, staring deep into her eyes.

In the dim light of dawn, his gaze was dark, anguished.

An ache rose under her breastbone. "It's all right," she whispered, covering his hand with hers. "I'm here now … where I belong."

Cailean stared down at his wife's lovely face. The pale morning sun highlighted the freckles that dusted her nose. Frank hazel eyes, filled with centuries of knowledge, stared up into his.

The curves he remembered well strained against her leather vest and tight leggings. She was much shorter in her Marav form. Of late, he'd gotten used to his wife hardly having to lift her chin to meet his eye; she felt a little different in his arms. More fragile, softer. She no longer smelled of rose. But the husky timbre of her voice was the same as before.

"You are," he replied, wishing his voice didn't sound so naked, so vulnerable. Gods, he'd worried about her these past two days. He'd tortured himself with visions of her captured and executed. He hated feeling so useless. His wife had been running for her life, and he'd been standing around, freezing his balls off, while he waited for her.

Bree's full lips curved then, even as her eyes gleamed. "It's done, Cailean," she whispered. "I'm Marav again … like you."

"I would have loved you the same, even if you'd remained Shee," he reminded her, his voice catching.

She swallowed. "I know."

Silence fell then, The Whistle shrieking around them as the snow swirled. A blizzard was rising. However, they remained locked in each other's arms.

The pressure in Cailean's throat tightened. He wanted to catch hold of this moment in his hand, like a snowflake. But just like the delicate fragment of ice, time couldn't be held prisoner. Nonetheless, the exhilarating relief that swamped him, under the looming shadow of The Ring of Caith, ignited a warmth deep in his chest—one not even the biting wind could dull.

He had his wife in his arms once more, and now their life together could start properly.

He became aware then that he could no longer feel his feet.

They needed to get out of this bone-numbing chill. While he'd been waiting for her, he'd built a shelter out of pine boughs on the edge of a clearing within the woods. He couldn't wait to take his wife into their shelter and love her long. Heat ignited in the pit of his belly as he anticipated entangling himself in Bree and sinking deep into her.

Dragging himself out of distracting thoughts, ones that had turned his prick to wood inside his breeches, Cailean focused on practical matters. He needed to move before his feet turned to lumps of ice. "Are you hungry?"

She nodded. "Starving." She lifted a hand to stroke his jaw, shadowed now by a few days' beard growth. The night before, he'd cleaned himself with handfuls of snow—a bracing experience that left his teeth chattering like dice. However, he hadn't bothered to shave. "I've barely eaten anything since we saw each other last … there wasn't any time."

"Aye, well, luckily for you, I've been busy," he replied with a wry smile. "I've got a fire burning nearby … and a haunch of venison roasting. It was Mid-Winter Fire, after all."

She rewarded him with a grin. "Welcome news, indeed." She paused then, glancing around at the swirling snow. "I suppose we should build a shelter. We won't be going anywhere in this blizzard."

Cailean smiled. "Fear not … that's already taken care of too." With that, he scooped her up in his arms once more and turned, heading toward the tree line.

Silently, Feannag and Skaal followed.

Bree laughed, even as she wound her arms around his neck. "What are you up to?"

He grinned down at her. "You'll see soon enough."

And with that, he carried her into the woods.

EPILOGUE: HOLDING FAST

Four moons later ...

"DON'T GRIP THE blade so tightly, Lara."

"Very well ... like this?"

"Better ... but hold it lower, and closer to your body. Otherwise, I can do this."

Like a striking adder, Bree's hand shot out, her fingers folding around Lara's slender wrist, holding it fast. Aye, she no longer had Shee reflexes, but she was still quick.

Lara made a frustrated sound in the back of her throat. "Cods!"

"I made the same error, Your Highness," Mirren quipped. The maid, who was busy folding clothes in the corner of the wide alcove, wore a solemn expression, although her blue eyes twinkled. "We all think waving a blade in an assailant's face is the way to scare them off."

The High Queen flashed her handmaid an irritated look yet didn't contradict her.

Swallowing a smile, Bree moved Lara's wrist down so that it was level with her belly and pushed it closer to the High Queen's torso. She then adjusted her grip on the handle. "The trick," she added. "Is to keep moving. That way, you'll be much harder to stab."

Lara muttered an unqueenly curse, causing Mirren to still in her folding and Bree to raise an eyebrow. "Maybe I should give up these lessons … I feel like a bumbling fool."

"Everyone does when they start," Bree reminded her. "But you've already learned how to defend yourself with your fists … and do so well. Don't be so hard on yourself."

Lara nodded, although her expression remained strained.

In the moons since Bree had stepped into the role of her warder and advisor, she'd noticed Lara had grown increasingly critical of herself. The woman barely slept. Every eve, she stayed up late studying the scrolls that Gil dug up for her or meeting with her druidic council.

The Shee still held the north, although they'd been silent ever since the battle just after Gateway. Ominously so. Aye, they hadn't expected an attack during the bitter season—for moving an army through snowstorms would have been foolish indeed— but now that the weather was warming up, the atmosphere in Duncrag grew tense.

Lara knew that Mor was preparing herself for another campaign—as such, she'd spent the winter and most of the spring, so far, rebuilding her armies. New overkings sat on the thrones of Braewall and Baldeen, cousins of those who'd fallen at Cannich. Lara had worked hard to conscript more men and women, to replace the many warriors Albia had lost. They'd also had to train them swiftly to strengthen the defenses at the new border forts of Dulross and Doure.

No word had come from the northern Uplands though—Strath, Rothie, and Morae—so it seemed that those places too had fallen to the Shee.

It had been a difficult time. Lara had yet to prove herself as the High Queen. Word arrived regularly of just how low morale was throughout The Wolds; especially since those in southern Albia learned that the hill-tribes and faery creatures had sided with the Shee.

"I feel as if I'm standing still when I should be running," Lara admitted then. "The waiting is getting to me."

"Your people are calling for you to take back The Uplands, Your Highness," Mirren said then, her brow furrowing. "Will you?"

Lara's lips thinned, a hard glint appearing in her pine-green eyes. "Aye." Not for the first time, the look reminded Bree of the High Queen's father, Talorc mac Brude. She'd inherited little from her sire—save a stubborn streak and a vindictive edge that surfaced occasionally.

The latter concerned Bree a little. Talorc mac Brude's insatiable hunger for reckoning had been his undoing, and striking off his former master's head hadn't brought Cailean the satisfaction he'd craved either. Revenge was a double-edged sword.

Aye, their recent defeat had caused something dark to take root inside of Lara, and if she wasn't careful, it would consume her.

Bree was considering warning her about this—for although Lara didn't always welcome her bluntness, it was part of her role—when a female voice carried through the curtain. "Your Highness … the new enforcers have arrived!"

Lara stepped back from Bree and handed her the blunted knife they'd been practicing with. A relieved smile flowered across her face, making her resemble the princess Bree had met a year earlier—a lass full of curiosity and spark. "Come then," she said, motioning to both Mirren and Bree. "Let's go out to meet them."

Wordlessly, Bree and Mirren obeyed, following their queen down the stone stairwell to the bottom level of the broch. Emerging through the iron doors—what a relief it was not to worry about accidentally touching it—they halted on the top step before the yard.

It was a bright and blustery spring afternoon. Fluffy clouds scudded across a blue sky. The Gales of Complaint were doing their best to scatter straw and dust. Pushing a lock of hair out of her eyes, Bree's gaze swept across the yard, to where her husband walked before a line of black-clad figures. As always, Skaal stalked at his side.

Behind Cailean, Torran and the three other 'senior' enforcers looked on.

There were twenty new arrivals. Young, tattooed, and arrogant. And to Bree's surprise, one of the new enforcers was female. Tall and broad-shouldered with dark hair tightly braided down her back, she observed the chief-enforcer with a veiled expression, her strong jaw set.

Bree's lips curved. Of course, this lot would try to test their leader.

She'd enjoy watching Cailean deal with them.

Her gaze settled on him now, greedily taking in every detail of her chief-enforcer husband. His expression was inscrutable, those woad-blue eyes as dispassionate as they'd been on the day they'd met. Only now, his coldness was a ruse—designed to let these recruits know their place. When his gaze settled on her, it always thawed.

"Twenty!" Mirren gasped at Bree's side. "I didn't think the arch-druid would send so many."

"Let's hope they're ready," Lara answered, her attention never straying from the line. "Some of them look very young."

Bree's gaze narrowed as she viewed the recruits once more. Aye, Lara had a point. Two of the male enforcers looked as if they hadn't yet shaved their chins. All the same, there was bullishness in their stance. The earth magic in their veins brought out aggression. It was what made enforcers so deadly.

Below, Cailean was now addressing some of the recruits, questioning them about their training. The rumble of his voice reached them, although the Gales of Complaint made it difficult to catch the words.

Bree glanced over at Lara once more, noting her proud profile as she watched Cailean. She'd once thought that Lara harbored a secret longing for her father's chief-enforcer. However, these days, she realized that it was merely a deep respect. She'd partnered with him in the blood-letting a few times, a ritual that forged a closeness between participants.

A ritual that Bree could now share with her husband.

Still watching Lara, she frowned, wondering what the future held for her friend. "Will you marry again?" she asked finally. She was the only one who addressed Lara so informally. The two women had developed a closeness that allowed her to get away with it.

Lara glanced her way, a groove etching between her brows. "I think not."

The response held an edge to it, and beside Bree, Mirren shifted in surprise. "Isn't it expected, Your Highness?"

Lara pulled a face. "Perhaps, but since I'm the High Queen, I can change the rules." She paused then, her gaze shadowing. "I've already had a taste of marriage … and didn't find it to my liking."

Bree stiffened. Over the past moons, Lara had spoken little of her brief union to King Dunchadh of Braewall. Had he lived, she'd have moved to the southern capital to bear his children. But The Gods had intervened. Nonetheless, from what little she'd gleaned, she'd put a picture together—of a vicious man who'd already buried three wives.

Whenever Bree had tried to discover more about how he'd treated her, Lara clammed up. And her insistence now, that she wouldn't marry again, made Bree suspect he'd used his fists on her.

"I suppose a queen doesn't need a mate," she said after an awkward pause. Lara wore a brittle expression now, and she wished to ease it. "*Mor* has never taken one."

Lara nodded, her jaw firming. "Aye. If I take a husband, I will likely be fat with his child within a few moons. Albia needs a *ruler*, not a broodmare."

Below, Cailean finished his inspection of the recruits. He then sent them away, watching as they followed Torran down the wynd that led around the broch and toward the barracks behind it.

Bree caught Lara's eye. "Can I go down to my husband?" she asked.

"Of course." The High Queen's mouth quirked. "You don't need to ask permission for such things."

Nodding, she descended the steps.

Hearing her approach, Cailean turned, his mouth curving into an intimate smile that he reserved just for her.

Warmth kindled in her belly in response.

Skaal moved forward to greet her, pushing hard against Bree's side and nearly knocking her off balance. "Careful," she greeted the hound fondly as she stroked her neck. "You don't know your own strength." She'd missed not being able to touch minds with animals since her return to Duncrag—and she still thought often about Tivesheh—but it was a small price to pay for the contentment she'd found.

"So," she greeted her husband. "Are they up to scratch?"

He pulled a face. "They'll do."

Bree inclined her head, halting before him. "I remember you saying something similar to me … on the eve we met. Do you remember?"

"Aye," he murmured, grimacing once more. "I was an arse."

She smirked. "You were … but fortunately, you've grown on me."

He caught her by the arm and drew her close. "What … like a wart?"

She grinned. She felt playful today, with the spring sun on her face and a blue sky overhead. The winter had been long and bitter, although easier to bear as a Marav. Life was good, and she was enjoying teasing her husband. "Aye … but one I'm fond of."

He snorted. "Fond? Now you make me sound like your grandmother."

Bree threw back her head and laughed, the noise echoing off stone.

In response, he muttered another curse and tugged her close.

They had an audience—for Lara and Mirren hadn't yet gone indoors, and members of the Fort Guard milled around them—but she didn't care.

Cailean's expression softened then, tenderness igniting in the depths of his eyes. "Gods, I love you, woman," he said huskily. "So much it terrifies me."

Her breathing hitched. Such words didn't slip easily off his tongue, yet her heart fluttered whenever they did. "It scares me too," she whispered back. "But here we are, facing our fears … and holding fast."

His gaze grew limpid. "Always." And with that, his mouth descended upon hers for a searing kiss.

The End

AUTHOR'S NOTE & GLOSSARY

I've been writing books set in Ancient and Medieval Scotland for years now … and have always wanted to create a fantasy world based on this setting, steeped in Scottish history and myth. So, I finally did!

I created Albia and filled it with everything I've discovered, all the lore I've wanted to put into my Hist Roms. And you can probably tell, I had a lot of fun with it.

Scottish folklore has a dark and foreboding quality to it—full of dangerous creatures that will foretell your death or lure you to your doom. It's just crying out to be used in Fantasy. Not only that, but Scotland's cold, rainy, misty climate lends a certain brooding atmosphere.

I moved to Edinburgh in January 2024, and since then have immersed myself even deeper into the setting of my books. This country has it all: forgotten cemeteries, lonely ruins, ancient stone circles, mist-wreathed mountains, dark woodlands, and desolate moors. There's so much to be inspired by.

When I created Albia, I wanted a Fantasy world reminiscent of Ancient Scotland, and the Pictish kingdoms that once thrived here—a world where I could bring mythology to life.

Of course, because it's fantasy, I've played with folklore a little and made several flourishes of my own!

Many of the names within this duology come from Scottish Gaelic. It's a beautiful language yet written quite differently from how it's pronounced. As such, I have changed some of the spelling in the novel, to make it more phonetic, and therefore more accessible to readers.

Below is a glossary of people and places from the novel and a bit of background on meaning and the original spelling:

Albia: a variation of 'Alba', the Scottish Gaelic name for Scotland

Ben Neeya: the Bean Nighe (see note below about 'the Washerwoman')

Caisteal Gealaich: the Shee queen's stronghold. It means Moon Castle. (pronounced *castel galeech*)

Sheehallion: Original spelling is 'Schiehallion'. Located in Perthshire, it's one of Scotland's most prominent mountains and rich in legend. Its name derives from the Gaelic Sith Chaillean meaning 'The Fairy Hill of the Caledonians.'

Feannag: Cailean's black stallion (The name means 'crow' and is pronounced *feearnarg*)

Skaal: Cailean's Fae Hound ('sgàil' means 'shadow)

The Marav: the name for the mortal race that inhabits Albia. Comes from 'Marbh' or 'mairbh', which means a dead person/people

The Shee: the name for the fae race that inhabits Sheehallion. This name is based on the Daoine sìth (pronounced: *doonyuh-shee)*, the Scottish name for the fairy race.

Tivesheh: is the name of Bree's white stag (the name means ghost and is pronounced *tiyv-sheh*).

In this novel, I use 'mac' with Malav names. Of course, this is from Scottish Gaelic, which meant 'son of'. In Pictish times, 'mac' was used as a separate word in a name with the father's name following. This was the origin of many Scottish surnames we see today.

The dice game 'Liar', is based on an ancient game:
https://www.lore-and-saga.co.uk/html/dice.html

The protection charm used in Chapter 11 was inspired by a Celtic blessing:
https://www.faithandworship.com/Celtic_Blessings_and _Prayers.htm#gsc.tab=0

The plant 'whin' is mentioned a few times in this novel—it's the Scottish word for 'gorse'.

My inspiration for The Hallow Woods comes from Warriston Cemetery in Edinburgh. Partially overgrown, you walk through dappled shade, climbing ivy, and banks of nettles, past where headstones and crosses covered in moss peek out of the undergrowth. Built in 1845, this huge Victorian cemetery spans 11 hectares and consists of a large terrace, serpentine paths, catacombs, and a neo-classical bridge. And although there's some restoration work underway, it's literally a place time has forgotten.

The societal structure of Albia is based on the ancient kingdoms of Ireland and the Pictish kingdoms of Scotland, where a High King ruled several lesser kingdoms governed by 'Overkings'.

The creatures that are mentioned or feature in THE ENFORCER'S BRIDE duology, and their Scottish mythological origin:

Fae Hounds are a variation of the Cù-Sìth (pronounced *ku-shee*), a ghostly hound from Scottish folklore that roamed the Highlands. The name means 'Fairy Dog'. The Cù-Sìth were said to be the size of a bull with dark-green shaggy fur and a coiled or braided tail.

People believed the Cù-Sìth was a harbinger of death—much like the Grim Reaper. Although mostly a silent hunter, this giant dog would sometimes let out three blood-curdling howls. If you didn't get away before the third howl, you'd be overcome with fear and die from sheer terror.

Ben Neeya: The Bean Nighe (pronounced *ben-nee'-yeh*) also known as 'the Washerwoman', is an old woman seen wandering near streams and pools, where she washes the bloodstained clothes of those who are about to die. The bean-nighe is sometimes said to sing a mournful dirge. She is often so absorbed in her washing and singing that she can sometimes be caught unawares. If a person sees her before she spies them, she will reveal who is about to die and will also grant three wishes. In my tale, I've altered things slightly so that she grants you one wish.

Powries: also known as a Red Cap, or a Dunter, a powrie is a type of malevolent, murderous goblin found in Border folklore. He is said to inhabit ruined castles along the Anglo-Scottish border, especially those that were the scenes of tyranny or wicked deeds, and is known for soaking his cap in the blood of his victims.

Find out more: **https://folklorescotland.com/the-fearsome-redcaps-of-the-scottish-borders/**

Trows: these creatures feature in Shetland folklore. They are similar to humans but smaller and uglier, and they live in the hills, particularly the heathery peatlands inland from the sea. They would only come out at night, to work mischief in the human world.

Find out more: **https://shetlandwithlaurie.com/the-blog/shetland-folklore-series-trows**

Aughisky: The each-uisge (Scottish Gaelic, meaning "water horse") is a water spirit found in the Scottish Highlands (anglicized as aughisky or ech-ushkya). It usually takes the form of a horse—similar to the kelpie but far more vicious. Unlike the Kelpie (which inhabits streams and rivers), the each-uisge lives in the sea, sea lochs, and freshwater lochs. The each-uisge is a shape-shifter, disguising itself as a fine horse, pony, or handsome man. If you mount this creature while it's disguised as a horse, you are only safe out of sight or smell of water. Otherwise, your skin will stick to the creature, and it will pull you down to the deepest part of the loch and tear you apart.

Find out more: **https://about-mythical-creatures.weebly.com/each-uisge.html**

Corpse candles: also known as will-o'-the-wisps or fairy lights. In Scottish folklore, will-o'-the-wisps are variously depicted either as mischievous spirits (typically fairies), or even the ghosts of the dead, eager to lead travelers off their path and to their death. The lights typically appear close to a bog, marsh, or swamp, places where straying off the beaten path can become dangerous – or even deadly.

Find out more: **https://folklorescotland.com/will-o-the-wisp/**

Bavaan: The Baobhan Sith (pronounced Bavaan-shee) is a vampiric creature of Scottish origin. Beautiful, tall women with pale skin and icy breath, they dress in flowing green robes and are said to dance in the moonlight, seducing men, in order to kill them and drain their blood.

Find out more: **https://folklorescotland.com/the-baobhan-sith/**

The Unforgiven/The Slew: The Sluagh Sidhe, or 'Fairy Host': spirits of the unforgiven or restless dead who soar the skies at night searching for humans to pick off. They always approach from the west and often prey on those close to death.

Find out more:

https://folklorethursday.com/folktales/the-sluagh-spirits-of-the-unforgiven-dead/

The Botach: The Gaelic word bodach (pronounced bot-ach) can mean 'old man' and also 'specter, ghost'. In ancient Scotland, it was the name of a mythological 'bogeyman' who comes down chimneys to steal children. He was also seen as an omen of death. The bodach was said to slip down the chimney and steal or terrorize little children. He would prod, poke, pinch, pull, and in general disturb the child until he had them reeling with nightmares. According to the stories of most parents, the bodach would only bother naughty children. A good defense would be to put salt in the hearth before bedtime. The bodach will not cross salt.

Find out more:

https://www.tumblr.com/bestiarium/65069709351159398 4/the-bodach-scottish-mythology-gaelic-mythology

Wulvers: a Scottish mythological creature that is part human, part wolf. The wulver kept to itself and was not aggressive if left in peace. They would often guide lost travelers to nearby towns and villages. There are also tales of wulvers leaving fish on the windowsills of poor families. Unlike their werewolf counterparts, the wulver is not a shape-shifter.

Find out more:

https://www.scotsman.com/news/people/scottish-myths-wulver-the-kindhearted-shetland-werewolf-2463904

Gods and Goddesses of Albia

The FIVE

The Mother: Goddess of enlightenment and feminine energy—the bringer of change

The Warrior: God of battle, life, and growth, of summer

The Maiden: Young goddess of nature and fertility

The Hag: Goddess of the dark—sleep, dreams, death, winter, and the earth

The Reaper: God of death

Gods and Goddesses of Sheehallion

The Ancestors

The Great Raven

Festivities of Albia

Earth Fire: Salute to new life and the first signs of spring

Day of the Hag: Spring Equinox

Bealtunn: Passage from spring to summer

Mid-Summer Fire: Summer Solstice

Harvest Fire: Festival to salute the harvest

Gateway: Passage from summer to winter

Mid-Winter Fire: Winter Solstice

Five 'paths' of druids

Enforcers: wear black and are the warrior druids who serve the king

Sacrificers: wear red and carry out ritualistic sacrifices to keep the Gods happy

Counselors: wear white and are the sages, you go to them for wise advice

Seers: wear green and are masters at divination

Bards: wear blue and sing and entertain, and tell lore through song and music

The Arch-druid: wears gold and is the one deemed to be the most wise

Initiates: wear brown and must choose their path

The four winds of Albia

The Whistle: high and shrill

The Sharp Billed Wind: pierces the land like a sharp-beaked bird

The Sweeper: whirling gusts that strip branches from trees

The Gales of Complaint: scatters food and crops
Source: **https://weewhitehoose.co.uk/study/the-cailleach/**

DIVE INTO MY BACKLIST!

Check out my printable reading order list on my website:

https://www.jaynecastel.com/printable-reading-list

ABOUT THE AUTHOR

Multi-award-winning author Jayne Castel writes epic Historical and Fantasy Romance. Her vibrant characters, richly researched historical settings, and action-packed adventure romance transport readers to forgotten times and imaginary worlds.

Jayne is the author of a number of best-selling series. A hopeless romantic in love with all things Scottish, she writes romances set in both Dark Ages and Medieval Scotland, and Romantasy with a Celtic vibe.

When she's not writing, Jayne is reading (and re-reading) her favorite authors, cooking Italian feasts, and going on long walks with her husband. She's from New Zealand but now lives in Edinburgh, Scotland.

Connect with Jayne online:
www.jaynecastel.com
www.facebook.com/JayneCastelRomance
www.instagram.com/jaynecastelauthor/
www.tiktok.com/@jaynecastelauthor

Email: **contact@jaynecastel.com**